Photo by Darren James

Kate Solly is a writer, a mother of six and really quite good at getting the bubbles out of plastic book wrap. While most of her time is spent finding lost shoes and investigating what's making the car smell bad, Kate frequently escapes to write entertaining things. She has penned many articles, columns and reviews for various publications, but when she is not writing, she enjoys starting crochet projects and never finishing them.

For my grandmother, Aileen Patricia Moriarty.
Ma Ma, you believed in me long before I ever did.
I am grateful for all of the years you were part of my life.

First published by Affirm Press in 2023
This edition published by Affirm Press in 2023
Boon Wurrung Country
28 Thistlethwaite Street
South Melbourne VIC 3205
affirmpress.com.au

10 9 8 7 6 5 4 3 2 1

Text copyright © Kate Solly, 2023

 A catalogue record for this
book is available from the
National Library of Australia

ISBN: 9781922992291 (paperback)

Cover design by Louisa Maggio © Affirm Press
Typeset in Adobe Garamond Pro by J&M Typesetting
Printed and bound in China by C&C Offset Printing Co., Ltd.

TUESDAY EVENINGS

with the

COPETON CRAFT RESISTANCE

KATE SOLLY

affirm
press

CHAPTER ONE

Claire tried her best in the supermarket, she really did. The trick, when shopping with two babies and a toddler, was to power quickly through the 'red zones' of lollies and chips, to distract as much as possible and to never double back. The only way was forward, ever forward. But even if you followed all of the rules, even if you completely bypassed the centre aisle of lawnmowers and guitar cases, things could go wrong quickly. So it was that she found herself at the checkout queue with an overloaded trolley and an overloaded brain.

Harry was on the floor. He wanted everything that was on the shelves by the checkout, from the breath mints and lollipops to the AA batteries and beef jerky. When she refused to accommodate these demands, he laid himself out prostrate, protesting the violation of his human rights. Claire did her best to ignore this demonstration and set to work unloading the trolley onto the conveyor belt. Lily, meanwhile, had reached behind her seat to discover a carton of eggs in the trolley, and had set to work unloading these onto the floor.

As other customers joined the queue behind her with mere armfuls of groceries, Claire waved them ahead, and they stepped around Harry, and the eggs, to make their purchases. After she had cleared out the entire trolley and had waved the fifth customer ahead of her, she scooped up Harry, took him through the checkout and placed him on the floor under the packing bench.

'You can finish having your tantrum here, darling,' she said.

A new customer had joined the queue behind her when she returned. He raised his eyebrows. Claire knew he was hoping she'd let him ahead of her, but she couldn't – she just couldn't. Studiously avoiding his eyes, she steered her trolley to its position at the end of the register and prepared for the onslaught of packages.

Spaghetti. Butter. Tinned tomatoes. Ice-cream. She grabbed the items as they shot through and attempted to fit them back in the trolley. Apples. Cornflakes. Toilet cleaner. Chocolate. Just ignore Customer Man with his sighs and disapproval. Nappies. Coffee. Milk. Wool wash. By this point, Hope was over it. She wriggled her legs up into the trolley seat and attempted to stand. 'Out!' she said. Celery. Brown sugar. Tuna. Frozen peas. Claire worked with her left hand as her right tugged Hope's foot back into place and held it there. Hope began to cry. Lily paused briefly in her egg tossing to cast a disdainful look at her noisy twin beside her. Beef mince. Baking paper. Bananas. Oil. Harry had grown tired of his tantrum and came over to inspect the commotion. 'Why is Hope crying, Mummy?' Toothpaste. Raisin toast. Tissues. Bread. 'You're hurting her, Mummy. STOP HURTING YOUR DAUGHTER, MUMMY!' Lettuce. Teabags. Depleted eggs.

Claire fit the last of the groceries into her precariously packed trolley. Time to pay.

Except that her handbag was nowhere. Nowhere.

'I, um, appear to be missing my handbag,' she stammered. 'Might I go back and see if I put it down somewhere in the store?'

Register Man nodded blandly.

'You've gotta be kidding me,' huffed Customer Man to no one in particular. Then he stepped in the eggs.

Awake. As soon as Yasmin realised, before she reached full consciousness, her hand was scrabbling down the side of the bed, grasping for the cardboard box. Quick, quick. Her eyes still closed, she shoved the flaky cracker into her mouth and forced herself to chew. Salt and starch. She swallowed and opened her eyes. Okay. Slowly, she sat up and cautiously ate a few more dry biscuits. Okay.

She got up, stumbled through her wudhu and managed to complete Fajr prayer. A little absently, it must be said, but still better than the half-asleep fumbling that had passed for morning prayer in the past few weeks. And she was definitely on time. Things were starting to get better.

She munched another dry biscuit as she dressed after her shower. The nausea was there, but it was in the background. Good. Better. Clean teeth. Makeup. Hijab.

Watching her reflection in the mirror, she fastened the soft, brown georgette fabric under her chin with a pair of rose-gold magnets. Oh, how she loved her magnet clips. They were a miraculous design, a no-snag, game-changing feat of engineering. She swept one end of her headscarf behind her head and made another fastening, folding the fabric so that the magnets remained invisible. Good. Breakfast.

She didn't really want to eat anything, but she made herself some tea and toast. She didn't even butter the toast, but it would do. It was something. She thumb-scrolled idly through her socials. So many ads for crochet patterns, yarn, craft supplies. That's what happens – you buy one pattern online, just one pattern, one time, and that's all it takes:

you will be bombarded with ads for the remainder of your natural life. Still, it was a break from the bizarre fifty-shades-of-werewolf ads that kept popping up in her feed.

A print-out of the digital download in question, the patient zero that had sparked the epidemic of crochet-themed banner ads, was sitting in a plastic pocket in a bag on the kitchen bench. Yasmin glanced across at the bag. It looked innocent enough. A shopping bag from the local yarn shop, also containing high-quality yarn and a new, soft-grip hook. She had even found a card of ancient pearly yellow buttons in her mum's button tin and stowed them in the bag too. It was all ready to go. Yet somehow she couldn't bring herself to cast the first stitch. Her eyes lingered on the bag as she nibbled her toast.

The pattern she'd bought was a vintage one. Classic without being dated or fussy. Yasmin knew that the rich, warm tones of the yarn she'd chosen would give it a modern twist. She needed to get started. She would get started. It was just that—

The front door opened with a clatter and Omar walked in. He called out a greeting and tossed his gym bag into the laundry. As he disappeared to shower, Yasmin got up and flipped on the coffee machine.

The flier was all typed up, formatted and ready to be printed. Meredith had put her skills to good use. The promotion was clear and easy to read. The graphics were eye-catching and visually appealing.

Her work day had not yet started, even though she was in her office. It was permissible to work on personal projects outside of work hours. While, technically, she was using office resources (the computer, the word-processing software, the electricity required to power her computer), Meredith felt confident that she had not committed an offence. The impact on the company was almost negligible and could perhaps be considered part of the 'fringe benefits' of her role as director of marketing at Rivergum Estate. She drew the line at printing and photocopying though. Using the printer or photocopier for personal items was theft, pure and simple.

Meredith liked rules. She enjoyed learning new rules. Road rules, company policies, codes of conduct, rules of etiquette. Meredith pored over these the way another person might devour a good novel. Following clear rules made Meredith feel happy. And the rules had to be clear. They had to be straightforward. 'Grey area', 'wiggle room', 'white lie'. Meredith abhorred these terms. How could a lie be 'white'? What did that even mean? Surely 'honest' and 'dishonest' were a strict binary, otherwise what was the point? As soon as there were exceptions, the concept lost all meaning.

Meredith also enjoyed reminding others of the rules when they forgot. She considered herself a bit of an expert. It was her duty to share her knowledge.

Two panicked laps of the store yielded no results. Claire had needed to pull Lily and Hope out of the trolley, which she had abandoned at the register, and the two toddlers were greatly enjoying their newfound freedom, grabbing packages to show each other and clambering into the shelves to sit on a throne of paper towels. The handbag was nowhere.

She returned to the checkout, where Register Man was in the zone, scanning at breakneck speed. 'I couldn't find it,' Claire said. 'I'm going to check the car.'

Register Man gave a tiny blink of acknowledgement, his scanning never wavering.

As she trudged towards the carpark, it hit her. Of course! The toilet door! The hook!

When they'd first arrived at the supermarket, Harry had taken one look at the man/lady toilet sign and made his announcement.

'I need to go to the toilet!'

Going out with a child who is toilet training was kind of like carrying around a grenade with the pin drawn. That thing could go off at any time. You needed to have your wits about you.

After manoeuvring the trolley into the ladies' toilets, Claire had pushed up her sleeves, slung her handbag on the hook on the back of the door and hoisted Harry onto the toilet seat. Then she stood, slightly crouched, ready for anything. It was a false alarm. Harry, it turned out, didn't need to go to the toilet after all. He was fast becoming a connoisseur of public toilets, and the restrooms beside Aldi were a set he had not yet sampled.

She rushed back to the bathrooms now, smiling. She had definitely left her handbag on the back of the toilet door.

Except, it turned out, the handbag was definitely no longer there. Claire stared blankly at the unencumbered hook as Harry, Lily and Hope investigated the hand-dryer situation. Her mind raced. Perhaps some kindly stranger had handed it in? Or perhaps some lady with a gambling problem had seen it as an answer to her prayers? The toilet was next door to a TAB after all. Perhaps a woman was plonking the handbag on the counter this very minute, saying, 'Put it all on horse number twelve.'

Claire's heart started thumping. Lily started crying. What was she going to *do*?

Omar was chatting about the receptionist at his practice as he prepared his coffee and made toast. He'd spoken about Brenda before. Middle-aged and formidable, she had been working at the practice for longer than any of the GPs.

'I mean, if it was just that she was snarky to the doctors and the other receptionist, I wouldn't mind so much. What gets me is when she's rude to the patients. She treats patients like they've just turned up to ruin her day. And nobody's brave enough to talk to her about it.'

Yasmin was still looking at the bag of yarn with the pattern and hook. She needed to do this. She had everything she needed. So why couldn't she get started? She blinked and looked at her husband. 'Perhaps she is doing the people of Copeton a favour? People will be too scared to get sick. They don't want to deal with her.'

'It's more likely …' Omar was slapping Vegemite on his toast in thick brown stripes, 'it is more likely that people will avoid going to the doctor when they need to and their condition will get worse as a result.'

Yasmin wrinkled her nose. 'How can you eat that? That's far too thick!'

Omar proffered the toast with a grin. 'Salty goodness!'

It's not like she didn't know the stitches. Chain stitch, double crochet, treble crochet, slip stitch. In her mind, she still used the Urdu terms even though she never spoke Urdu anymore – she wasn't even sure she still could. It was always English. Even her dad spoke only English now. 'If you were to say something to her – the doctors are the ones in charge, she'd have to listen to you.'

Omar laughed. 'No. Doctors don't know anything, apparently. She considers us inferior. Or perhaps it's just brown doctors. It's like she doesn't trust my medical training. I'm like, dude, I went to Monash. But so what if I did train overseas? There are excellent universities all over the Middle East. Top class. I just wouldn't go there because I am *from Australia*. Anyway …' He screwed the lid onto his coffee mug, gathered up his toast and bag and, after planting a kiss on Yasmin's mouth, he was out the door.

Yasmin finished her tea and began gathering her things for work. She cast one last look at the bag of yarn. The bag of yarn gazed reproachfully back at her.

Tomorrow, she thought.

Claire asked at the gift shop and the post office. She even ventured into the TAB. Nobody had turned in a handbag. 'Go check Centre Management,' suggested the $2-shop man.

Centre Management, it turned out, was at the opposite end of the shopping centre. By now, she had commandeered an empty trolley and put Harry, Lily and Hope into the body of it. She trudged on, pushing the trolley ahead of her and keeping her eyes forward to avoid meeting any disapproving glares.

As she pushed her unwieldy load ever onwards towards her distant goal, Claire thought. Her handbag. Her handbag with her wallet. She was going to be late for school pickup. She couldn't call the school to let them know. Her phone was in her handbag. Her phone … and her KEYS! Her keys were in her handbag! She was stranded here with no keys and no phone and no wallet and no lovely red handbag with the pretty striped lining.

It was a very white-faced Claire who sidled into the Centre Management office with her cartload of offspring. She rang the bell and waited.

A woman in a navy blazer appeared. 'Can I help you?'

Claire's lip wobbled ever so slightly. 'I've lost my handbag.'

The woman smiled. 'Can you describe it for me?'

'It's, um, red, and—'

'Here it is!' The lady jubilantly produced the handbag. Claire had to stop herself from throwing herself at the woman's feet and kissing her pointy red shoes.

Claire drove her baby-laden trolley straight to the car and drove her car straight to the school. Ben and Piper were waiting at the school office. Claire gave the school secretary a strained smile. Then she rushed everyone back to the car, they all drove back to the shopping centre, all got out of the car and all traipsed into the supermarket.

Register Man was still there, swiping and bleeping for all he was worth.

She approached him. 'I found it!' she exclaimed. 'My handbag, I mean. I found my handbag. I can pay for my groceries now. Where's my trolley?' She pulled out her wallet.

Register Man looked uncomfortable. 'We didn't think you were coming back,' he said. 'All of the stock is back on the shelves.'

Claire stared bleakly at the labyrinth of aisles and queues and half-price specials. She couldn't go back – she just couldn't.

'Mummy,' said Harry, 'I need to go to the *toilet*.'

The office supplies shop had its usual lunchtime crowd, but the queue moved quickly enough. Meredith sat in her car and looked over the stack of printed fliers, warm in her hands. She had spent a little extra on colour printing, but there was room in her budget – she'd checked. Meredith was on track with all of her goals this year.

She tried to set goals in every area of her life. There was her Career, of course, but there were also Fitness, Finance, Education, Social and

Entertainment/Hobbies. This endeavour would cover both Social and Entertainment/Hobbies. She had put so much planning in, she was sure to nail it. She already knew the format for the first six meetings as well as location, logistics, supplies. That was how she operated. That was why she was so successful, even though she was still young.

She didn't put her name on the flier, and the phone number she supplied was not her work number (using a work phone for personal reasons would be a breach of company policy). She didn't want anyone to know about this. She didn't want anyone to know about this until she was ready.

Meredith carefully stowed the fliers in her plastic document wallet and placed it on the passenger seat of her car. When she picked up her lunch box, it was still cool from a morning spent in the office fridge.

Vegemite and lettuce sandwich with a yoghurt that was supposed to promote bowel regularity. Of course, she probably wouldn't need the bowel-stimulating yoghurt if she made her sandwich on brown bread, but she'd never liked brown bread. She had only ever wanted white bread. Plus, it gave her lunch a pleasing aesthetic. A sort of minimalism. White sandwich, white yoghurt, white boiled egg. It would be nicer if her yoghurt spoon were also white. Tomorrow maybe. Her lunch box was teal green, but that was right. A white lunch box would be too much. Teal was the perfect backdrop to set off the white tableau. She ate it slowly in her car in the Officeworks carpark. Meredith did not enjoy lunch-room banter.

She was early. For the first time that week, Yasmin had actually arrived at work early.

It felt good to unzip the jade-green book protector and pull out her hardcover bullet journal and black-ink pen. She had neglected this for too long. She flipped past the pages with random notes, meal plans, prayer intentions and lists of books she planned to read. Time to get her swirling thoughts out of her head and onto the page.

In the top left corner, she wrote the tasks she needed to get done ('Treasury report', 'Stage three proposal', 'Tuesday meeting notes'). In the top right, she wrote a list of the people she needed to contact ('Skype Meesha', 'Email Mum', 'Text Marion', 'Call plumber'). In the bottom left, she wrote a shopping list ('milk, bleach, dry biscuits, BIN LINERS!'). In the bottom right, she wrote errands and appointments ('Op shop run', 'Cake for Qur'an group', 'Meal for Dad', 'Baby doc 5.30pm'). When everything was written down, Yasmin sat back and surveyed her work. Her entire life, reduced to neat black dot-points. It was very satisfying.

At 10.30, she felt like she could manage a cup of tea and a muesli bar without throwing up. In the tea room, she fell into conversation with Jeremy from Approvals. To be fair, it wasn't her fault. She didn't see him coming before it was too late. And once you were in, it was hard to find a way out, short of pointing and saying, 'What in the world is that?' and dashing away while he wasn't looking.

'Ms Malak.'

'Hello, Jeremy.' *Oh my goodness, we've talked about this: call me Yasmin. Yasmin. It's not hard. Rhymes with 'Kathleen', maybe, if you have a lisp.*

'I just wanted to ask you a few questions about the rezoning of the retirement village.'

She summoned a smile. 'Fire away.' At least this conversation was work related. Last week it had been a full fifteen minutes on the comparative benefits of E1-class and C2-class trams.

'So, the Catholics run the nursing home now, and they need council approval to turn it into a refugee processing centre.'

She blinked and swallowed a mouthful of muesli bar. 'Um, no. Not a refugee processing centre. The units in question are in a residential area zoned for seniors. Max Kolbe are applying for a two-year permit to house families and single women in these units. These refugees have already gone through all the paperwork. They've been processed.' She winced. She hated that word. It reminded her of plastic cheese and lunch meat.

Jeremy squinted and frowned. 'Okay. Wait. Who is Max Kolbe?'

Yasmin sipped her tea. 'He was a Catholic priest who was interned, and later executed, in Auschwitz in the Second World War. He volunteered to die in the place of a young father.' She was being deliberately obtuse, but she couldn't help herself: he should know all this. 'St Maximilian Kolbe Ministries, however, is a Catholic agency that deals with social welfare. They're the people who have been applying for the zoning approval.' *We've talked about this already. I know we have.*

'Wait, I thought it was the nursing home people who wanted that.'

Allah, give me strength. 'Okay, yes. This is a joint initiative from two independent agencies. You have Aikenhead Healthcare – they're the ones who run Vincentian Hospital and this nursing home – and you have Max Kolbe. Two agencies, one project.' *Just like in the clearly set-out email I sent you last week. It's all there, buddy.*

'So, what do we say to residents who are worried about their rates being used to house refugees?'

'We say it's fully funded by these agencies. There are no rates involved. They're just asking for zoning approval.' *Is he TRYING to get under my skin? Surely he's not actually this stupid?*

'Okay, well, should we really be kicking our old people out to make room for refugees? Shouldn't we look after our own first?'

'The units have been empty for a while now. And they're designed for independent living, not assisted. That's why they want to use them.' Perhaps, if she concentrated hard enough, she could will the conversation to be over. *Oh, no: here it comes. There's the stupid smirk. Let's hear it.*

Jeremy scrutinised Yasmin's forehead, studying her light-brown hijab. 'It's funny, I always think that maybe you have bright pink hair under there and we wouldn't even know. Maybe you have a mohawk! And nobody would know!'

Yasmin smiled weakly. Why the same joke every time? And why was he always asking the same questions about her use of the sick bay room for the Dhuhr and Asr prayers? Did he feel like she needed him to point out the ways in which she was different from everyone? Maybe he wasn't happy with her lukewarm response and was trying again in the hope that he might get a better reaction. Next time, she would burst into hysterical bouts of laughter, clutching her sides, slapping the bench, unable to speak except to croak out the words 'Pink … hair …' in appreciation. *Stop it. No, really, stop it. You're killing me.*

CHAPTER TWO

After her disaster day at Aldi, Claire shut herself in the laundry. The laundry floor was hard and cold. She hardly noticed. Her back against the washing machine, in a miniature city of crumpled clothing towers, she sat in a pool of brightly coloured yarn, intent on her task. This was going to look awesome. And it made up so quickly. The yarn slowly unravelled as it slid through her hands: DC, DC, increase, DC, DC, increase, DC, DC. She pulled out her phone to double-check the pattern. Yes. All good. She was flying along.

There was a knock at the laundry door. She froze. 'Claire?' It was Peter's voice, Peter was home. What time was it? The laundry door opened. Peter peered down at his wife. The yarn spilled away from her in all directions. She probably looked like a murder victim in some performance art piece that used wool to symbolise gore. He blinked. 'Claire, why are you knitting on the laundry floor? Are you hiding from the children?'

She looked up at him. 'First of all, this is not knitting, it's crochet. You should know that by now. One hook, see? Not two needles. It's a completely different craft. Second of all, this is a new pattern I just discovered. They're like rainbow stacking cups, but they're crocheted! I'm going to make a whole bunch to give as presents.'

He raised his eyebrows. 'And third of all?'

Her smile wavered. 'Third of all, I'm definitely hiding from the children.'

'Did you know they're watching *The Simpsons*?'

'Kind of.'

'And they're eating cereal straight out of the box.'

'Oh.'

'I thought you said *The Simpsons* was off limits?'

'Mmmm.'

'And where are the twins?'

'Asleep.'

'But it's six o'clock!'

'Mmmm.'

'They're never going to sleep tonight!'

She resumed stitching. DC, DC, DC, increase, DC, DC, DC, increase.

Peter disappeared from the doorway. Claire finished the base and began building up the sides. One DC stitch in each stitch, all the way around.

In a way, you might say it all began when Ben was three years old and got gastro. Waiting in the twenty-four-hour doctor's surgery, Claire picked up an ancient copy of *Lovely Homes* with a five-page crochet special. Surrounded by blank white walls and bland corporate furnishings, she was transported to a world of colour and texture. Her fingers itched to create such lusciousness.

When she'd stopped at the supermarket afterwards to buy sports drinks and children's paracetamol, she'd also bought red 8 ply yarn and a 4mm crochet hook. That night, as she stroked her son's sweat-damp hair, she looked up YouTube tutorials on her phone. It wasn't long before she had hooked up her first wonky granny square. That was the beginning.

And now she was obsessed. No trip to the shopping centre was complete without a pilgrimage to the haberdashery store. Of course, not all shopping centres have haberdashery stores these days, which is why she'd started shopping at Highton Hub, which had a Discount Craft. It was worth the extra distance to go to a place where she could immerse herself in the aisles of yarn, hooks and patterns, before doing battle with the supermarket.

She was surprised at the intensity of her own fervour. She would glimpse a pattern on Pinterest or Ravelry, a baby hat with rabbit ears or a nifty basket or an adorable stuffed dinosaur, and she would be seized with an intense desire to bring it into being. Perhaps it was her repressed creativity striving for an outlet; perhaps she just wanted to achieve a little success in her life and have something to show for her efforts. At any rate, she always crocheted while she sat in a waiting room, watched a movie or travelled any distance (as a passenger, that is – although, even when driving, she was sometimes tempted at red lights to grab her workbag and get a few stitches done).

It was the rhythm she loved. Somehow, the steady building of stitches, the predictability of following a timeworn pattern, smoothed her tangled thoughts. For once, her fingers were at work making something, instead of swiping a glowing screen.

When she wasn't crocheting, she was looking at what to crochet next. Apart from her jaunts on Ravelry and Pinterest, she discovered a wealth of blogs where people shared pictures and patterns of the things they made. Some of them talked about their lives as well, and Claire found herself being drawn into these personal worlds. It was a comfort to know there were others like her. She found herself wondering if Jane from *Confessions of a Yarnaholic* had chosen colours for her blanket yet, and when Sara from *Adventures in Hooky Land* would have her baby.

Her favourite blog of all was *Beautiful World*. It was pure visual inspiration. Siobhan, the blog's writer, didn't publish as often as some of the others, but she could usually be relied upon to post every Thursday afternoon, around four o'clock. To Claire, Siobhan seemed to be the perfect blogger, the perfect mother, the perfect *woman*. She was more guarded about her personal life than some of the other bloggers, but that only made Claire more intrigued. She imagined Siobhan had long dark hair and mysterious eyes. And her home would be decorated so tastefully, and it would always smell of baking artisan bread. And she would be thin, but effortlessly so. The images on her blog were so beautiful. In some perverse way, Claire took comfort in the thought that, despite her own many failures, somewhere out there, somebody was doing domesticity right.

Beautiful World gave Claire the pattern for crochet snowflakes. Claire loved to make these because they looked so intricate, yet hooked up so quickly. She could finish one in a little over ten minutes. There was no risk of them ending up in the Drawer of Shame.

The Drawer of Shame was the place where Claire eventually hid all of her unfinished projects. And there were a lot of them: those ridiculous pink slippers she had tried to make for Piper, but the fluffy yarn was almost impossible to work with and now they would be too small for her anyway; the poor little toy Labrador, lying in pieces with his polyfill guts hanging out; three blankets that Claire had eventually lost patience with; and various other sad objects, some with balls of yarn still attached, many with only ten minutes more work needed before they would have been complete. The problem was the constant deliciousness of a new idea. It was always more exciting to start a new project than to plod away with one whose appeal had gone stale. And there were so many luscious new ideas out there.

Claire didn't know anyone else who liked to crochet. She fantasised about living in an Anne of Green Gables novel where women got together to sew and knit and crochet and gossip. They would swap patterns and show each other new stitches, and it would be okay just to knock on someone's kitchen door and have a cup of tea with them without making an appointment. But then, there were no washing machines or vacuum cleaners in an Anne of Green Gables novel. Or indoor plumbing, for that matter. Claire struggled enough as it was to keep a tidy house; she would never have managed in Anne land.

When Peter reappeared, he was wearing a T-shirt and tracksuit pants. 'Sooo,' he ventured, 'what's the plan for dinner?'

Ugh! That question!

Peter tried again. 'You went to the shops today?'

'Yes.'

'So we have dinner options?'

'No.' Claire thought of her groceries, swiped through the bleeper and stacked in the trolley and now neatly returned to the supermarket shelves. She could feel the tears coming. There was no stopping them.

'What's the point of me? What is the point of me?' she hiccupped. 'What's the *point* of being a stay-at-home mum if I can't keep a tidy house?' She looked around for a tissue, then wiped tears away from her eyes impatiently with a pink sock. 'I just feel like I'm failing at everything. Everyone else has these perfect homes and jobs and families and I keep getting it wrong. I'm getting it *all wrong*!'

Peter stepped awkwardly around the piles of clothing and sat down on the floor beside her. 'What do you mean "everyone else"? All your Facebook friends?' he said.

'Not just my Facebook friends! My blog friends, too!' she shot back.

Peter was quiet for a minute. 'I think you need some real-life friends,' he ventured at last.

She sniffed. 'I know. I've been trying with the school mums, but it's hard work. We just don't have that much in common.'

Peter stood up suddenly. He strode out of the room and came back in with his laptop case, fishing around in the pocket. 'I saw this flier at the supermarket,' he said, retrieving a small piece of paper and presenting it to her. 'Crochet. That's what you do, isn't it?'

She looked at the flier. *Copeton Crochet Collective (no knitters please).* The group met at the scout hall on the other side of town. And it was on a Tuesday night, once a month.

'I'm free to look after the kids this Tuesday, if you want to go,' Peter said.

Claire sniffed and nodded. Then she picked up her crochet. Only three rounds to go.

Stuart Willis was having a bad day. He'd cut himself three times when shaving (he didn't normally shave on a Friday, but today was important) and Gareth had eaten the last of his margarine (he knew it was Gareth – it was always Gareth). His bus had been cancelled, and when he finally trudged into the gleaming glass offices of Rivergum Estate Holdings, he discovered the photocopier was jammed. Shaking the rain out of his hair (it *would* rain today, and of course he didn't have his umbrella), Stuart tapped frantically at the photocopier control panel. Not today. Please not today. At 10.30am, he had to give a presentation to his boss. The first presentation of his first job out of school. Stuart hated speaking in public, but he would gladly have given a speech to a sports stadium full of jeering Collingwood supporters if it meant he didn't have to spend ten minutes talking about client engagement to the senior marketing manager of Rivergum Estate. The truth was, he was terrified of his boss.

The trademark clip-clip of Meredith James's heels echoed down the corridor. Stuart broke into a cold sweat. (Or maybe it was the rain? It was hard to tell. He was pretty soaked already.) He gave the photocopier one last desperate jab. The photocopier, for a wonder, bleeped meekly and came to life. Even photocopiers didn't dare misbehave before Meredith James.

Meredith loomed in the doorway. She was only five foot four and very slim, but still: she loomed. 'All set for ten-thirty in the Jacaranda Room?' she barked. Then: 'What on earth happened to you? Did you forget your umbrella?'

Stuart stammered something incomprehensible about rain and buses and photocopiers.

'Right.' Meredith gave her blazer a snapping tug. 'Well, you might want to comb that hair before ten-thirty.'

And she was gone. He released the breath he must have been holding the whole time. Meredith James was pretty young. She couldn't be more than ten years older than him. Still, she reminded him of his stern paternal grandmother. He walked off dazedly, in search of a comb.

At 10.20, looking neat and presentable, Stuart stepped into the Jacaranda Room. Meredith was already sitting at the table, tapping on her laptop computer. He gave a small start, which he quickly suppressed, but she did not look up when he entered. Nor when the other members of his team started arriving. At 10.29am, Meredith closed her laptop and picked up her pen. At 10.30, she fixed her sharp green eyes on Stuart expectantly.

He stood up. 'Thanks for coming, everyone. Today, I'm going to present you with some ideas about, erm, client engagement. Basically, how do we get people to come to our display village?' He flicked the remote and his slide-show presentation lit up the screen. He took them through a few slides of pie charts and statistics about the current status of client engagement. He had been careful to keep the slide show simple and straightforward. Meredith had savaged a colleague a few months ago for making the mistake of using cute animation gimmicks and sound effects as part of his presentation.

Meredith was looking impatient. So far, he was only covering old ground. He gulped and flipped through to the crux of his presentation. 'On Saturdays and Sundays, from eleven am to two pm, we can have a free sausage sizzle in the village.'

'With onions!' Jared chipped in. 'You need onions to make it smell good.'

'And don't forget veggie burgers,' said Steph the Vegan.

Stuart grinned. 'The initial outlay, for bread, sausages, gas, will be—'

'Do you have any other ideas?' It was Meredith. Stuart's blood froze.

'Erm, sorry, what was that?'

'Do you have any ideas apart from the – the sausage one?' He didn't. The next twelve slides were all about the costs and logistics of running a free barbecue.

'Well, I—'

'Because it won't do. Whatever venture we go ahead with will need to speak to the character of the village. This is not some car dealership. What next? An inflatable Mr Blowy with waving arms? This is simply not good enough, Stuart. As soon as stage one of construction is complete, we will need to present our plans to head office. We will need more than this. We need to think about who we are, what sets us apart from the others. If you don't have anything more, Stuart' – he did, but it was useless now – 'I suggest you all get back to work.'

Stuart's arms wobbled a little as he packed up his things. Later, Steph plonked a cup of tea on his desk. 'Don't let Cyclone Meredith get you down,' she said with a sympathetic grin.

He couldn't think of anything clever to say in response, but he smiled back and sipped the awful-tasting herbal concoction. It needed milk.

There was an ad on the television that had somehow taken up residence in Claire's head. It showed a group of busy school mums dashing about, being capable. Then their phones beeped with a message: *Time for coffee?* (Except, of course, they didn't say 'coffee', they used the brand name. Who does that? Nobody, that's who.) The next thing you know, four good-looking mums are laughing and chatting in someone's kitchen, happily sipping the advertised brew. Claire hated the ad. The peppy music, the lame slogan, the fake, upbeat tone of the voiceover lady (she sounded just like she was about to step into the kitchen with them to join the fun). She *hated* it.

And yet, as she watched the curly haired TV mum double up with laughter, clutching hold of her brunette friend's shoulder (and her coffee, of course), she felt a small inward twinge. A quiet voice in her mind said: *that's what I want.*

It wasn't like Claire didn't have friends. She had plenty of friends. Some had moved to Sydney or Brisbane. Some were travelling overseas. She followed their lives on Facebook and Instagram, acknowledging their achievements with likes and cheerful comments. But there was nobody nearby. Nobody whose house she could visit or whom she could have at her house. Nobody like the coffee sachet ladies.

She had been sure things would be different in Copeton. It wouldn't be like the city, where everybody was uptight. Their unit in Melbourne had nasty wallpaper and a tiny courtyard. Peter worked as a project manager at one of the major universities. When he was offered a promotion at the university's outer-suburban campus, Claire had jumped at the chance. At Copeton, they could afford a four-bedroom house with a proper backyard. The schools were excellent and they all had ovals. And it was almost the country. People were sure to be friendly when it was *almost the country.*

But it was over a year now since they'd moved to Copeton. The garage still had fourteen unpacked boxes, and Claire was yet to make one new friend.

Of course, she would always say hello to the school mums at pickup time. But it was hard to get beyond the smallest of small talk. She found the netball mums of Piper's year level rather intimidating, and she was only just getting to know the prep mums.

It would be easier, maybe, if she could just relax and be herself. But she had to be on her guard, so she wasn't the Weird Mum With Too Many Kids. Because, you see, there was Ben, who was five, and also Piper, who was nine. They had a younger brother, Harry, three, and twin sisters, Lily and Hope, who were eighteen months. That made five children. Five of them. This was why people sometimes treated Claire with mild concern. This was why it was imperative that Claire held it all together at all times.

'Hello, Jocelyn.' Claire adopted a bright tone as she approached Hunter's mum, standing outside Ben's classroom. Jocelyn looked agitated, but then, Jocelyn often looked agitated. Maybe that was just her face?

'Hello.' Jocelyn was peering in the classroom window, through the gap between two Blu-tacked posters. 'Hey, Claire – what level words is Ben on now?'

'Um … orange, I think …'

'There is no orange. Do you mean amber? Or tangerine?' Jessica's mother, upon hearing they were talking about word levels, had joined the conversation. 'Jessica's on violet words, but she should really be up to lime. The teacher needs to test her more often. She knows all her violet. She's supposed to be on lime. At the very least.'

'Hunter's still on lavender,' Jocelyn murmured in a worried tone, 'but Muriel said that Georgia's on heliotrope already.'

Miss Evans, Ben's teacher, had employed a system where the children were taught to read eight words at a time. These word lists were stapled to the inside of the children's reader covers and named after colours. When Ben could read all of the words on his list to the teacher, he would be given a new colour word list. Claire wasn't sure how many word lists it would take before Ben could read every word in the English language, but Miss Evans seemed to have an endless supply.

'Hunter knows all of the lavender words,' Jocelyn continued dolefully, 'he just gets stuck on "said" sometimes. And he gets nervous when the teacher tests him. That's all. He does know them, really. I think I need to talk to Miss Evans.'

'I want to talk to her too,' murmured Jessica's mum. 'How is Jessica supposed to move up if the teacher never tests her?'

Claire nodded brightly and tried to find an opportunity to fall, laughing, on Jessica's mum's shoulder, but the moment just wasn't there.

'Here comes Muriel.' Jocelyn's voice dropped to a whisper. 'That woman is obsessed with reading levels. Obsessed.'

'*Totally* obsessed,' Jessica's mum agreed in a hushed tone. 'Do you know, I caught her one time outside the classroom going through the kids' school bags to *check their reader covers?* I bet she wanted to make sure nobody else had heliotrope words yet.'

Claire leaned in and shared in the communal scoffing. It wasn't exactly a coffee-sachet moment, but it was better than nothing.

CHAPTER THREE

The 3rd Copeton Scout Hall was a modest double room with a kitchenette and walls sparsely adorned with pennants and photographs. Today, eight chairs stood in a circle in the middle of the dusty wooden floor. At one end of the circle was a free-standing double-sided whiteboard with a fresh packet of dry-erase markers and an eraser propped in the tray at the bottom. A small table with a clipboard and money tin was strategically positioned next to the door. In the kitchen, three plates of plain biscuits rested beneath cling film shields and the urn grumbled out steam.

Meredith James paced from the circle of chairs to the kitchenette to the door. She smoothed her skirt, pulled out her phone again and gave the screen a jab. 7.03. People should be here by now. On the A5 flier, which she had distributed to all of the local libraries, doctor's surgeries, churches, supermarkets and community centres, '7pm sharp' was printed in plain bold type. She would get a glass of water. She would get a glass of water and bring it to the table by the door and she would sip it and wait.

It was as she was filling a plastic tumbler at the sink and frowning at the misspelt laminated notice (*All patrons must clean there own cups*) that she heard a tentative voice.

'Hello?'

Somebody was standing in the doorway. She must have been Muslim, with her patterned headscarf, and Meredith's sharp eyes detected a neat baby bump under the woman's stylish, flowing tunic.

She took down her name (Yasmin), collected her money ($3 to cover expenses) and invited her to sit down (the aforementioned circle of chairs). Another person had arrived in the meantime. She was large, noisy and middle-aged. Her name was Lottie. This made three. Three was enough to make a group. The door opened again. It was an elderly woman and a young man.

Meredith flinched. She didn't like men, as a rule, and she hated good-looking ones. The older woman's name was Edith. She was the one who was attending the meeting. The young man, who was maybe thirty, was merely providing transportation. To be fair (and, for all her faults, Meredith was always fair), 'good-looking' didn't properly describe this man, whom Edith introduced as her grandson. His features weren't regular, he needed a shave … and yet there was something about him. His eyes perhaps? She darted a quick glance at his eyes. That was it. Just an ordinary person with nice eyes. So what? Still, she was glad when Edith had paid and the grandson went away.

'Don't forget you've got your thing tonight,' Peter had called as he left for work in the morning. But for all that, Claire had forgotten within the next ten minutes, somewhere between the lost library bag, burnt toast with subsequent smoke alarm and single black school shoe that seemed to glare at her insolently, refusing to disclose the whereabouts of its missing comrade. She hurtled through the day, battling the discount supermarket, navigating the labyrinthine bureaucracy of driver's licence renewal and preparing a beef casserole with a small child attached to her leg. It was only at five to seven, as she cleared the plates from the table, that her phone gave a cheerful notification bleep. She looked up at Peter, startled.

'I've got that thing!'

'You've got that thing!'

She started dashing about, gathering her bag and random crochet projects that were scattered about the living room. She kissed Piper, Ben, Harry, Lily and Hope (who, sensing an imminent departure, had reattached herself to Claire's leg) and told them to be good for their dad. Peter prised Hope off her mother's leg and tossed her to the ceiling. Hope tried to look unimpressed. Claire closed the front door and ran, cringing, to the car, with the sound of Hope's wails echoing in her ears.

She was ten minutes late when she pulled into the scout hall carpark. She had managed to scribble on some makeup using the rearview mirror at the two red lights she'd encountered on the way. She drew a deep breath as she stepped into the old hall. The meeting had already started. Four people were in a circle; three were sitting and one was standing up and speaking as she burst in. She felt so foolish. She stumbled to a spare seat and collapsed with her bags. She blushed an even deeper red when she realised she'd sat down next to a Muslim woman. She was wearing a headscarf and everything. Claire was certain that she would say something offensive to her. She didn't know how to talk to a Muslim person!

As soon as she got over feeling flustered, she took in the room. It was obvious who the boss of the group was. An attractive blonde woman in chic corporate wear sat facing the lady who was talking, listening with an intense focus. She sat in front of a whiteboard – a *whiteboard* – on which an agenda was neatly written. If everything was running on time (and Claire had a feeling that it was), then they must be up to *1.1: Introduce Yourself to the Group*. She did some quick calculations. Boss Lady would have gone first (obviously), followed by Old Lady, now this brightly coloured woman with the loud voice was talking, then it would be Muslim Lady, then Claire.

'I work in aged care and I just love handmade things with a passion. Crochet, patchwork, knitting, sewing – even daggy old macramé! There is something so wonderful about something that's been made by hand. I don't know what it is. I love it.'

'Thank you, Lottie,' said Boss Lady, 'Although I do want to point out that this group is only for crochet. There will be no discussion of other crafts here.'

Claire giggled loudly at Boss Lady's joke. Boss Lady looked at her blandly. She wasn't joking. Claire's laughter evaporated as she felt her face turn crimson yet again. Muslim Lady stood up.

'Hello, my name is Yasmin. I work for the local council as the community engagement officer. My … my mother taught me to crochet when I was eight, but I haven't been doing it much until recently. At the moment, I am working on a set of baby's clothes.'

Muslim Lady sat down. Cripes, that was quick! Claire still hadn't worked out what she was going to say. And it was her turn already!

Yasmin took a deep breath. Thank goodness that was over. If there was one thing she hated, it was 'Stand up and introduce yourself to a bunch of strangers'. Why did every group, every training day, every antenatal class need to include this bizarre torture ritual? So unnecessary. She was glad, not for the first time, that she had gone back to wearing hijab. It meant she didn't have to explain herself. It meant she didn't have to see the light in a stranger's eyes change when she said, 'I'm Muslim,' when she needed to politely decline certain foods. The way they would recalibrate their facial expression as they mentally adopted a new set of assumptions. At least when she wore hijab she was being clear from the start.

The woman who had come in late was now speaking. 'Um, I'm Claire and um, I'm really just happy to be out of the house without the kids!' She swallowed and nodded. 'But, don't get me wrong – I love crochet. It's my favourite thing! And I didn't know anyone else who liked crochet before now. I mean, not in real life. I know lots of people on the internet. But nobody I can, um, talk to. So I hope we can all be like in *Anne of Green Gables* together …' She trailed off and sat down with a thump, her cheeks a brilliant scarlet. This woman had no problems with blood supply to the face.

Even while Yasmin's dread of introducing herself had been mounting, she had felt a rush of warmth for this woman when she had blundered her way into the meeting. She reminded Yasmin so much of her sister, Meesha. She felt the familiar pang of distance. Skype and email were wonderful things, but New York was still so far away. She'd tried to give the woman a conspiratorial smile when she sat down, but it was difficult to catch her eye.

She glanced around the room. It looked like everyone had brought their work with them. Some used tote bags; some had zip-up pouches. The lady with the vivid crocheted wrap – was it Lottie? – had a large wicker basket filled with richly coloured yarn.

Introductions now over, the organiser, Meredith, stood beside the whiteboard with the agenda. She seemed nervous, for all her brisk, take-charge demeanour.

'This group has been formed as my personal project to connect with other people who share a common interest in crochet. I have a lot of knowledge and expertise in crochet that I am willing to share with you. Perhaps, in time, we can even start a group project together. Here are the group rules …' Yasmin wondered if she ought to take minutes.

When they finally reached Agenda Item 4.1: Crochet and Chat, Yasmin carefully opened the shopping bag at her feet. It contained several balls of yarn in a rich, buttery yellow; a crochet hook, still in its packet; a card of pearly yellow buttons; a curling paper receipt; and the pattern she'd bought online with a baby on the cover. Drawing a deep breath, she took a ball of yarn out of the bag and held it in her hands. It was so soft. She could do this. But as she pulled out the pattern, she felt her breathing become shallow. She shoved the yarn and pattern back into the bag and dropped the bag onto the floor.

Meredith paused from her industrious stitching and frowned. 'Is everything okay?'

Yasmin summoned a bright smile and squeaked, 'Bathroom?'

In a creaky old bathroom, in the cloying redolence of lavender disinfectant, Yasmin washed her face. Her breathing steadied as she locked eyes with herself in the mirror. She was being silly. She patted her face dry with paper towel and touched up her makeup. She could do this.

When she returned to the group, she did not go back to her chair. Instead, she sat beside the older lady, Edith, and began a conversation.

'What are you working on?' she asked brightly.

Edith held up her work. It was eggshell coloured and lacy, with a tiny hook and a large ball of fine mercerised cotton. 'You can ask me what I'm crocheting any day of the week and I'll give you the same answer,' Edith said with a twinkling smile. 'I love making doilies. They are so satisfying.'

Yasmin smiled. 'But don't you get to a point where you have enough doilies in the house?'

Edith shook her head. 'Do you stop going to the movies because you have enough ticket stubs? No. I like the experience of making doilies and I'm not going to stop. Besides, my granddaughter has taken it into her head to adopt them. She sews doilies onto children's clothes and play rugs and goodness knows what else.' Edith cast a look at the abandoned shopping bag underneath Yasmin's previous seat. 'How about you? What do you like to crochet?'

Yasmin shrugged. 'I haven't crocheted in a while. I bought a pattern and some yarn, but, well …' she trailed off.

Edith paused and lowered her work. She peered at Yasmin with a shrewd expression. 'If you haven't crocheted in a while, don't start with some complicated pattern. What you need to do is make some washcloths. They're very satisfying to make, and it will help you get in your groove. Here,' Edith fished in her bag and pulled out a pen and small notepad. She wrote on the paper for a minute and then tore it off to hand to Yasmin. 'Very simple, you see. And you can never have too many washcloths. Get started on some of those, and soon you'll be ready to tackle something more – well – something more overwhelming,' she said, with a nod to the shopping bag.

As Yasmin cast her eye over the neat, swirling handwriting, she felt a sudden urge to weep. She swallowed, smiled and nodded. 'I'll give these a try.'

CHAPTER FOUR

From: yasmin.malak@threerivers.vic.gov.au
To: esma_sharif58@excite.com
Subject: Happy Friday!

As-salaamu alaykum, Mum. How are you? I'm doing all right. My morning sickness is getting a bit better, but I still gag at the smell of mangoes. Ugh. I don't know what it is. It's just gross.

I also can't stand the smell of the bright pink hand soap in the bathrooms at work. It's the worst. And then you're stuck with that smell on your hands for ages afterwards. Can't deal.

Did you have any weird aversions when you were pregnant with Meesha and me? Or weird cravings?

Meesha is all over the place at the moment. You know how she gets when she's preparing for an exhibition. I'm happy for her. Of course I am. I definitely don't feel like the boring older sister, pregnant in the suburbs. Going to gala New York events where your name is up on posters is fine, but it doesn't really compare to working for Three Rivers Shire Council in Copeton, Victoria. Why have art and glamour when you can have surveys and bureaucracy?

Does Dad seem a little weird to you lately? He was really distracted on Sunday. Not, like, *Meesha*-distracted, but still, not himself. It's not like *he* has an exhibition coming up and is lost in a frenzy of creativity. I mean, unless he's quit being an engineer and just hasn't told us yet. But it's the same sort of vibe. And he's definitely lost weight over the past few months. I mean, that's probably a good thing – it's not healthy to carry too much weight around the midriff at his age – but still, I worry.

I wonder if he's getting enough iron?

Make dua for me on Wednesday, Mum. I've got a check-up at the dentist and I'm almost certain I'm going to need a filling! I need all the prayers I can get. Gah!

Love you lots,

Yasmin

Yasmin stood, knife in hand, over the cutting board. She could do this. Two pale pink chicken breasts leered back at her, glistening moistly.

Five minutes later, she was still standing there in grim determination, locked in a bizarre poultry-versus-woman standoff. Her nostrils were full of the stench of the meat as keys rattled in the front door.

'Daddy's home!' Omar, it seemed, never entered a room without announcing himself in some way. She found it both charming and baffling. She herself would much prefer to be unobtrusive, to observe and test the waters before plunging into a social interaction. But she couldn't help smiling. *And of everything We created you in pairs that you remember the Grace of Allah.*

Omar dumped his bags and kissed his wife. 'You have to see what I bought in my lunch break,' he crowed, fishing among the pile he'd made on the couch. 'Here it is!' He produced a small packet and presented it to her with a flourish.

It was a baby's bib with *we both know that's not an aeroplane* emblazoned across it. The thing was tiny. It was *tiny*. Suddenly, there wasn't enough oxygen in the room. The air was thick with the smell of the raw chicken, and Yasmin's head grew hot. It was happening again. 'Gimme a sec,' she muttered as she pushed past Omar and rushed to the bathroom.

She dry-retched a few times even though she knew she wasn't going to vomit. She lowered herself shakily onto the toilet seat. Her breathing was all over the place. Focus. She tried to detach herself from the surge of panic that threatened to take over her body. She retched again.

Only when she had tamed her ragged sobs and dried her eyes did she emerge from the bathroom. Omar had cut the chicken and was washing his hands. 'Sit,' he commanded, pointing to the armchair.

He stepped out of the kitchen carrying a glass of water and some ginger biscuits. She offered a wobbly smile. 'The smell of the chicken was too much for me,' she said. It was true and it was not true.

Omar didn't smile back. His playful demeanour had been replaced by a doctor's shrewd concern. 'I'm cooking dinner,' he said. 'You rest and grow our baby.'

She nodded and picked up her crochet work from the basket behind her chair. Omar was talking about his visit to the new mosque site with their imam earlier that day. 'The planning permission sign has been graffitied. And there was this sticker on it, "The Union of Concerned Residents". Concerned residents! I said to Imam Jamil, "This mosque is being built for residents. And they are 'concerned' about practising their faith!" And he said, "Let's just hope they used up all of their spray paint on this sign." But I dunno. Think we're gonna have to stock up on Goof Off and eucalyptus oil.'

If she just focused on the stitches, the other thoughts would be crowded out and the panic would pass. She didn't need Edith's instructions any more. She could stitch each row without thinking about what came next. She watched Omar slice carrots in that industrial-style apron that made him look so sexy. She felt like such a fraud.

From: yasmin.malak@threerivers.vic.gov.au
To: esma_sharif58@excite.com
Subject: The Office Kitchen

Mum, you should see what's going on in the lunch room at work. It's the best. Somebody has appointed themselves the Kitchen Police. I don't know who it is yet, but they seem to have full access to the colour printer and use it liberally. The notes just appear overnight. It started out with a small one on the fridge. It has this little poem about how there are no 'dish fairies' in this kitchen and everybody has to clean up after themselves. Oh, and did I mention that all of these notes are illustrated? The fridge one has a picture of one of those yellow cartoon aliens looking bewildered in a fairy costume. If you ask me, nothing screams 'passive aggression' like a print-out of a Minions meme.

There's another above the tea-towel rack. It's telling us to stop using paper towels to dry the dishes and instead use the tea towel this person has lovingly provided from home. It has a picture, a close-up of a child's face. She's a white girl with blonde hair, about nine years old. Her lips are slightly parted in a look of desperate entreaty; her large blue eyes glisten. On her clear-skinned cheek sits a single tear. Inside that tear is the earth, glowing turquoise, streaked with clouds. The implication is clear. Use the tea towel or the kid will cry planets.

On the microwave, there is one of those cheerful 1950s housewife illustrations warning against heating 'heavily fragrant ethnic food'. I think this is a little unfair, given how many people think it's fine to eat curried eggs and tinned tuna at their desks. If I'm lucky, there will be a new note soon about that, too. I can only hope.

Stay tuned, Mum.

Yasmin

The shiny purple document wallet was sealed with a plastic press-stud. Yasmin pulled it open and shook out all the print-outs and pamphlets. Safe sleeping. Gestational diabetes. Avoiding Listeria. Her left hand drifted up absently to stroke the outer corner of her eyebrow. She blinked and pulled her hand away. She re-read the information about soft cheeses, sushi, cold meat. Her hand drifted back to her eyebrow. There. One of the hairs felt wiry and out of place. She longed to pull it out. It would feel so good to just yank the sturdy little hair out, feel its roughness between her fingertips, then feel the smoothness of her eyebrow once it had been liberated of that nasty mutant hair.

But no. She needed to let them grow back. She knew that. Self-control. She forced herself to read a leaflet about alcohol in pregnancy, even though she never drank. She stroked the errant brow-hair with her finger. She could feel her heart beating faster and her breaths shortening. Self-control. Think of something else.

Although – it was just one hair. She didn't care about the others. If she could just pull the stupid hair out she could relax. It would be such a relief, and then she wouldn't have to think about it anymore. One hair wouldn't make a difference. She would leave the rest alone.

She pinched her fingers around the offending hair and gave an experimental yank. So satisfying! Her fingers came away pinching several plucked hairs. Did she get it? She traced the edge of her eyebrow. No! It was still there! This time she took a firmer hold. She pulled again and again. How was she not getting it? Her grip was slipping. She had started now. She might as well keep going until she got the stupid rough hair out. It didn't belong. It bothered her. It had to go.

When the tough little hair finally yielded, she felt a rush of satisfaction. She bounced the springy brow hair between her fingers and stroked the now-smooth edge of her brow. So smooth. So much better.

Only … wasn't it a little *too* smooth?

Yasmin rushed to the bathroom and gazed at her reflection in dismay. There. On the left side of her face. She had half an eyebrow. She heaved a deep sigh and started hunting for her eyebrow pencil. Not again.

From: yasmin.malak@threerivers.vic.gov.au
To: esma_sharif58@excite.com
Subject: The Office Kitchen

ASA, Mum.

Time for an update on the office kitchen. There have been some developments on the tea towel situation. I am here for this.

1. Somebody has coloured the little girl's eyes in red. It is magnificent. She looks like some demonic, earth-spawning child.

2. People keep using the tea towel to get their food out

40

of the microwave. It constantly has food stains on it. I'm not sure this is entirely accidental.

3. There is a new note that has been put on the wall next to the original tea-towel note. This one has a different author. It's long. It's all about the health implications of using tea towels. It even has a little table ('fig 1.1') with evidence of bacterial reproduction over an eight-hour period.

4. Now there is a fresh print-out of the original note. The little girl's eyes are no longer red. And there's extra information on it: 'Studies show, with regular washing, tea towels are as hygienic as paper towels. Kindly DO NOT use this tea towel to handle food. This tea towel is provided for dish drying ONLY.' The other note, the one with the table, has disappeared.

5. Now there's a new note next to the tea towel note. I can't work out if it's the same author as last time or not. It talks at length about the environmental impact of washing tea towels – chlorine in the water supply, water wastage issues, electricity, carbon footprint. Also, somebody's written on the new print-out of the original with a thick black pen. The words 'studies show' have been circled with 'PLEASE CITE' written beside it. And Earth Child now has black, curly eyebrows, giving her a sinister expression.

It's such a treat. Things can only get better from here.
Love you, Mum,
Yasmin

The fragrance of something rich and gingery greeted Yasmin's nose as she opened the front door. She was ravenous. She was always ravenous these days. She was glad it was Tuesday. Tuesday was Omar's early day; he didn't take appointments after 4pm even though the clinic itself ran late.

'Something smells amazing!' she sang down the hall. 'Have you been watching *MasterChef* again?'

Omar had a fascination with food that was belied by his lean frame. While Yasmin saw cooking as a rather mundane means to an end, Omar revelled in finely chopping chillies, basting potatoes in duck fat and blow-torching crème brûlées. He leaned back from the stove to give her a kiss, then he crouched down to talk to her belly. 'And how is your day going, Harun al-Rashid?'

Yasmin smiled. 'Harun al-Rashid?'

'Totally. Silly Mummy doesn't know your name, Harun al-Rashid!' Omar gave the baby a new name every day. Yesterday, the baby's name was Madge.

Yasmin started to forage in the pantry as Omar stirred the wok and checked the rice.

'Don't go filling up on potato chips before dinner!' he scolded, in a sing-song imitation of his own mother.

She closed the pantry door behind her. 'I'm just tidying!' she said, with her mouth full.

Omar spooned the fragrant rice and colourful 'Superfood Stir-fry' into bowls. He had been cooking a lot more often since Yasmin had become pregnant. She still remembered the look on his face when she showed him the two blue lines on the pregnancy test. When your husband's face is so transfigured with joy, it is not right to tell him that you feel despair.

It was not so much that she did not *want* children. Of course she

42

did. She and Omar had talked about it often. It was just that the Yasmin she always pictured having kids was more mature than she was, further along in her career, better organised, emotionally stable. Yasmin-who-had-kids was *ready*.

So she'd smiled brightly when Omar rushed to find his obstetrician friend's number and she smiled brightly now, as he chatted about omega-3s and leafy greens. She could feel the panic bubbling to the surface. She swallowed and pressed it back down.

From: yasmin.malak@threerivers.vic.gov.au
To: esma_sharif58@excite.com
Subject: The Office Kitchen

As-salaamu alaykum, Mum.

Did you fast for Ramadan when you were pregnant? I'm trying to plan what I'm going to do. It wouldn't be the same to have iftar without fasting first. It wouldn't be like Ramadan at all. I hate not fasting when everyone else is and I'll hate fasting later when nobody else is. It's lonely. Omar doesn't want me to fast at all, and he says he'll fast with me again later when I'm making up the days. This is the ultimate sacrifice for love. You know how grumpy he gets when he doesn't eat.

I finally started crocheting the baby clothes. The bonnet wasn't as hard as I thought it would be. My theory is that if I can make clothes for this baby, I can somehow make myself into a capable mother. It's as if hooking together a bunch of yarn can magically bestow feelings of self-competence. It hasn't worked for the bonnet, but maybe making the jacket is what's going to do it for me?

Update on the kitchen notes: I THINK I KNOW WHO IT IS. I

43

might be wrong, but one of the women from HR, I think her name is Susan, is hanging around the kitchen A LOT. She just seems to be constantly making herself hot drinks and hovering.

There's a fresh tea towel and, I don't know, but I think it might be racist. It's an old illustrated map of Australia, with pictures of landmarks on it like Sydney Opera House and 'Ayers Rock'. There are also some generic kangaroos, dingoes and ... Aboriginal people. They're black silhouettes, holding spears. I don't know why I have a problem with it exactly. Is it because it's a stereotype? Is it because they don't seem like people, but exotic landmarks? Can a square of fabric used to dry dishes really be racist? I don't know. I don't think I know enough to argue about it.

Susan from HR was in the kitchen this morning when I was getting a cup of tea. I was chatting with Steve from Accounts. He was having a go at the whole tea towel situation, just riffing, you know, like, 'What's with the tea towels?'

I joined in. 'I don't know, what do you think: is this tea towel racist?'

Susan interrupted from the other side of the kitchen. She was all irritated. 'That tea towel is *classic Australiana*. You wouldn't understand!' Because I'm not Australian, apparently.

Update 2: Just went past the kitchen again. The notes were gone. The fridge note, the microwave note and all of the notes around the tea towel rack. They are in the bin. All of them. So is the tea towel.

I feel like we've all been on a journey.

CHAPTER FIVE

Edith settled into her seat and arranged her bags around her. She was really enjoying these crochet meetings. She pulled out her work and peered at the crumpled pattern.

'Is that the same doily as last time, or is it a new one?' It was the nice girl she had been speaking to the month before – the Muslim girl, Yasmin.

Edith smiled warmly. 'I think this might be doily number five since last month. My granddaughter is abroad this year, so they're beginning to pile up!'

Yasmin sat down in the chair beside her. 'And who is your handsome chauffeur?' She nodded across to Luke, who was in an animated conversation with Lottie.

Edith looked at him approvingly. Pure charm, that boy. And a born talker. 'That's my grandson, Luke. He's the youngest. He has moved back to Copeton for a bit while his sister is overseas. I told him I can get along just fine on my own, especially since his brother only lives half an hour away, but Luke insisted. I don't know. He seems at a bit of a loose end lately and happy of the distraction.' She frowned, then sniffed. 'But it's not such a bad thing. I probably wouldn't have joined this group if Luke weren't here. I don't drive at night.' She looked across at Yasmin unzipping her workbag. 'Now, what do you have there?'

Yasmin pulled out a dainty little bonnet made up in warm yellow wool. She smiled. 'I'm expecting a baby in September. I thought if I crocheted some baby clothes it might help me. Mentally, I mean.'

Edith nodded. Then she picked up her own work and began a new round. These square stitches laid the groundwork for the pretty lace section after.

Yasmin smoothed the bonnet across her knees. Such a tiny thing. 'I wanted to thank you, Edith,' she said quietly. 'That pattern for washcloths was exactly what I needed.'

Edith eyed Yasmin's belly. 'I'm sure they'll come in handy soon enough,' she said, with a significant arch of the eyebrow.

Yasmin bit her lip and nodded. 'The next piece is a matinee jacket,' she said, 'but I'm getting a little confused as to how it will make up.' She held up the beginning rows, a flat strip that curved around in four places, shaped a little like the outline to half a hexagon. 'How will this ever be a jacket?'

Edith smiled. 'A matinee jacket is one of those things that is impossible to do until you actually make one. It seems overwhelming, but once you're in there doing it, things will begin to make sense.' She took the work from Yasmin and pinched two of the corners together. 'You see, eventually, these corners will join and form the sleeve hole. And the same over here. Then you can continue working this section to make it longer, only you bypass the sleeves. After that, you join the yarn here and here to add the sleeves.' She handed the work back to Yasmin. 'But you don't have to worry about that yet. For now, just focus on building up the yoke. You'll get there. And you can always ask for help if you get stuck later.'

Yasmin began to work a few stitches into the yoke panel. 'Thank you, Edith,' she said.

Edith reached over and squeezed Yasmin's hand impulsively. 'You're not the first woman in history to feel overwhelmed at the thought of having a baby,' she said with a brief nod. 'There is a reason that pregnancies last for nine months. You will need that much time to get used to the idea. And it's impossible to know everything at the start. Just dive in and learn as you go.'

If this were a work meeting, Meredith would insist on it beginning at 7pm sharp. That was the time of the meeting, everybody knew that was the time of the meeting, and any delay in starting would only serve to encourage latecomers. But this crochet meeting was different. It was a social endeavour. This made everything a lot more complicated. She finally decided to schedule five minutes of 'Settling-in Time', allowing people to chat and find their seats. She, meanwhile, could sit safely behind the registration table, taking money and ticking off names.

It was 7.04pm. Yasmin and Edith were sitting in their chairs with their work out and chatting to each other. Good. Lottie was talking and talking and laughing and talking to Edith's grandson. Claire was nowhere to be seen.

Lottie needed to stop talking so that Edith's grandson could leave and they could start the meeting. And where was Claire?

It was now 7.05pm. Meredith stood up from behind her desk. 'Okay, everyone, time to get started.' She tried to do the thing where she made her voice sound hearty instead of stern, but it always came out wrong.

47

She walked over to the whiteboard, where she had everything ready for the presentation part of the evening. Tonight, she was going to teach them all about the properties of plarn – yarn made from plastic bags. Yasmin and Edith were shifting in their seats towards her. Lottie looked like she was trying to insist upon something despite the reluctance of Edith's grandson, but now she was finishing up and moving towards the chairs. But what was this? Edith's grandson was moving towards the chairs too!

'I told Luke he should stay and learn how to crochet. It doesn't make sense to be driving back and forth in this rain!' Lottie said, by way of explanation. No. This was not good. But there was no time to argue. It was almost 7.06pm.

Meredith was a professional. She could give a presentation smoothly and confidently even when her mind was racing. Not even the sound of Claire clattering in the door at 7.15pm put her off.

She looked around the room as she talked. Edith and Yasmin, both listening politely; Claire, red-faced and fidgeting; Lottie, smiling broadly and nodding; and Edith's grandson, leaning forward with his eyes fixed on her. Meredith lost her place.

Late. Late. Late. Why could she never be on time? Claire felt everyone's eyes on her as she entered the room. They had already started, of course. She wanted to sit down quickly and turn invisible, but she remembered her mistake from last time and took a moment to scan the room. There. The chair between Meredith, the Boss Lady, and Lottie, the chatty middle-aged lady, was her target. She had nothing against the Muslim Lady (she had forgotten her name!). She was *glad* the group had a Muslim lady in it. It made everything so much more cosmopolitan. But she wouldn't risk sitting next to her. Things were sure to get awkward. Claire never knew what to say.

At 7.30pm, it was time for Crochet and Chat. Meredith was looking forward to burying herself in her ripple blanket and tuning out all the confusion by focusing on the orderly repetition of stitches. But what was Lottie doing now?

'Meredith will have to teach Luke to crochet,' Lottie announced. 'She's the only other left-hander in the group.'

What? No, this was too much. What was that insane Lottie thinking? Meredith's fingers scrabbled around the inside of her new ball of yarn. Where was that stupid end? Luke sat down in the seat next to her. She attempted a brusque smile, but she had a sinking feeling that she came across more like a startled marsupial than a capable woman of the world. This was a disaster.

Lottie had equipped Luke with a ball of yarn and a hook, but they didn't match. Fingering weight wool and a 7mm hook! Lottie needed to spend less time hijacking meetings and more time paying attention to important things, like appropriate stitch tension. Meredith sighed and fished a 3mm hook out of her zip-up pouch.

Luke smiled broadly as she helped him set up. He seemed to be thoroughly enjoying the experience. She had no idea why. He didn't have a clue what he was doing. First, he tried working with the wrong end of the yarn. Then he was holding it all wrong. She leaned in to thread the yarn around his little finger and over the top of his index finger. Her own fingers accidentally brushed his and she drew them back quickly. The hook was just too small. Luke's hands were large and strong-looking. They looked ridiculous trying to manoeuvre a tiny hook and thread-like yarn. She drew in a deep breath and tried to talk him through the steps. Someone had been fiddling with the heater settings again. It was hot in here. It was far too hot.

Claire was happily stitching away at her pink and yellow bunting as she watched Lottie strongarm Meredith into teaching Edith's grandson how to crochet. It was very entertaining. Lottie sat back down and immediately began chatting to Claire. She moved from topic to topic so quickly, Claire found it difficult to keep up. Soon, though, she found that she didn't really need to. Lottie's conversations were self-powered. For the most part, it was enough for Claire to smile and nod.

Lottie was talking about a new program at her work. 'We're getting new residents in the independent living units. They haven't announced it officially yet, but word gets around. They'll be my new neighbours. I live just down the road. I can't wait – they've been empty for so long. And here's what I've been thinking.' She leaned forward, so Claire did the same. 'The people who are settling there are refugees. So they're starting out with nothing: no furniture, no appliances – nothing. We need to find a way to help them to feel welcome. They'll be our new neighbours after all. Can you guess what I have in mind?'

Claire paused in her stitching and opened her mouth to speak.

'Blankets!' said Lottie with triumph. 'There is nothing like a handmade blanket to warm up a space. I've noticed it with the residents at the cottages where I work. It makes all the difference. Perhaps, if we all worked together, we could make enough so that each unit has one before the refugees arrive. Just a small welcome gesture.'

Claire smiled. She loved the idea of welcoming the refugees, but she was herself yet to complete an entire blanket. 'Perhaps some people can contribute squares, and they can be sewn together to make blankets? And it doesn't have to be just us. Maybe we can put a shout-out on social media or something?'

Lottie beamed. 'Yes! I am liking this idea more and more!'

Yasmin crocheted to the end of the row before she realised her error. She'd sailed right past the corner without putting in an increase. She would have to pull the stitches out until she got back to the part she got wrong.

'Oh no! I'm going to have to frog this whole section!' She showed Edith her mistake.

'What's that?' Luke looked across at them in interest.

Yasmin grinned. 'I mucked up and missed a stitch. So I'm going to have to do a bit of frogging.'

Luke tilted his head to the side. 'Why is it called "frogging"?'

Yasmin began pulling apart her stitches in demonstration. 'Because you rip-it rip-it!'

By the end of the meeting Luke had managed a basic stitch and had created a long green chain. 'It's a bookmark!' he announced. 'I'm a genius!' Luke handed the chain to Meredith with a flourish.

Claire approached Meredith. Her crochet bag still had some yarn poking out of it; her shoulder bag was slipping off her shoulder as she scrabbled for her wallet. Claire always looked like she was about to drop something important. 'Meredith! I'm sorry I was late. I still need to pay you.'

Luke gave a start beside her. 'Oh! I should pay too!' He pulled out a battered wallet from his back pocket.

Meredith frowned. She did not want Luke to pay. If Luke paid, then she would need to write his name down on the registration list. If Luke paid, he would become a *member*. But how could she take the money from Claire and not from Luke? This was getting complicated.

'No, that's okay, Luke, you don't need to pay,' Meredith said crisply. She hoped she could leave it at that.

'It's fine. I don't mind,' he replied. He extracted a $5 note. 'Here. You can keep the change.'

Meredith shook her head. 'You don't need to pay,' she repeated.

Luke held out the money. 'I don't see why not. I had a great time. I'm happy to pay.'

Meredith crossed her arms and ignored the pink shiny note in his hand. 'No,' she said.

He fixed his eyes on hers. 'Meredith, please.'

His eyes were clear and hazel. Meredith looked down. 'No,' she said.

Claire finished counting out $3 worth of odd coins. She looked from Meredith to Luke. 'Special introductory offer,' she said with a grin. 'Your first taste is free. That's how we get ya!'

Luke smiled and then shrugged. He put the note back in his wallet. 'In that case,' he said, 'I'll pay next time.'

Meredith swallowed. Her mouth had suddenly gone dry. She had won this small social battle, but why did it feel like she had lost? And what did Luke mean by *next time*?

CHAPTER SIX

Lottie's computer pinged. 10.25am. Time for her Monday walk-through. She shot off her last email, reapplied her lipstick and fastened her wrap. It was her favourite wrap today, alpaca wool, dusky grey-black, with vivid crocheted autumn leaves sewn on, golden and rusty and deep red, falling down the edge of the front panel. Lottie liked to look nice for her ladies. Though, she mused, as she closed her office door and strode towards Cottage One, 'ladies' wasn't the most inclusive term to use. She mustn't forget George, or Pat, or Frank, or Howard. But they were *mostly* ladies. And, she noted with a wry smile, it would only be the ladies who noticed what she wore.

She pulled out her cheat sheet for Cottage One and ran her eye down it stealthily. She knew the names of all the staff and residents here by heart, but it didn't hurt to run her eyes over the list. Cottage Two had a new girl in the kitchen, and Cottages Three and Four had a new resident each. Lottie breezed through each cottage, greeting the staff and residents and taking note of where the residents were and what they were doing. Some were sitting in the dining room and chatting through the servery to the girls in the kitchen as they prepared lunch, some were watching TV in the living room and some, Lottie was pleased to note, were sitting happily in the sensory garden that had recently been set up. A few were still in bed. She took note of who they were and popped her head in to say hello. Of course, it was important for the residents to have the freedom to sleep in sometimes if they felt like it, but she didn't like for them to spend too much time in bed. 'Get up and get active' was her motto.

At the door of Cottage Five, she heard a welcome sound. Jack, Howard's four-year-old great-grandson, was bellowing in fury. 'No! Nanna! I – can – do – it – my – self!' His tortured expression split into a broad grin when he caught sight of Lottie stepping through the door. 'Mrs Lottie! Mrs Lottie! Look what Nanna Carmel gave me!' he exclaimed, brandishing a half-fastened Thomas the Tank Engine wristwatch.

'Well, look at that!' Lottie replied, crouching down to examine Jack's small wrist. 'Your Nanna Carmel is very good to you!'

Jack's Nanna Carmel was very good to the whole of Cottage Five. Mondays were Carmel's day with Jack, and she never failed to bring him in to visit Howard. Everybody cheered up when Jack and his nanna arrived. Jack knew the names of all twelve residents and all the Monday staff. And he didn't have a cheat sheet like Lottie!

'Mrs Lottie? Do you have a white Tic Toc in your bag?'

Lottie gasped in surprise, as if this wasn't a question Jack asked her every Monday. 'A Tic Toc? Why would I have a Tic Toc?' She reached into her handbag and produced a snap-lock bag with an iced clock biscuit inside. 'Check with Nanna that it's okay to have,' Lottie said.

'I already did! I already did!' Jack was bouncing on the balls of his feet. 'Ask me the time! Ask me the time!'

Lottie solemnly removed the biscuit from the bag and presented it to Jack, clock face up. 'Two o'clock!' Jack exclaimed. 'That one's too easy!'

Lottie smiled. 'I'll try to find a trickier one for next week.'

Jack had a fascination with clocks and clock faces. He loved to look at the large clock in the kitchen and always asked politely to look at the residents' watches. Some people might not have understood why Lottie went to the trouble of purchasing a particular kind of biscuit especially for a single resident's great-grandchild. Lottie would have bought out the entire biscuit factory if it would have encouraged more children to visit. For the residents, one visit from Jack was worth three bus rides, five music sessions and a fully landscaped courtyard all smelling of rosemary.

On Tuesday morning, Lottie plonked a box of raspberry and white-chocolate muffins onto the table and pulled out and took a seat in her regular chair. Lottie liked to bring baked goods to their Tuesday-morning meetings; everybody was more cheerful when they had access to sugar. She always grabbed a butter knife from the kitchen on the way. The team were all women. They liked to slice the treats into smaller portions, even when they planned to eat the whole thing.

Lottie could always hear Barbara and Frida approaching long before she saw them. They chattered loudly as they approached down the hall before bustling in the door and grinning broadly at Lottie. Dorothy and Peg weren't far behind.

Peg leaned over the table and sliced herself a piece of muffin. She'd already made a mug of tea on the way there. 'Are we all here? Should we get started?'

'Yes,' said Lottie, 'we might as well. Cate said she'd stick her head in at some point, but that we should get started without her.'

They set about their usual meeting formalities – although 'reports' often seemed more like 'gossip session'. They could have been five friends chatting at a cafe. It was the muffins that did it, Lottie was sure of it.

The meeting door opened again, and their new manager came in.

'Cate! Welcome! Sit down! Have some muffin!' Lottie was aware that her team were still getting used to Cate's way of doing things, which was why she may have overdone the warmth in her welcome just a little bit.

Cate smiled at everybody and said the usual greetings. She looked as if she wasn't going to have any muffin, but then, seeing that they were cut into pieces, allowed herself a small portion. Lottie breathed a tiny sigh of relief. She knew the only way her team would truly accept Cate as one of their own was if she was complicit in their calorie consumption.

Cate set herself up at the table. 'I wanted to fill you in on an exciting new development we have planned for the independent living units we have on the property.'

Lottie looked up in interest: she really wanted to know more about these plans.

'As you would know, these units have been sitting vacant for some time,' Cate continued. 'We have been having talks with St Maximilian Kolbe Ministries about their refugee settlement program. They have been looking for some affordable housing, close to public transport and shops, that they can rent out to refugees who are new to Australia. They're very interested in leasing our units for this purpose.'

'So, wait: they're going to turn Copeton Gardens into a refugee camp?' Frida interrupted. She looked less than impressed.

'Not at all,' Cate reassured her. 'These refugees have already been processed and are living in the community. This would simply be a low-cost rental option for them to get started. I was talking to Fiona from Max Kolbe about it. Apparently, it's really tricky to find a place to rent these days without a landlord's reference. Our units will help new arrivals to get access to the rental market. After they've rented here for a couple of years, they will have experience and a reference to help them find another place.'

Frida did not look convinced. Lottie suspected the nuance of 'processed' versus 'unprocessed' refugee was lost on her. 'Yes, but is it safe? It doesn't sound safe to me. We need to think of our own residents.'

Cate offered a brisk smile. 'Max Kolbe are only planning to settle women and families. No single men. It will be much safer than leaving those units vacant. And we could certainly use the extra income. If you ask me, this is a great idea. What do you think, Lottie?'

Lottie gave an extra enthusiastic response to balance her staff's quiet suspicion and Frida's all-out resistance to the idea. Lottie didn't like to admit it, but she was embarrassed by Frida's comments. Frida was a lovely person, warm and chatty. She worked hard and genuinely cared about the residents. Lottie didn't want Cate to think that Frida was *racist*. Frida was just a little outspoken. Just a little uneducated in some of her views, that's all. But what could Lottie do? She smiled to counter Frida's suspicious scowl and nodded till it felt like her head would fall off. When Cate left the meeting, Frida had some choice comments to make about 'boat people' and 'Muslims'. Lottie winced and sighed quietly into the steam of her tea.

Lottie brought her mug of tea and cryptic crossword out to the table on her front veranda. One-across at first glance was far too difficult.

She cast her eye about for an easier clue. Five-down had eleven letters. It would be hard to get without any cross letters, but then again, if she got the answer it would open the crossword up nicely: 'Small procedure with harmony involves drink shot'. Lottie scratched her nose with her pencil. She sipped her tea. Was 'small' the definition? Or 'drink shot'? Was it an anagram? A container clue?

A mother walked past the front of Lottie's house with an assortment of noisy children. Young families often passed the house on their way to the park. It took Lottie a moment to recognise that the lady was Claire, from her crochet group. She called out a greeting. Claire looked up and smiled as Lottie walked over to the fence.

They chatted a while, and Claire introduced her to the identical twin girls, strapped in their double stroller, and her golden-haired little boy, who glared at Lottie suspiciously as she smiled at him.

'I've had some more ideas about the Welcome to Copeton group,' Claire said. 'Somebody from Max Kolbe came to talk at Ben and Piper's school, at assembly. There's actually heaps we can do to help, but I think the blankets would be a really good starting point.'

Lottie ushered Claire and the children through the gate. Soon, Claire and Lottie were sitting at the veranda table with a fat brown teapot and a plate of banana bread between them, while Harry marched around the front yard brandishing a Tic Toc biscuit. The twins stayed in the stroller, Lily dozing and Hope regarding them both solemnly. Claire and Lottie pored over the draft – what was it? Website? Social media whatsit? Well, whatever it was – that Claire had put together.

Welcome to Copeton.

This is a place for Copeton residents to meet and discuss ways to welcome our refugee neighbours. This is not a place to post about your multi-level marketing schemes. Nobody wants to hear about your miracle supplements or magic milkshakes.

'That bit's necessary, trust me.' Claire helped herself to a piece of banana bread. 'So, I'm thinking we could approach local businesses to help out, talk to the local churches, and if we need to source something specific, we could put a shout-out on the page here.'

Lottie pointed to a link that reads *Become an English language teacher*. 'What's that?'

'Oh, Max Kolbe are running training courses for English language teachers – and they're also looking for people willing to give driving lessons. I'm putting links to all of their programs here.'

They drifted into companionable silence, watching Harry shout at a magpie. Lottie poured herself a second cup of tea. 'If we can get each family one blanket, I'll be happy,' Lottie said. 'A welcome gift that's been handmade with care. That transcends language.'

Claire nodded as she pressed her finger into each crumb on her plate. 'Hopefully we can get enough. Otherwise maybe some of them can be lap blankets or baby blankets.' She ate her finger crumbs. 'Or, like, coasters. Anyway, I better get these kids to the park.'

Lottie walked Claire and the children to the gate, and they chatted a little longer. When she finally sat back down with her crossword, the answer jumped out at her. A small procedure was an 'op'. Could it be 'Opportunity'? Yes! Because the definition would be 'shot', the drink is 'port' and harmony, well, harmony is 'unity'. Lottie filled the letters in with a rush of satisfaction. Now everything was opening up.

Harper pushed the door open and stepped into the cluttered office.

Sue, her community corrections officer, stood up and shook hands with her. 'Make yourself at home, Harper,' she said with a smile.

Harper did not smile back.

Sue consulted her file. 'So. Harper. Let's see. You were experiencing some homelessness before your time in prison, but now you have temporary accommodation through the assistance program. You are not in contact with any family members. Currently estranged from your mother and stepfather.' Sue watched Harper carefully as she said this last sentence, as if looking to confirm what was clearly written on her file. 'When we last caught up, you were planning on finding a job. How has that gone?'

Harper grunted at the filing cabinet. She did not want to be here. What was she? A child? And why was there so much pressure for her to get a job? Didn't they realise what it was like out there? It wasn't like there were any jobs to go for. And the ones she did go for didn't want her. Even the worst jobs didn't want her.

The week before, she had sat through a whole hour of staff induction at the supermarket for a job stacking shelves. A burly woman with a clipboard had stood at the front shouting a list of instructions. She wasn't angry at them or anything, and it wasn't even like she had to speak up for them all to hear. She was just loud. It was like her voice had no volume control – or if it did, it was stuck on max. Harper was willing to bet this woman sent all her text messages in ALL CAPS.

The woman had been talking (shouting) about the staff discount card, time sheets and industry super funds. The next part she tacked on, as if an afterthought.

'Oh, and if you have a criminal record, you can leave right now.'

Harper had sat there for another minute, but when the bitch at the front had started barking about 'bathroom breaks' she stood up. 'This is bullshit,' she announced to the room and trudged to the exit.

Now, in Sue's office, Harper glared at the outdated metal cabinet in silence.

'I'm guessing that's a no,' Sue said, with a wry smile. 'It's normal for there to be some difficulty getting back on your feet. There is a not-for-profit service near here that works to match up young people with offence histories with suitable employment opportunities. You remember Sister Pat?'

Harper shifted her gaze from the filing cabinet to Sue's face, peering cautiously into the woman's soft brown eyes. Then she shrugged and looked away.

'Well, Sister Pat is one of the coordinators of this program. I forget what it's called exactly ...' Sue was shuffling through the papers in the file in front of her. 'Ah! Here!' She produced a pamphlet and handed it over. Obviously choosing to ignore Harper's eye-rolling, she went on, 'Here's another one, while I'm at it. Something like this could be good for your community engagement.'

It was a flier for a crochet group. *Whatever.* She fixed her eyes on the clock on Sue's desk. *Can I go now?*

CHAPTER SEVEN

Meredith had made a decision. For this meeting, she would not hide behind the registration table. For this meeting, Meredith would sit in her place at the head of the circle of chairs. For this meeting, Meredith would participate in the 7.00–7.05pm Settling-in Time.

People started to arrive. Lottie was first. Lottie might be loudmouthed and overbearing, but Meredith had to credit her punctuality. She was talking about some AM radio program she'd been listening to in the car. Meredith didn't say anything, but Lottie chattered on. Lottie had the ability to carry on a conversation with very little input from the other party. Would she be yammering on in the same way if Meredith wasn't in the room? Probably. Perhaps she'd strike up a conversation with young Queen Elizabeth on the wall and share opinions with the small portrait of Robert Baden-Powell.

Soon Yasmin joined them. The plan was working well so far. When Yasmin and Lottie arrived, they had simply dropped their money into the tin on the table and sat down. Lottie was still talking, so it felt like they were all in a conversation.

At 7.02, Edith arrived with her grandson. Edith dropped her money into the tin, but then Luke put money into the tin as well. He looked right at Meredith as the coins dropped with a clink. Meredith frowned.

It was not that she *minded*. Everyone was welcome. Except for knitters, of course. Meredith knew that the minute she allowed a knitter to join, they would take over and it would become a knitting club. Knitters always took over. Meredith was surprised that Lottie was not a knitter; she was so good at taking over things.

But part of the reason Meredith had been attracted to the idea of a handcrafts group was because it was unlikely to have any male members. And yet, here was Luke, *looking* at her and striding over to the circle of chairs. Like he was a regular member. Like he *belonged* there.

Luke sat down next to Meredith, actually *next* to Meredith, without asking her or anything. Which was okay. There was no rule against sitting beside her. That seat was sure to be taken up sooner or later. But the room was still relatively empty. There was a protocol: didn't Luke know? She had learnt this from an early age. When strangers (or near-strangers, as in this case) congregate, they must settle at an equal distance from each other, so as to preserve the maximum amount of personal space. As more people arrive, this space will necessarily decrease, but the strangers will continue to distribute themselves equally across the available space until all have arrived.

Luke had defied this protocol. With Edith on his other side (it was okay for Luke to sit next to Edith; they were not strangers and thus operated as a single unit in this case), the circle was unbalanced: three of them in a clump together. It made Yasmin and Lottie, who had correctly sat on the opposite side of the circle, an equal distance apart, look like castaways, adrift on a sea of empty chairs.

But now Lottie was standing up. 'C'mon, Yasmin! We're too far away: let's move a little closer.' Meredith wondered if Lottie's brain was subconsciously trying to correct Luke's mistake by making them all equidistant in spite of the available space. Lottie plonked down on the other side of Meredith, but, with the whiteboard between them, she had retained the required personal space. Even Lottie had the sense to do this. Not like Luke. Luke's upper arm was almost touching Meredith's upper arm. He was very close. Meredith could even smell him. It was barely discernible, but it was there. It wasn't a bad smell. He actually smelled rather nice. But how on earth was Meredith supposed to concentrate when a man (who shouldn't even *be there*) insisted on sitting right next to her and smelling nice and flexing his biceps every time he moved his arm? It was sensory overload. And it wasn't like *Meredith* could move: she needed to be next to the whiteboard!

Yasmin also shifted a chair closer. There was now only one chair space between Yasmin and Edith. While the average space between participants had evened out, there was now a large bank of empty chairs between Lottie and Yasmin. Meredith had set out twelve chairs for the meeting. This would allow for both newcomers and personal space. It didn't make sense to have six empty chairs in a row. When Claire arrived and paid, she sat in the empty space between Yasmin and Lottie, with three empty chairs on one side and two on the other. This was fractionally better. They were now, more or less, equidistant. Meredith stood up to start the meeting.

The door opened again ten minutes later, when they were in the middle of discussing the possibility of a group project. A pale, dark-haired girl stalked in. Meredith noted the tattoos on her arm, and the piercings in her eyebrow and the tops of her ears, and realised the misunderstanding.

'Hello, you must be looking for the guide hall next door.'

'What?' the girl barked.

'The guide hall is next door.' That's where the Alcoholics Anonymous

65

meeting was held. Meredith felt quite proud of her discreet handling of this awkward situation.

The girl frowned in consternation. 'What are you on about?' She pulled an A5 flier out of her shoulder bag. 'Is this the crochet group or not?'

'Oh.' Meredith paused, opened her mouth and then closed it again. 'Oh. Take a seat.'

This would usually be the point where the new person was asked to introduce herself to the group. But this surly delinquent was twenty minutes late. There was no time for that sort of thing now.

'Hello! I'm Lottie! And this is Edith, Luke, Yasmin, Claire and, of course, Meredith. Why don't you tell us a little about yourself?'

Damn that interfering Lottie! There was no time for this. And at any rate, Meredith was reluctant to hand control of the meeting to this unpredictable, angsty teenager, even if it were only for five minutes.

The newcomer cleared her throat self-consciously. 'My name is Harper.' She sat down.

Lottie beamed. 'Welcome, Harper! So: where did you learn to crochet, Harper?'

Harper dropped her bag on the floor with a bang, glared at Lottie and then swivelled to face Meredith. 'Can we get on with the meeting?' she said pointedly. It was rude. It really wasn't acceptable behaviour. Meredith should call her on it. But she decided to let it pass. They should be getting on. Besides, it was satisfying to see Lottie put in her place.

'Absolutely. We've been discussing front-post and back-post stitches. These can be used to give your work a more textured appearance ...'

Harper, now seated, was tapping her foot rhythmically on the floor and staring out the window. If it weren't for the yarn spilling out of her shoulder bag, Meredith could still have sworn she belonged next door and was suffering withdrawal symptoms. When Meredith paused mid-sentence to direct a raised eyebrow at her, Harper shrugged and scowled, but she stopped tapping.

For the rest of the presentation, Harper sat slumped halfway down on a plastic chair between Claire and Yasmin, occasionally tipping the chair back onto two legs. Her satchel was dropped unceremoniously next to her, the straps a clear tripping hazard for anyone walking past. For somebody so small and slight, Harper had a way of taking over a lot of space. As Meredith spoke, Harper glowered. It was as if Meredith had *forced* her to be there.

Edith had been right, Yasmin realised. The matinee jacket remained a mystery until the part in the pattern where she formed the arm holes. After that tricky manoeuvre, which really wasn't that tricky when she got there, it somehow became something that she could work in rows without any trouble. This was nice: she didn't have to check the pattern, just row after row of repeating stitches. She smiled across at Edith and held up her work for her to see. Edith mimed applause.

Lottie had stood up and was talking to the group. 'We've had an idea. We want to start making blankets to welcome the refugees into Copeton. You could contribute a whole blanket or just a square. If we get enough …' Lottie continued talking, but Yasmin's mind drifted. She wondered if her washcloths would work as blanket squares. She would ask Edith. She watched Edith now, smiling and nodding as Lottie explained the plan. Luke sat beside her. It was funny, Luke and Edith did not look at all alike, you couldn't pick them as being family members, but right now, their mannerisms were exactly the same. They both had the same slight tilt of the head, the same attitude of whole-body listening. Yasmin smiled to herself.

Next to Luke was Meredith. Yasmin was curious to see how she would respond to Lottie addressing the group like this. It didn't seem like the sort of thing Meredith would stand for. *Welcome to the Copeton Crochet Collective. All ideas welcome, so long as they are Meredith's.* But Meredith was steadily crocheting, her face impassive. Yasmin took up her own work and resumed stitching.

Meredith did not know what Lottie was going on about, but she did not like it. This part of the meeting was 'Crochet and Chat' not 'Stand up and Address the Whole Group on a Whim'. Meredith had already pulled out her large workbag with the half-made ripple blanket inside. She had hoped she could just crochet and not chat. She had planned to start quickly and look absorbed in her task, but when Lottie stood up and started talking, it threw her off. This wasn't part of the plan. When Lottie finished, Meredith did not respond, but applied herself to the blanket with renewed vigour. Crochet. Crochet and not chat.

'So, how's the ripple blanket going?' Luke was talking to her. But if she didn't look up, he might stop. After all, he might have been asking someone else that question. They had not made eye contact. It was possible she hadn't heard him.

She took in the room surreptitiously. Yasmin was still working on her set of baby clothes; Claire was working on something different from last month – she always seemed to have something new on the go; Lottie was untangling yarn and talking fit to burst; Edith was making a lace doily with thread and a tiny hook; and Harper ... was that a skull? Harper looked like she was making a skull motif out of grey yarn. That girl was an odd unit. Meredith hoped she wouldn't come back.

'Hey. Meredith.' Luke nudged her. With his *elbow*. She looked up, shocked. Luke repeated his question with a smile. Meredith wordlessly held her blanket up for Luke to inspect. Luke picked up the edge of it and spread it across his knees. 'I like this blue bit,' he said matter-of-factly, as if there was nothing strange about them sitting side by side with a blanket across their knees. Almost like … almost like they were in *bed* together. Meredith felt her face getting hot. With a few sharp movements, she gathered the blanket back into her bag.

'Listen, Meredith.' Something in Luke's tone had changed. Meredith couldn't help looking up. He was looking right at her. 'Did I say something wrong at some point? I get the feeling I've done something to annoy you.' That searching look again.

She took a moment to collect her thoughts. 'It's not your fault,' she said slowly. 'It's just that I don't like men.' She tried to infuse a tone of finality into her statement, to verbally emphasise the full stop at the end of the sentence.

Luke's brow wrinkled in confusion. 'I don't understand,' he said.

'I don't like men,' she repeated.

'You don't like men. That can't be a thing,' he deadpanned. 'You can't just *not like* men!'

Meredith shrugged. 'I don't see why not. It's my life. I'm entitled to my own preferences.'

He still didn't get it. She could see that. What was so hard to understand? Then he made a sound of dawning realisation. 'Ohhhh, wait: *preferences*. I understand now: you're not saying you don't like men, you're saying you prefer women. You're a lesbian.'

Meredith rolled her eyes. 'I'm not a lesbian,' she said, in a long-suffering tone. 'If anything, I'm asexual. It's simple: I don't like men. That is all. I don't like mushrooms on my pizza, I don't like aisle seats on the plane and I don't like men. Why can't people just accept this?'

Luke was still frowning in consternation. 'But surely you have men in your life?'

She picked up the blanket and began working a few treble stitches into the row. 'Of course. I work in the building industry. I can hardly avoid it.'

He shook his head. 'Not work colleagues. They don't count. Don't you have any brothers or cousins? Any male friends?'

She pursed her lips and shrugged. She continued stitching.

Luke raised his eyebrows in surprise. 'You've never had any male friends? Ever?'

She shook her head. As a matter of fact, Meredith didn't have much time for friendship in general. It took too much effort and it got in the way of things. But she wasn't going to say that to Luke. She'd learnt that it was one of those things about her that people found hard to accept.

But what was he doing now? He'd put his backpack on the floor beside him and was rolling his shirt-sleeves up to his elbows with a mock-rueful expression. 'Well, I guess that's it. I've got my work cut out for me,' he said, almost dolefully. 'It won't be easy, but I will answer duty's call.'

She frowned. 'What are you talking about?'

He grinned. 'I'm going to be your friend. As an ambassador for the males of the species, it's my duty to befriend you.'

'You don't have to do that.'

'Oh, but don't you see: I must. I would be letting the side down if I didn't at least try.' Luke was becoming more and more animated as he warmed to his theme.

She shrugged. 'Suit yourself, then.' It wouldn't last. Friendships never did with Meredith. In the end, people rejected her. These days, she had no patience for friendships or a 'social life'. Why would she waste all of her energy on something she just wasn't talented at? She

70

was on a good trajectory right now: a successful career, independence, people who respected her. She had no time for distractions. On the other hand, she could see that Luke was not going to give up easily. It would be more efficient to agree with him and let the friendship run its course than to waste time arguing about it.

'Good. That's settled then.' Luke rolled his sleeves down again. 'And now I want to show you something.' He dug into his backpack and produced a piece of crochet work and a fat plastic hook. The work had four balls of 8 ply yarn attached, three brown and one red. He had made a thick crocheted disc and, as he set himself up with the hook and yarn, Meredith could see that he was treating the four strands of yarn as one thick strand.

'I find it easier to work with a larger hook,' Luke explained. 'It's less fiddly that way.'

'What are you making?' she asked.

'Well, if I stop now, it could be a frisbee,' he said, 'but I'm hoping to make a snow beanie.' After a pause he added, 'It feels good – making things with my hands. Knowing it's the only one of its kind. It's satisfying.'

Meredith was surprised. He seemed in earnest. She never expected Luke would like crochet. She thought he was only tolerating it to be polite. 'That's exactly how I feel,' she offered, in a small voice, 'and it lets me fidget in a productive way.'

He laughed and pulled a pen and battered exercise book out of his backpack. 'I need to write that down,' he chuckled. 'Can I use that?'

Okay. That was weird. What was he planning? A handcraft-themed stand-up tour for the Melbourne Comedy Festival? She nodded mutely.

He put his pen away and picked up his work. 'So, Meredith, what sort of work do you do in the building industry?' he asked, as he struggled to wedge his hook into the stitch.

'Marketing,' she answered. 'You should really work your stitches looser. It will make everything easier in the next round.'

'Marketing?' He pounced on this information. 'Listen, could I pick your brain some time over coffee? I have a new project' – he gestured to the exercise book poking out of his backpack – 'that I need some help with. And you're my friend now. Friends help each other,' he added, with a lopsided grin.

She shrugged as Luke got out his phone. As he programmed in her number, she wondered, what had she got herself into?

When Claire got home from the meeting, all of the children were asleep except for Lily. Peter rocked the fussing baby on his lap as he watched *SBS World News*. Claire scooped her up and took her to the change table. It was as she had suspected. What was it with Lily and her 9pm nappies? And had Peter not thought to check her himself?

After she had settled Lily in her cot, she took the small stink-parcel to the outside bin. The stars were out and the air was cool on her face. Peter had pulled the bin to the kerb, ready for tomorrow's collection.

There was someone walking along the street. It looked like the new girl from the meeting: what was her name? Harper. It was Harper. Claire called out to her, and Harper looked up, startled.

'Harper! Did you walk to the meeting? It's pretty far.'

Harper shrugged. 'I don't drive,' she said shortly.

'Are you planning on coming to the next meeting? I could give you a ride if you like?'

Harper said nothing. It seemed like she wasn't going to answer at all. Then: 'Lit.' And she walked off.

CHAPTER EIGHT

From: yasmin.malak@threerivers.vic.gov.au
To: esma_sharif58@excite.com
Subject: Fail.

Hi Mum,

In the 'recently deceased' section of the prayer notices last week, I read that Bahnam Astarabadi had died and there was a big funeral for him this week. I didn't know Bahnam at all but I knew his wife Souma Astarabadi to be a tall, older lady who had a lot to do with the mosque planning committee. I would nod at her and say 'Souma' and she would nod back rather aloofly and this was the full extent of our relationship.

When I spoke to Najma, from my Wednesday Qur'an group, about Bahnam and Souma, she said that they lost a child many years ago and did a lot of ministry for parents who had lost children. My heart went out to Souma and I realised why she sometimes seemed rather distant.

So this morning, we had prayers and a fundraising drive for the drought. And Souma was there. I always feel awkward in this kind of situation, but you have always told Meesha and me it's better to say something than to avoid the person and make them feel even worse. And that it's better to say something sooner rather than later because it will only get more awkward. This was definitely true for me when – well, it's helped me lots of times.

As people were packing up after the service, I found myself side by side with the woman in question, so I seized my opportunity. I turned to her, gave her a little hug and said, 'Souma, I'm so sorry about Bahnam.'

In the moments that followed, I discovered the following useful facts:

1. Bahnam wasn't actually her husband.
2. Her husband is still alive and at home at the moment.
3. This woman was not Souma Astarabadi.
4. This woman's name was Ann.

I also discovered:

5. There may be another reason why this woman was so unresponsive when I called her 'Souma' all these years.
6. Sometimes 'sooner rather than later' does not avoid an awkward situation if soon is too soon to confirm a positive ID.

She was really quite gentle and lovely about it. It was like she wished she could be Souma for my sake but she could not escape the fact that she was in fact Ann and she did indeed have a live husband.

Whatever. Just tell Souma I said hi.

The noise invaded Yasmin's dream before it woke her. She had been dreaming that she was in the pharmacy where she'd worked before moving to Copeton. She'd been carefully writing a name and address on a sticker to go onto the pills, even though she was wearing her pyjamas and Donald Trump was at the counter asking for head lice treatment. She stepped out of the pharmacy, and she was in Karachi for some reason. And the call to prayer was playing. It was really loud. Then she woke up, and the call to prayer was still playing.

She rubbed her eyes and stared at the ceiling in confusion. Then she rolled over and gave Omar a shove. He grunted. She shoved again. That man would sleep through anything.

'Hghg ... whah?' Omar growled.

'Am I going crazy? Do you hear it too?'

'Ugh. It's all I can hear. What gives? Did you tune into The Muslim Hour on, like, Muslim FM?'

'Muslim FM? Really? Not your best work.'

'Hey, I just woke up. You're not gonna get champagne comedy at 7am on a Sunday.'

They both stared at the ceiling for a minute.

'I think it's getting louder,' murmured Yasmin.

The music kept playing on a loop. Then a voice resonated out over the top of the music, as if through a loudspeaker. 'IS THIS WHAT YOU WANT?' it boomed. It was a man's voice, flat and monotonous, and it spoke slowly and deliberately – just amplified to ear-splitting volume. Omar, now wide awake, stepped across to the bedroom window and peered through a crack in the blinds. Yasmin got up and peeked through on the other side. Some sort of van, with a loudspeaker rigged to the top, was crawling along their street. Yasmin squinted. It had been decked out with flags and banners and the words *NO MOSQUE FOR COPETON.*

'IF YOU ALLOW THESE PEOPLE TO BUILD THEIR MOSQUE, THEN YOU BETTER GET USED TO THIS NOISE. YOU BETTER GET READY TO BE OVERRUN WITH ISLAMISTS.'

The van rounded the corner and trundled away. The blaring noise began to fade. Omar and Yasmin stared blankly at one another in the dim morning light.

'Is it just me,' said Omar, 'or did ice-cream trucks suddenly turn feral?'

From: yasmin.malak@threerivers.vic.gov.au
To: esma_sharif58@excite.com
Subject: Pregnancy Questions

Hi Mum,

So, I'm in week 20 of my pregnancy. Baby is now the size of a banana. I got this app on my phone that measures Baby's development. But a banana? That's not a very standard size. Are we talking ladyfinger? Cavendish? Those ones with the red wax on the end? Baby has spent time as a grape, a walnut, a poppy seed and a pea. I think they'll get through the entire inventory of the fruit shop before it's time to give birth. According to the app, Baby is now old enough to have eyebrows, and has fingerprints on his fingers. Or they might be *her* fingers. Omar and I have decided not to find out until the baby is born. Allah (SWT) infuses our world with mystery. I'd like to keep this a mystery too.

But there are some things I definitely want to find out, which is why I need your help.

1. Feet. Did your feet get enormous when you had Meesha and me? I swear I've gone up two shoe sizes. So weird and gross. Perhaps I should start wearing clown shoes?

2. Hair. I have so much hair now. And it's so shiny. I could be a model for a shampoo commercial. Except they don't have Muslim ladies who wear hijab on shampoo commercials. Not ever. It's a conspiracy.

3. Okay that last one wasn't really a question. But this one is. How much does it hurt? No, really: how much? I try to ask other women and they always smile and talk about how wonderful it feels to hold your baby and how you forget all about the pain. Ugh. Spare me. I just want to know the facts. How much did it hurt?

4. I'm scared I'm going to stop being a person when I have the baby. Will becoming a mum make me invisible? Will I become irrelevant?

5. I feel like I'm about to lose everything. What if I'm terrible at this? How on earth am I going to learn everything I need to know? And what will happen to the old me? The me who was good at things?

Yasmin stopped writing. Her breathing was becoming ragged. She already knew that she wasn't going to send this email, but even seeing the words written down was confronting. She wasn't supposed to feel this way. She was supposed to feel overjoyed and hopeful. What was wrong with her?

'Action, comedy, rom-com? What do you want?' Yasmin asked.

She was curled up on the couch, her dark hair tumbling in glossy waves over her shoulders. Omar was loading the dishwasher and watched her from the kitchen as she flipped through the menu of the streaming service with the remote control. He'd like to watch an action movie. Work had been busy, with back-to-back appointments, and he'd barely managed a lunch break. By the end of the day, all of the patients had been grumpy because he was running late. Mrs Ferris had said something cranky about all doctors being 'foreign' these days. Omar was born in Bendigo. He'd like to watch something with lots of explosions that didn't make him think too hard. On the other hand, a rom-com might be a good investment, might set the mood for romance ...

'Omar!'

'What?'

'OMAR!' Yasmin was pointing to the rug in front of the TV.

The thing was tiny. One of those medium-sized spiders, not even a huntsman – Omar forgot what they were called – was ambling across the rug towards Yasmin.

'Kill it! KILL IT!' Yasmin shrieked.

It was such a funny thing about Yasmin. She was so fierce, so fearless. Yet somehow, when it came to small arachnids, she was completely irrational.

'It's just a little fella. Nothing to worry about.'

Yasmin had edged up onto the back of the sofa. Her voice was becoming more and more high-pitched. 'It's getting closer. Omar!'

'There is no way that spider can hurt you. Calm down.'

'Do not tell me to calm down! The whole point of a phobia, Omar, is that it's an irrational fear. Your argument is valid and cogent and has absolutely no place in this conversation. Kill it!'

Omar strolled over to the rug. He didn't mind. He actually kind of liked it. When somebody was as intensely capable and independent as Yasmin, it was hard to do things for her. Spider management was easy, but gave him so much cred.

Yasmin's spider phobia was next-level. It was like all of her anxieties were concentrated onto these small creatures with their odd shambling gait. And Yasmin had been really anxious lately. She thought Omar hadn't noticed, but he had.

Her trichotillomania was back. Most people wouldn't notice that the far corner of her left eyebrow was pencilled on, but Omar knew that Yasmin only started pulling her hair out when she was deep in an anxious state. He knew he couldn't draw attention to it without making her feel worse. He wished she would talk to him. He wished he was better at asking what was wrong.

Omar bent down and picked up the spider with his fingers.

'EW! NO! KILL IT!'

'I'm going to take it outside, the poor thing,' he said.

Yasmin was actually shaking. Her breathing was ragged. 'You should kill it. If you take it outside, you have to take it all the way over the back fence, otherwise it might come back. Maybe you should just kill it. I think it needs to die.'

If it had been one of his sisters, Omar might have teased her, letting the spider crawl up his arm, holding it out for her to see. But Yasmin was not his sister, and Omar did not want to live the rest of his life in celibacy, so he said calmly, 'I'm going to drop it over the back fence. Pray for my safe return.'

When Omar came back inside, he attempted to put his arms around his wife. Yasmin shifted away from him sharply. 'Don't hug me! There could still be a spider on you! Take your jacket off first.'

'You're the boss.' Omar took his jacket off. Then he started unbuttoning his shirt. 'Just to be extra sure.' He pulled his shirt off, sucking in his stomach and clenching his muscles. He was a master of seduction. Was that a gleam in Yasmin's eye?

'Maybe I should take my pants off too. You can't be too careful!'

'Omar! The curtains are open!' But she was giggling.

'Safety first. The pants must go. And I think we should go to the bedroom. The bedroom is definitely spider-free.'

Yasmin was starving. She'd ordered avocado toast twenty minutes ago. Had they forgotten her? Her obstetrician appointment was in fifteen minutes, and while Dr Modi never ran on time, she didn't want to turn up late. Where was the waiter? The cafe was crowded, but the wait staff were nowhere to be seen. She couldn't even see anyone behind the counter. There was a queue of three people waiting. Hang on – her dad was in the queue! How funny! What was he even doing in Highton? She tried to wave, but it was obvious he was in his own little world. She tried calling out to him, but still no reaction. She could see he had his earbuds in. He would be listening to one of his podcasts, no doubt. She would try to catch his eye after he finished ordering. They could sit together.

When it was his turn to order, her dad took his earbuds out and put them away in their little pouch. She smiled, watching him. Khalid Sharif always treated people who worked in service with politeness and respect. She was too far away to hear what he was ordering, but she was willing to bet he'd ordered the free-range Spanish baked eggs. Yasmin had considered ordering them herself, but then figured the avocado toast would be quicker.

She tried to catch her dad's eye as he turned around in search of a table in the full cafe. He would need to share with someone. She tried giving a little wave, but he was completely oblivious. Her dad walked across to a nearby table where a woman was sitting alone. She tried waving again. This was so silly. Then her hand froze mid-wave.

The woman at the table had stood up, and Khalid was greeting her warmly. His eyes were locked on hers. He was trying to say something to this woman over the noise of the cafe. She leaned forward and Khalid cupped his hand, speaking into her ear.

That one movement. That was enough. It would be difficult to explain it, especially to a non-Muslim. But there was intimacy in the way he spoke in her ear, in the look they exchanged. Yasmin was certain she was looking at two people in love. Her stomach churned.

Yasmin snatched the menu up and hid her burning face behind it. This couldn't be happening. She lowered the menu a fraction. The woman was only in her forties, surely? Her dad was sixty-two!

'How can I help you?' Yasmin jumped in alarm. The waiter, nowhere to be found for the past ten minutes, was suddenly *there* at her table. She blinked up at him. The waiter raised a weary eyebrow. 'You were waving at me?'

'Oh, no, that's okay,' she fumbled. 'Actually, no, wait: I'm waiting on avocado toast!' She spoke in a rapid undertone. She definitely didn't want to draw attention to herself. She kept the menu in front of her face.

'What? Sorry, what did you say?' The waiter was loud, he was so loud.

'Avocado toast. I ordered and paid twenty minutes ago.'

The woman was talking to her dad; they were in earnest conversation. She was rather pretty. She wasn't wearing a headscarf, but her clothes were very modest. Yasmin suspected she was Muslim. Another person had joined their table. It didn't matter. The cafe could be even more crowded than this and the couple wouldn't even notice. It was as if they were the only two people in the room.

'And was there anything else you wanted to order?' Where was this waiter before, when she needed him?

'Just the toast, thanks.' Yasmin continued to peer over the top of the menu. But something was happening. The waiter was tugging the menu from her hands.

'If there's nothing more you want to order, I can take your menu, thanks.' The waiter continued to tug.

She tugged back. 'No! Wait! I need the menu! I – uh – I'd like to order a drink!'

The waiter pointed with one hand to the small laminated card wedged between the salt and pepper shakers, his other hand still firmly grasping the menu. 'The drinks menu is just there.'

Her face fell. 'Dessert?'

'Desserts are on the back of the drinks menu. I'll get you your toast.' The waiter expertly twisted the menu out of Yasmin's hands and was gone. She shrank into her seat. She had nothing left to hide behind. Her dad could look her way at any moment.

Not that this seemed likely to happen. Khalid's eyes were locked on the mystery woman. It looked like he was telling some funny story. She was laughing a lot and touching her face.

The cafe's owner appeared among the tables. Yasmin could tell he was the owner because he made it his first order of business to make sure everybody in the cafe was aware of two things. Firstly, that he had arrived, that he was present in the building. Secondly, that this was his cafe, that every latte-sipping patron was a beneficiary of his marvellous hospitality. He erupted onto the scene in a cloud of noisy bonhomie, shaking hands and booming out pleasantries. Now he was approaching Yasmin's table. Why on earth was he approaching her table? The waiter was with him, carrying what looked like her avocado toast.

'I've just discovered that you've been waiting on your lunch for twenty minutes!' The man was bellowing, there was no other word for it. 'This is terrible! Let me make it up to you. A glass of champagne? On the house, of course!'

Yasmin shook her head demurely. It was 11.15am, and she was both pregnant and Muslim. She would not be drinking champagne today. On the other hand, her avocado toast had finally made an appearance, which was certainly a cause for celebration.

'Something soft, then? An orange juice? Yes?' This man was so loud! Several people from neighbouring tables were looking across at her. Her father, however, was so rapt in his date that he hadn't noticed anything. Yasmin looked at her again. She was telling some funny anecdote, and her dad was doing that thing he did, leaning back as he laughed and clapping at the funny parts. Who was this woman? Who was this *usurper*? What was her father *doing*?

Yasmin gave a hasty nod. Orange juice gave her reflux, but she'd suffer anything to make this man shut up and go away. This whole time, her dad had not looked up, not taken his eyes off the woman. They were smiling at each other, as if they shared some secret.

CRASH! 'Ho ho ho! Clean-up in aisle six!' The owner had bumped into one of the waiters and sent a tray of empty coffee cups flying.

Khalid looked up, startled, and then his eyes finally locked on Yasmin's. They stared at each other for a moment. Yasmin's gaze hardened into a glare of seething scorn. She stood up and swept from her table, ignoring his calls.

When she reached the door, she stopped, turned on her heel, returned to her table, snatched up the avocado toast and swept away again. She was starving, after all.

CHAPTER NINE

Haemorrhoids (also known as 'piles') are varicose veins in the rectum and anus ('back passage'). They can be internal, external or a combination of both.

Yasmin's phone rang again. Her dad. She pressed the 'decline' button and continued to read the information sheet on the wall of Dr Modi's waiting room.

The best treatment is prevention. A healthy diet, adequate water intake and a lifestyle enabling regular bowel habits are essential.

Omar walked in. He offered a slightly concerned smile as he sat beside her. 'So, your dad called me,' he said.

Yasmin frowned and turned back to the notice board. *Go to the toilet when you feel the urge, not just at a time of convenience. Do not linger on the toilet reading books or magazines.*

Omar shifted in his seat. 'Do you want to talk about it?'

Haemorrhoids occur more frequently in women in their reproductive years. During pregnancy they are most common in the second and third trimesters and are caused by hormonal changes, pressure from the growing uterus, changes in blood flow, and constipation.

Omar took her hand. Yasmin pulled it away and pressed it to her head. 'Did he tell you he was on a *date*? Did he tell you he was there with *another woman*? How could he do this to me?' she hissed. 'How could he betray Mum like this?' She felt the panic bubbling up again. She closed her eyes and paid attention to her breathing.

'He told me he was having lunch with a lady and that he hasn't told you about her yet. He said you seemed upset.'

'Upset? Sure, let's go with "upset". I was upset. I was disgusted. I felt physically sick.'

Omar began rubbing her back in small circles. 'How are you feeling now?'

Yasmin fixed her eyes on the poster again (*Section 6: Suppositories and Ointments*). 'Better since I ate something.'

Omar paused as if he were choosing his words carefully. 'Don't you think, maybe, your reaction is a little strong?'

Yasmin glared at Omar in shock. 'How can you say that?'

Omar sighed. 'Do you want your dad to be alone forever?'

'Dad is not alone. He has me. He has Meesha. He has heaps of friends.'

Omar squeezed her hand. 'Just because your dad has started courting' – Yasmin looked up sharply at this word – 'doesn't mean he doesn't miss your mum.'

Yasmin paused. She began to answer and then stopped. Finally, she said, 'I just miss her so much.' Her voice cracked a little. She looked down at her lap and shook her head. A tiny 'no'. 'It's stupid. I should have moved on by now. It's been eleven years. Why does it feel like it was yesterday?' She sniffed and rubbed her eyes impatiently with the heel of her hand. 'I can't deal with the thought of Dad seeing another woman. It makes me sick inside.'

Omar hesitated. 'It was a halal meeting. The lady's brother was there as well.'

Yasmin blinked at Omar. The other person at the table. He wasn't a stranger looking for somewhere to eat his lunch. He was a chaperone. Why did this make everything so much worse?

'I can't deal with all of this. I mean, Dad's moved on. Obviously. Meesha's moved on. What's wrong with me?'

Omar put his arm around his wife. 'Nothing is wrong with you. Don't talk like that.'

Yasmin sat rigidly in his arms. Her fingers pulled agitatedly at the hem of her tunic. 'There is something wrong with me. I haven't told you this, but I haven't been so great lately with my anxiety.' She cast a nervous look at Omar, expecting him to look shocked, but his brown eyes gazed steadily back at her. She took a careful breath and continued. 'I'm just really scared. I'm not ready to be a mum. I'm not ready. Everybody expects me to be happy and excited and I'm just terrified. I can't see how I can do this without Mum here to help me. Plus, I was scared that if I had a baby to look after, there would be nobody to take care of Dad. Who's going to take care of Dad?' She was babbling now. She thought she saw the receptionist shoot her a concerned look.

Omar took Yasmin's hand in his and used her fingers to count. 'Number one: grief is not a running race. You can't get a gold medal in competitive mourning.

'Number two: your dad is a fully competent grown man. Khalid can take care of Khalid.'

Omar took a breath and looked at the poster on the wall. Yasmin looked at him. 'And number three?'

'How do you know there's a number three?'

'You always have a number three.'

Omar paused. 'Number three: do you mean to tell me that the whole reason you've been anxious all this time is because you thought you might not get an A+ in parenting?' Omar kissed Yasmin's hand and made the little half-shrug he did when he wanted people to think what he was saying was just incidental. His voice dropped a fraction of a decibel. 'I was convinced that you were upset about having a baby because you didn't want to be trapped in a relationship with me. That's what I thought it was this whole time. And I didn't want to ask because, well ...'

Yasmin leaned her head on Omar's shoulder. 'Of course you thought it was all about you,' she murmured.

Omar straightened his shoulders. 'I'm an only son in a desi family,' he said, 'of course *everything* is *always* all about me!'

His face brightened slightly at the sight of Yasmin's small smile. 'Anyway,' he continued, 'do you think I'm not also terrified I'm going to do a bad job? We can be crap parents together!'

Later, Yasmin took some nihari in a casserole dish to her dad's house, even though it wasn't Monday. Khalid stood next to the refrigerator as his daughter flitted around the kitchen, wiping and tidying. She fired questions at him as she worked. So far, she had discovered that the woman's name was Noor, that she was in her late forties, that Khalid had been introduced to her by a mutual friend from his Qur'an group.

Yasmin stopped her interrogation and was now cleaning silently. She lifted the cast-iron grate off the stovetop and wiped the near-immaculate surface underneath. Khalid cleared his throat. 'I think your mum would be happy for me.'

'You don't know that!' Yasmin had found a water stain and was rubbing at it with a cloth.

'There are lots of things I don't know,' Khalid said. He watched his daughter as she waged war on his spotless stovetop. 'But there are things I do know. I know that I love you and your sister more than life itself. And I love your mother, of course I do. I think about her every day. And

I think she would want me to be happy.' He sighed and straightened the stack of mail at the end of the bench. 'When your mother died, I thought that was it for me. I fell to pieces. I – well, you know what I was like.' He looked at Yasmin, who had paused reluctantly to look back at him. 'But now ...'

'Now what? Now you've forgotten all about Mum?' She replaced the grate on the stove with a clatter.

Khalid spoke with the same tone of unruffled calm he had used on Meesha when she was nine years old and had screaming tantrums about going to school. 'I could never forget your mother. But I couldn't remain a helpless mess forever. It's been eleven years. And just like I had to learn how to get up in the morning and how to feed and dress myself after your mother died, more recently I've discovered there's room in my heart for love again.'

Yasmin paused and looked warily at her dad. Then she looked back at the dishcloth in her hand. When she spoke, she spoke to the Chux Kitchen Wonder Cloth. 'It just hurts because you've obviously moved on, and I am stuck.'

Khalid shook his head. 'I haven't "moved on". I don't think those are the right words.' He stopped, frowning out the window. 'Imam Jamil said that when his wife died, he had to learn to make friends with his pain. That's what I have done. I made friends with my pain. I will never get over losing your mother. That is a part of me now. But I can function like a human being again. Just in a different way. And the pain still jumps up and bites me in the butt sometimes.'

Yasmin rinsed out the cloth carefully in hot water, then turned to face her dad. 'I miss her so much. I mean, I've always missed her, but lately it's been so much worse. There's so much I want to ask her. I'm so angry that she's not here. She *should* be here.'

Khalid stepped across the kitchen. He stood beside her, carefully put his arm around both her shoulders and gave her what Meesha called The Khalid Sharif Patented Side Hug. 'Of course she should. Can you imagine her as a nani? She would have bought so many baby clothes, the credit card would have broken in two from all that swiping and tapping.' He scanned her face for any hint of a smile. 'Do you still send your mother emails?'

Yasmin nodded. 'I know I'm not supposed to. I know I'm supposed to trust in Allah azzawajal.' She folded and refolded the clean dishcloth. 'It's just been really hard lately. I hadn't sent her any for ages, but lately, there's been so much I've wanted to ask her. So much I wish I could talk to her about. Does that make me a bad Muslim?'

'I don't think that you're a bad Muslim for writing letters to your mum,' Khalid said. 'But don't forget there are people here on earth who love you very much. We can help you with your questions too.' Khalid brightened as he considered this. 'You could ask me. I know lots of things. And I'm very good at researching the things I don't know. And don't forget, your husband is a doctor. There's plenty of questions we could answer for you.'

Yasmin smiled. 'You don't have to solve all my problems, Dad. But the moment you or Omar have first-hand experience of giving birth, let me know and I'll pepper you with questions!'

From: yasmin.malak@threerivers.vic.gov.au
To: esma_sharif58@excite.com
Subject: Fwd: Office Kitchen

Dear Mum,
    Enjoy!
    Y
    – – – – – Forwarded message – – – – –

From: management@threerivers.vic.gov.au
To: Copeton Offices: all
Subject: Office Kitchen

Good morning everyone,

RE: OFFICE SHARED SPACE

The office kitchen is a convenience that allows us to share food together in a collegial, convivial space. This is essential to a harmonious workplace.

It has come to our attention that there has been some confusion around the operation of said kitchen. This is to remind all staff that personal items should not be provided for shared use in the workplace.

In addition, notices, informal memos et cetera displayed in public areas must first be approved by management. Any unauthorised notices found displayed in shared public spaces will be destroyed.

Please allow dishes to air dry using the dish racks provided.

Thank you for your continued cooperation on this matter.

Regards,

Management

CHAPTER TEN

Meredith shifted in her seat. She'd agreed to meet with Luke at a cafe to discuss ideas for some business venture of his. She had arrived early so that she could choose the table. She arranged the sugar packets in their little jar. Her chair was against the wall, she had a good view out of both windows, the bathrooms and the noise of the coffee machine were a proper distance away and her table had the exact number of chairs required. She could not have handled it if the two of them were sitting at a table for four or six. Unused seats at a table itched at her. If there had been three of them meeting, she would have found a table for four and quietly moved one of the seats away before the others arrived. That was one of the benefits of arriving early.

A waiter ambled over to the table and handed her a menu. 'Can I start you with a drink?'

She shook her head. 'I'm meeting someone. I'll order when he gets here.' She wasn't going to *start* with a drink. She was *only* going to have a drink. She was not having a drink because she was thirsty. She would purchase a drink in order to rent this meeting space for the time taken to drink it. Thus, it would be foolish for her to order this beverage *before* Luke arrived.

'You beat me here.' It was Luke, sliding easily into the chair opposite, placing his backpack on the ground. It was then that she realised that she'd made a mistake in selecting the table. It was too small. It was far too small. The whole *cafe* seemed smaller. Meredith had forgotten how *big* Luke was: tall and broad-chested, he seemed to have his own gravity, his own atmosphere. Their knees were almost touching, she was sure of it. His T-shirt displayed a picture of Astro Boy alongside some words in Japanese and 'The Mighty Atom' in English. It was a little tight. It was, perhaps, a medium. He should have bought a large. Or perhaps it was large and he should have bought extra-large. Meredith didn't know about men's T-shirt sizes. She could definitely tell he had muscles with this inadequately sized shirt. It was distracting. He placed his forearms on the table and leaned forward. The table really was too small. He gave a half-smile. 'What are you in the mood for?' he murmured.

Meredith blinked.

Luke reached over to her side of the table. His hand was *right there*. He retrieved the menu from in front of her and studied it. Meredith quietly released a breath she hadn't known she'd been holding. 'Let's get something to eat,' he said, without looking up. 'They do great wedges here, or maybe some Turkish bread and dips. Or maybe both.' Luke shrugged with a lopsided grin. 'I'm always hungry.'

'I'll just have a mineral water,' she said.

After the waiter took their order, Luke pulled his exercise book out of his backpack. 'Here's what I wanted to talk to you about. I've been playing around with this idea of selling make-your-own beanie kits, and marketing them especially to men. Each kit would contain thick wool, a large hook and instructions. I figure I can't be the only man out there who enjoys making beanies.'

She studied the exercise book full of sketches and notes. 'So you're not selling the beanies, but kits with instructions?'

'That's the idea. It will be fairly straightforward to source supplies and package them. The main challenge will be in marketing. I don't know. Should I make the letters look like they've been crocheted?'

'Ugh. No. That's stupid,' Meredith said, still frowning down at the pages. She looked up suddenly. 'Was that rude? Sometimes I'm rude when I don't mean to be.'

Luke's face broke into a broad grin. 'Not at all! I need your honesty. Tell it to me like it is!'

She continued to study the notes. 'Your angle is not that it's a crochet kit. Your angle is that it's a crochet kit *for men*. You need to emphasise masculinity. If anything, you should downplay the handcrafts side of things. Behave as if this is a new product that hasn't been tried before. Also, think about your market. Who do you imagine will buy this product?'

The waiter arrived with their order. She frowned as she moved the notes out of the way to make room for the food and drinks. It was silly, meeting in a cafe, really. They could get so much more done in a library.

Luke was trying to grasp a potato wedge by one of its corners. 'Ow! Hot! C'mon, Meredith, have something to eat.'

She shook her head. If she were hungry, she would have ordered something. Besides, she'd already eaten her chickpea salad at her desk before she came. Meredith was allocated a full hour for lunch. If she ate quickly, she could use the rest of the hour for errands or exercise, or mysterious meetings in cafes.

Luke shifted the dip plate across the table. 'I mean it, Meredith. You're doing me a big favour here. It would make me feel better if I could treat you to some food.'

She sighed and looked at the Turkish bread and dips. She made a quick mental calculation of the bread-to-dip ratio and used this calculation to determine the size of the piece of bread she tore. This was important, so as not to end up with too much bread or too much dip. It was actually pretty delicious.

Returning from his lunch break, Malcolm had the lift to himself as he ascended to the top floor. He took the opportunity to burp richly. He really shouldn't have had onions on his burger. His wife had packed him a kale salad for lunch. That was the problem with marrying somebody young and fit: Heidi took far too much interest in his health. Having said that, the salad wasn't half bad. It made a good side dish to his burger-with-the-lot with chips and a large Coke. It was important that he ate the salad. This way, he could answer truthfully when Heidi asked him about it. Honesty, he believed, was critical to a healthy marriage. Having been married three times, Malcolm considered himself an expert on the marital state.

He burped again and then yawned. Why did lunch always make him so sleepy? Perhaps he would close the door to his office, put his large chair on recline and spend some time ruminating on important work-related issues. Yes. With his eyes closed …

As he lumbered out of the lift towards his office, he suddenly stopped in dismay. What was *she* doing there? There: standing in his office like she had every right to be there?

Meredith James was smoothing out a large curling document onto his table. She was placing weights on the corners to hold it in place. Malcolm had little time for Meredith James. Of course, she was clever enough, he supposed, and productive. And there was no doubt she was good-looking: nice hair, great figure and that pert little arse. The issue was with Meredith's *personality*.

He remembered when she had been introduced to him as the new manager of marketing. They hadn't had a female in management before, though there were plenty of women in other roles. Malcolm had sensed from the start that there would be problems.

For one thing, you couldn't talk to her about anything except work. He had made some joke when they first met. 'Meredith, eh? Perhaps I could call you "Merry"?' Then he'd said something clever about 'Making merry'. He couldn't remember how it went now, but it had been very clever. Quite witty. Phil, who had introduced them, had definitely chuckled. Meredith had just looked at him levelly and repeated slowly, 'My name is *Meredith*.' As if he hadn't understood. As if he were an *idiot*.

It was like that every time. Any time Malcolm tried to be friendly or to put Meredith at ease, he was rebuffed. Meredith would meet harmless flirting with a scornful raised eyebrow and stony silence. She didn't respond with a giggle and a blush, like the charming girls at reception. It was like she didn't even *understand* wordplay. The woman had no sense of humour, just a bland stare and an impatient click of the pen. Meredith was one of those 'difficult' girls.

And now, there she was, standing in his office – *was she setting up her laptop?* Malcolm stepped into the doorway and cleared his throat authoritatively. Meredith looked up and gestured to welcome him in. She was welcoming him into his *own office*.

'Hello, Malcolm,' she said, giving him a compact smile (Malcolm had told her once that she really should smile more. She had frowned in response). 'Your two-fifteen?'

Ah. Damn. He remembered now. She had asked if she could discuss the site plans with him, and he had said 2.15. He looked at the clock on his wall. It was 2.25.

She raised a single eyebrow. 'Let's get started.' Had it not been Meredith, had it been some other girl, Malcolm might have given a wicked smile and said, 'Feeling toey, are we?' But Meredith was useless with that sort of thing. She had all the charm of a constipated librarian. So he merely put his bag down in silence. He did not like the way she made him feel like he was bumbling.

'I've been looking at plans for stage one,' she continued smoothly, 'and I think we need to make some changes.'

'Oh you do, do you?' This was unbelievable. The woman was so bloody opinionated.

'Yes,' she said briefly, as if she hadn't heard the edge to his voice. 'Firstly, the existing trees on the property. I believe the current plan is to bulldoze and plant afresh?'

Malcolm nodded sullenly. 'That's what makes the most economic sense,' he muttered. Was Meredith going to get all sentimental about trees? She didn't seem the type.

'I'm sure it often does make sense, economically,' she countered, 'but not in this case. If you look here, where I've marked the map in blue, there are some large trees scheduled to be taken down by an arborist. But if we look at the stage three site plan, we can see that this land is earmarked as a park anyway. Surely it would make more sense to retain these trees, rather than plant new ones. And here, where I've marked in pink, is a very large tree, expensive to remove. It's not on park land, but it's close to the boundary. A minor adjustment would be enough to retain the tree without major disruption to the original plans. The trees marked in purple form an avenue along an existing driveway. I'm sure you would agree that this avenue is too narrow to retain for our purposes. However, if we were to establish a median strip, the trees could run down the middle—'

'Meredith, are you one of our engineers?' Malcolm interrupted.

He didn't know why he hadn't interrupted earlier.

Meredith frowned. 'No.'

'Are you our chief accountant?'

'No.'

'What is your role here, Meredith?'

She held his gaze. 'I'm head of marketing,' she said.

'Marketing,' Malcolm repeated with a withering glare. 'So what does any of this have to do with you? Since when are you such an eco-warrior?'

Meredith placed both hands on the table and leaned forward. 'This is not about the environment, this is about saleability. I can't market wasteland.' She reached into her bag and produced a fat document. 'It's all in here. You'll see this approach actually saves money, as well as adding value to the site. I've also proposed retaining the existing farmhouse building, which is in good condition, to use as our site office and cafe.'

He picked up the document and gave it a cursory flick through. It looked like she had done her homework. He hated when she was right.

'I will look into this,' he said in a tone of dignified authority. 'But I must say it will take more than trees and old buildings to attract customers to our site. I hope you're not so busy doing other people's work that you've been neglecting your presentation. Perhaps you need to get back to your posters now?' He attempted a sneer, which faltered under Meredith's deadpan gaze.

Meredith had rolled up the map and was putting the laptop into her bag. 'You have the information. If you need to discuss anything further, you know where to find me.' And she was gone. Malcolm didn't bother waiting until she was out of earshot before he let out a resounding belch. Blasted onions.

Meredith strode back to her office. Things were on track. She had effectively communicated her feedback on the site development, using email, hard-copy and in-person conversation. She was already pursuing tenants for the farmhouse cafe. She was getting better at delegation. Managing people was a challenge, but she was on top of it. As she walked past her team's cubicles she could see the three of them gathered around Steph's desk, deep in conversation. It was clear that some effective collaboration was in progress, and she looked forward to hearing what cutting-edge proposals they came up with. Stuart, the one who was facing her direction, gave a start of surprise when he saw her approach. Meredith gave a nod. She considered giving a thumbs-up, but she could never quite get the hang of those. Still, she couldn't help feeling rather impressed with herself. As far as career goals went, Meredith was doing just fine.

CHAPTER ELEVEN

Meredith straightened the pen on the registration table so that it was parallel with the registration sheet and smoothed the skirt of her dress. She had decided to change out of her work clothes before she came to the meeting. This was a social event, after all. Why shouldn't she look nice? The door opened. She looked up sharply.

It was Lottie. Lottie smiled broadly at Meredith as she handed over her money. 'You look absolutely gorgeous tonight, Meredith! You should wear your hair out more often. Are you going somewhere after this?'

She shook her head. She felt foolish. She could never gauge the right level of formality in clothes, especially at the 'neat casual' level. Lottie leaned in and patted her hand. 'Well I think you look wonderful. Thanks for making an effort just for us.'

She swallowed. Lottie annoyed her sometimes, but she had the gift of always putting people at ease. Meredith had an absurd urge to put Lottie on a workbench and pull her apart like a clock. What was it that made her so adept socially?

The door opened again. Meredith looked up. But it was Harper. And Claire! She was glad that her policy of starting the meeting without waiting for everyone to arrive was beginning to have an effect on Claire's punctuality. She smoothed her dress again as they sat down.

The next people to come through the door were Yasmin and Edith. Meredith eyed the door nervously. If Edith were here, that would mean – but the door closed behind Edith and the two of them walked together to the registration table. It looked as if they had travelled to the meeting together. So. No Luke tonight.

Yasmin smiled. 'You look lovely today, Meredith,' she said, as she dropped her coins in the money tin. 'That dress brings out the green in your eyes.'

Meredith nodded distractedly. Yasmin and Edith sat down and started chatting with Claire.

Lottie was beside Meredith, talking about something she'd seen in the neighbourhood, but Meredith wasn't really listening. Her eyes were on the door. Had Luke stopped coming? Lottie chattered on. Meredith had assumed Luke was a member now. She had assumed he would be at this meeting. She looked at the door again. So he had stopped coming. So what? This was what she wanted anyway. This was perfect.

'Have you seen them?' Lottie's voice cut through her thoughts.

Meredith gave a start. 'What's that?' she asked.

'The spiders. Have you seen them? Do you know what they're about?'

Meredith shook her head. 'No,' she said. 'I mean, yes I've seen them, but no, I don't know what they're about.'

Lottie shrugged and went to join the others. Meredith wrote a small 'X' next to Luke's name and put the pen back down, parallel to the page.

Claire couldn't believe it. They were on time! She sighed and flopped into a plastic chair. Harper sat opposite, glued to her phone. They were soon joined by Edith and Yasmin. Lottie was talking to Meredith at the money table.

'Huge black spiders everywhere. Pretend ones. There are three near work, and I saw two more on the way here. I've no idea what they're about. I think they're protesting something …'

Lottie plonked down opposite them. 'Do you know what's going on with those spiders? They're everywhere.'

Claire had noticed spiders along the way as she'd walked Piper and Ben to school that morning. The first one had given her a fright before she realised it was plastic. 'I don't know. But I've seen them too.'

'They are protesting the mosque,' Yasmin volunteered calmly. 'There is a whole batch of them along the fence of the proposed mosque site. They've been put there by a group that calls itself the Union of Concerned Residents.'

Lottie blushed. Claire was certain she wouldn't have raised the topic of conversation if she'd known it was something so sensitive and controversial. 'Oh. But why spiders? What do they have to do with anything?'

'The spiders are supposed to represent Islam and its insidious spread across the globe,' said Yasmin. 'I've been on their website.'

'That's just creepy!' Claire exclaimed, then she blushed hotly. 'The spiders, I mean, the protesters. Not … I didn't mean … I don't think *Islam* is creepy!'

Yasmin smiled. 'They are creepy. I hate them.'

'What about you, Harper?' said Lottie. 'Do you know anything about the spiders?'

Harper looked up quickly. 'Why would I know anything about them?' she retorted, her tone sharp and defensive. Claire looked at Harper. She still didn't feel like she had a read on this intense, spiky teenager. She remembered how Harper had turned up on her doorstep earlier that evening.

Seven o'clock really is a bit early for a meeting, Claire had thought as she drained the bath water and wrapped towels around Lily, Hope and Harry. *It's obvious Meredith doesn't have kids.* The doorbell rang. Ack! Balancing a twin on each hip, she walked downstairs to open the door.

It was Harper. Claire managed to mask the surprise she felt at seeing the thin, dark-haired girl standing on her doorstep. Of course! She was giving her a lift to the meeting. She'd completely forgotten. Harper was early, too, not that it made much difference. Claire would probably still be scrambling about even if she'd been late.

'Harper! Come in!' Claire felt the familiar creeping shame as she led Harper through a hallway strewn with toys, shoes and a small heap of sultanas. 'Excuse the mess.'

Harry burst into the room, stark naked, and began marching around triumphantly. Simultaneously, Claire felt a spreading warmth on her left hip. Ew.

'Um. I need to go sort all of this out,' Claire said with a fingertip gesture that encompassed her two noisy hip-attachments, and Harry, who was now turning nude handstands on the couch. 'Maybe you could sit and read the paper for a bit?' She nodded at the kitchen table, its surface covered in debris and crumbed over like a chicken Kiev. Harper shrugged, and Claire dashed upstairs.

When Claire had re-emerged, fresh and clean, she heard a commotion in the kitchen. The crash of something being dropped. Harper's voice: 'DUDE, WHAT THE FUCK?' Then she could hear Peter's voice, more subdued, then Harper again, 'You scared me. Who are you? Where the fuck did you come from?'

Peter's voice came back, louder this time. 'I *live* here. This is my *house*!'

When Claire reached the kitchen, she saw Harry sitting cross-legged on the freshly wiped kitchen table, watching the drama play out. He wore a toy fireman's hat and nothing else. Harper was standing at the sink, rubber gloves dripping, glaring indignantly at Peter. On the floor between them was a saucepan lid, half covered in suds, the source of the crash. Harper caught Claire's eye, then pointed accusingly at Peter.

'He shouldn't sneak up on me. It freaks me out.'

Peter looked beleaguered. 'I didn't sneak … I just … headphones!' He pointed at Harper's earbuds. 'All I did was walk into my own kitchen in my own house to find this angry girl dropping dishes and shouting at me. And why is Harry naked?'

Claire looked at the miniature naturist, now standing on the table. 'Harry's always naked.'

Peter nodded. 'Fair point, I guess. But why is there a stranger in my kitchen? And why is she so angry?'

'I'm giving her a lift to crochet group.'

Peter squinted at Harper, then shifted his attention to Harry, who had climbed off the table and was searching the dress-ups bin for a new hat, digging through the costumes with his small bottom in the air. 'I'm going to try to convince him to wear pyjamas. If you've got your thing, you should probably head off now or you'll be late.'

Claire nodded and gave Peter a kiss. 'Twins are clean, fed and asleep. Ben and Piper are getting dropped home soon, but they'll need dinner. Bye!'

Peter made a game attempt to fix things with Harper. 'Okay then. It was nice to meet you …?'

Harper did not fill the gap Peter left for her name. She shot him an incredulous scowl and stomped out of the room.

Claire looked at Harper now, sitting in the scout hall, holding her backpack protectively on her lap, eyes narrowed in suspicion. What was her story?

Yasmin enjoyed chatting with Claire and Lottie. Later she would seek out Edith so she could check she was joining the sleeves correctly on her little matinee jacket.

Claire was talking about the spiders that had started appearing all over Copeton. 'The next thing you know, the media will get onto it and make it into a whole big thing. It's not fair. It makes it look like we're all racist, but we're not. We are multicultural. We love being multicultural. Australia doesn't have a problem with racism. Not really.'

A small, incredulous laugh escaped Yasmin's lips. To be fair, she thought Claire was making a dry joke. Too late, she realised Claire was being earnest.

Claire noticed her reaction and was quick to qualify. 'I mean, I know we have racist people, like the people who keep putting the spiders about, but they are outliers. On the whole, Australia is pretty accepting. We're not a racist country. Don't you think?'

The look Claire gave her was hopeful, almost pleading, and there was a faint echo of that expression in Lottie's face. This was a familiar role. It was Yasmin's job now to make them feel better. She felt that pull. That desire to please. But then she thought of the noisy van trundling through the streets every damn morning, the op-ed pieces printed in mainstream newspapers. The spiders everywhere. The more articulate racists presented as 'experts' on panel shows. Suddenly she found herself saying something quite different.

'You're not really in a position to decide whether Australia is racist or not, Claire. You're white and you're polite. You're in a well-meaning middle-class bubble. Racism doesn't happen to you and it doesn't happen in front of you. This is not your debate.'

She hadn't meant to shut things down so forcefully. She also hadn't expected the whole room to reach a conversational lull just as she began talking. Claire had gone quiet. Retreated a little. Yasmin valiantly tried to bring the conversation back around to more neutral topics, the urge to be seen as the easygoing one stronger than ever now. Then Meredith cut in over the top of her, calling the meeting to order.

At the end of her presentation about Tunisian crochet, Meredith cleared her throat. 'This is our fourth meeting together, and we still haven't settled on a group project. We really need to get a move on with this and make a decision.'

She positioned herself beside the whiteboard. It was currently covered with notes on 'cabled hooks', 'forward rows' and 'return rows'. With a deft tug, Meredith flipped the whiteboard to reveal the opposite side. This board had 'Group Project' written at the top, with 'Objectives', 'Key Outcomes' and 'Proposed Deadline' all set out in Meredith's neat handwriting.

She unclipped a black dry-erase marker and looked around the room. This was one of her key objectives for the group; she needed everyone's full attention. Claire was quiet and still. Yasmin was frowning at her baby jacket. Lottie and Edith were both looking at Meredith, smiling benignly, and Harper was scowling, but that seemed to be her normal face.

'We have a few options. It really shouldn't be too hard for us to set some goals and key parameters and get started. Now—'

'You gotta be kidding me.' Harper's voice cut in loudly over Meredith's.

She paused and looked at Harper. 'Was there something you wanted to say, Harper?' she asked, with a tilt of her chin.

Harper scuffed her shoe against the wooden floor. 'It's – whatever.' She subsided.

'Okay. Very articulate. Well, we really need to get cracking on this group project. This has gone on for long enough.'

'Why are you making everything so complicated? Why can't we just crochet together? That's pretty much all anyone wants to do anyway. Who made you the Crochet Police?' Harper again.

Meredith frowned. 'We can't just keep meeting up and aimlessly crocheting and nothing else. I've done the research. You're welcome to read it. Groups that share goals and projects survive in the long term. Groups that don't have a shared purpose fall apart. People will stop coming if they don't feel like there's a reason to be here.' Like Luke. Luke had already stopped coming. If the others followed Luke's example, it would just be Meredith and her whiteboard, alone in an empty hall.

'Don't you think people will stop coming if you are constantly ordering them around and treating them like fucking shit? We're not little kids. And you're not the boss here.'

'I thought we had a group project.' This was Lottie. 'The blankets, remember? I thought the blankets were going to be our group project.'

Meredith hesitated. 'The blankets are another thing. They aren't our group project.'

Lottie lifted her own chin a fraction. 'Well, I don't see why not.'

Meredith shook her head. 'They are part of another thing.' Why couldn't she form the words?

Lottie was looking at her steadily. 'Another thing? What other thing?'

Meredith tried again. 'I want the group project to be more complicated than just basic squares. I want it to be something that uses all of the skills I taught you.'

Harper spoke up again. 'Wait. We're all crocheters here. It's not a class. It's a group. We don't need some fucking assessment project to prove our skills.'

'Please do not use inappropriate language here.'

'Why? Why do I need to watch my language?' Harper turned to Claire. 'Do you have a problem with the way I talk?' To Yasmin, 'Do you have a problem with the way I talk?' To Lottie, 'Do you have a problem with the way I talk?' She wheeled back around to Meredith, in the wake of startled head-shakes. 'Nobody else cares how I talk, Meredith. I'll talk however the *fuck* I like.'

Meredith glared at Harper. 'Why do you even come here?' she said. 'It's obvious you're not enjoying yourself.' Harper stared levelly back, saying nothing. 'We will make a decision at the next meeting,' Meredith said, still looking at Harper. 'If you don't like this, you are welcome to not attend.'

Edith picked up her lace work and gave it a snapping shake before resuming working stitches into it. 'Well *I* would prefer a little less foul language, but it seems *my* opinion doesn't *matter*.'

CHAPTER TWELVE

Claire felt distracted after the meeting and didn't fall asleep easily. She stumbled about the following morning, barking out general-purpose hurrying commands. They needed to be ready in time to walk. Ben and Piper's school, in their latest effort to torment parents, had introduced Walk to School Month. It was not that she *minded*. Of course it was a good idea to get kids walking and being fit and learning about road safety. It was just that there were so *many* initiatives pushed by the school. No-Hat-No-Play-No-Fun-Today; nude lunches (not playtime without clothes, but wrapper-free food); and every manner of costume day, from Book Week to Come Dressed as Your Favourite Existentialist Philosopher. And, while Claire acknowledged that Piper made an *adorable* Kierkegaard, each drive and campaign seemed to send the same message: 'You're not being a good enough parent on your own. You need a little push.'

And so, she grunted away as she shoved the double stroller up the first steep hill. If they didn't walk to school, Piper and Ben wouldn't get a stamp on their special Walk to School cards, and if they didn't get a stamp on their special Walk to School cards, they wouldn't get a raffle ticket to win their very own Walk to School drink bottle, and, what's worse, they would be *different from the other children.*

The first spider was stuck against a high wooden fence. It almost looked real, except it was *too* large, *too* imposing. Beneath the spider was scrawled a URL. They saw six more spiders before they reached the school gate. Some were at eye level, but most were up high, out of reach. All seemed ugly and menacing.

It wasn't until Claire was walking back down the hill after dropping Ben and Piper at school that she realised she was still feeling angry about last night. Why did Yasmin talk to her like that? It had made her feel so small. And it wasn't even like she had said something bad.

As she opened her front door and hung up her bag, she thought back over the meeting. Later in the evening, when it came to Crochet and Chat, Yasmin had moved away and spent the rest of the night talking to Edith. So it was obvious she was annoyed with Claire. She turned Yasmin's words over in her head. 'Racism doesn't happen to you and it doesn't happen in front of you.' What? So Claire wasn't even allowed to have an opinion now?

Claire's earliest experience of racism was with schoolyard jokes about Aboriginal people. She couldn't remember a specific joke – wasn't there one about a seagull? or a pair of thongs? – but she remembered the premise required to make each joke work: the Aboriginal person in the joke was always stupid or naive, always poor and inarticulate, often shown to be the same as an animal. The joke didn't work unless you accepted this view.

Over time she would learn to wrinkle her nose, shrug and say, 'I don't really like those jokes.' It was a learned behaviour, a polite habit, but it was also true. Racist jokes made her feel yuck.

She didn't come across much racism these days. She had always fondly assumed that was because society had evolved out of the schoolyard. But what if what Yasmin said was true? What if she was 'too polite' to witness racism? Could it be that these things were happening, just out of sight?

She sat at the table and pulled out her tablet. She looked up the website she had seen scrawled next to one of the spiders. The organisation was called UCR, short for the Union of Concerned Residents, but it seemed connected to the groups 'No Mosque for Copeton' and 'Patriots League'. The whole thing was a tangle of Australian flags and random memes and quotes. It took her a while to navigate it properly. There were more spiders, often threatening adorable blond-haired children, and some pictures of a dark silhouette of a burqa-clad figure superimposed next to a lithe white woman in athletic wear. Whoever wrote the content seemed to have an overactive CAPSLOCK key.

Looking at the pictures and manifestos was like watching a clean, white fridge being pulled away from the wall, exposing all the horrible grime and dust behind. The worst was the cartoon halfway down the page. It depicted a version of 'The Evolution of Man', but it was back-to-front. On the left stood an upright fully evolved man, then each image from left to right showed man at an earlier stage of evolution, becoming more crouched and ape-like. The final figure on the right showed a Muslim man, prostrate in prayer.

Claire was so distracted by what she was seeing on the screen that she answered her phone without checking the number. It was Yasmin.

'Hi Claire. Meredith gave me your number. Look' – she drew a breath – 'I didn't mean to be so blunt with you last night. I hope you don't think I was having a go. It's not you. I think I'm just feeling worn down by all of the protests.' She paused. 'It's just this constant feeling of not being welcome in my own town. You know what I mean?'

Claire had the uncomfortable feeling that she didn't know what Yasmin meant, not really. 'I think I was wrong too,' she offered. 'I don't think I realised how bad things really are.'

'Yeah, well. I guess you didn't have to. That's your privilege,' Yasmin said, not unkindly.

'Oh. Okay.' Claire kind of understood the idea of 'privilege', but she wasn't properly across it. 'I feel like I need to learn more about this. I could probably learn so much from you.'

'Um, yeah. Look, I don't mind talking about all of this, especially with you, but …' Yasmin hesitated for a moment, as if she were choosing her next words carefully, 'it can be a bit of a burden being the one who has to be the local expert on Islamophobia. It would be really great if you could also look things up online, maybe, find some things out for yourself.'

'Oh.'

'And try to look for the resources written by actual Muslims. That's a biggie.'

Claire nodded, then remembered she was on the phone. 'Yep. Yep.' She was on the point of asking Yasmin for a list of websites when she stopped herself. She knew well enough how to google.

They chatted politely for a few minutes more. Claire eyed the UCR website as they spoke. Then they said goodbye. It was at this moment that Claire realised Harry had been merrily painting the table with yoghurt the whole time she'd been sitting there. She put her tablet away and went to fetch a cloth.

The crochet class had been Sister Pat's idea. It sounded stupid, and Harper had said no when Pat asked if she was going to join. But, for all that, she'd turned up in the prison activity room the next Wednesday. Because it was fucking Wednesday. What the fuck else was she gonna do?

Besides the inmates, Pat had a lady from outside with her. The woman was smiling brightly but she looked kind of terrified. Harper was willing to bet her whole week's chocolate allowance that 'Judy', as she was introduced, had never set foot inside a prison before. She smirked as she imagined Pat honing in on this tidy parish lady after Sunday mass. Nobody could say no to Sister Pat.

There being no black yarn, she'd grabbed a ball of purple and a hook and sat down. Nervous Judy had talked them through making their first stitch and then making a chain. It wasn't long before they were all trying to mutter and tangle their way through a basic square. Sister Pat moved among them. 'You look like you know what you're doing, Carly – would you give Skye a hand?' 'That's looking good, Harper. Keep it up.'

Each week, Pat would bring in print-outs from websites with free basic patterns on them. Some of the girls would look up patterns during their weekly turn on the computer. The mums made beanies to send to their kids, or you could make stuff for charity if you wanted. Harper never stuck to patterns. She was always testing new and different techniques. When she crocheted, she didn't have to think. Didn't have to play scenes from the past on repeat, imagining what she might have done differently. When Harper was creating, she could just be.

'She's never going to admit it.'

'She has to admit it. There's no way.'

'Nah, she's never going to admit it. She can't step down now.'

'I can't tell if she's upset or not. Her face is, like, *immobile*.'

'I don't think she can move her face at all.'

'Yeah. I reckon they just use the same reaction close-up for everything. Just reuse the same clip. Very economical.'

It was Saturday morning. Friday night in New York. Yasmin and Meesha were watching a trashy reality TV show together, via videocall. As the program played a recap, Meesha's gaze shifted to her sister.

'Are you in a fight with Dad?'

'What? No.'

'He says you're avoiding him.'

'I'm not avoiding – that's not – did you know he's seeing someone?'

'Noor? Yeah. She's okay, I guess.'

'What? You've met her?'

'Of course not. I've only seen her on videocall. We did a three-way chat.'

Yasmin frowned. That's what she'd meant.

Meesha peered at the screen. 'So am I right? Are you "not talking" to Dad right now?'

Yasmin shook her head. 'I'm not "not talking" to Dad. I just really miss Mum.' She pulled on a thread at the cuff of her pyjamas. 'It's like you and Dad have moved on, but I'm just … stuck. I'm a remedial griever.'

'I don't think I've "moved on". I mean, sometimes I do. Sometimes I think I'm fine. I'm totally on top of things. And then something stupid and random happens. Like when we got the consignment of materials for *aloft,* and we're all opening boxes and the *smell.* Something about the smell of that yarn reminded me of Mum and I just started *sobbing*. It was like she had just died a few days ago. And there are workmen and assistants, and I'm just ugly-crying. It was the worst. But I'm an artist. I'm allowed to be dramatic. That's my excuse.'

Yasmin gazed at the reality show without seeing. 'I think I felt like I was on my own, like I was the only one left who wasn't coping.' She blinked then looked at Meesha on the screen. 'Is it wrong to say I'm really happy you find it hard sometimes too?'

Meesha grinned and nodded. 'I get that.' Her smile faded and they drifted into a pause. 'Do you think Mum would have been okay with …?' Meesha's gesture encompassed her blue hair shaved on one side, free of hijab, her artfully torn designer T-shirt, her SoHo loft.

'What are you talking about? You are the success story out of us two. When we were teenagers, you were struggling at school and all the teachers wanted to have "meetings" about your behaviour. Now, when I type "Meesha" into Google, "Meesha Sharif" pops up as soon as I type the second "e". You won the MacArthur Fellowship. You are like one of the Influential People of our Time. And all the critics love you. It's like you can't put a foot wrong.'

Meesha's face had gone small and pensive. 'I'm not talking about the critics, though. I'm talking about Mum. I'll never know what she would think about me. About what I've done.'

Yasmin shifted herself up against the pillows. 'Well I can tell you. She would hate your hair. She would nag you about it all the time. She would worry about you eating enough. She would stress about you being alone in New York. And she would stress even more about you being *not alone*, if you know what I mean.' Yasmin waggled her eyebrows and Meesha gave a reluctant giggle.

Yasmin grinned. She paused before she continued. 'And she would save every review and tape every interview and she would bore Randa Khan and Demet Rasheed to death bragging about you. They would hate it. She wouldn't stop.' Yasmin smiled and quickly swiped at her eyes. 'You would give her one of your pieces as a present and she would put it in the entrance hall, right where you open the door, so that even Jehovah's Witnesses could see it. *She* would preach to *them* about her incredible daughter.'

Yasmin and Meesha laughed. They were both crying a little now.

For a while, they lapsed into watching the TV show. Then Meesha spoke. 'Dad says you've been emailing Mum again.'

'Yeah. A little bit.'

'You can email me sometimes, you know.'

Yasmin looked up. 'Oh, you don't want to hear about the stuff I email Mum about. It's pretty mundane. Like, office politics and stuff. Nothing like your glamorous life!'

'I love that stuff. Mundanity is life. And anyway, glamour is an illusion. I mean, publicity can be glamorous, but that's just a little part of what I do. Most of it's just me in my studio scratching my head and glaring at the wall. If that's not mundane, I don't know what is.'

Yasmin smiled. 'Yeah, okay, but— Oh. Wait. Wait. Look. Look. Bombshell.'

Both sisters turned their attention back to the TV show.

'Haye Allah! But did you see Ralph's face when she did that?'

'We don't know for sure that he was making that face when she said that. Maybe he's reacting to something else and they spliced it in there. Maybe his dinner is gross. How do we know that's his genuine reaction?'

'No. No. Don't do that, Yasmin. You always do that.'

'Do what? I'm just asking the question.'

'Don't over-analyse the editing of it. We need to accept it as it's presented to us. This is art. We need to suspend our disbelief.'

'I'm trying. I'm trying. But the harnesses are straining. So. Much. Disbelief.'

Meesha cackled and snuggled back on her pillows. She looked at Yasmin. 'I love you, sister.'

Yasmin smiled comfortably. 'Yeah. I know. I love you too.'

CHAPTER THIRTEEN

Yasmin sat at a long table in the conference room next to the library. The council had arranged this community Q and A session in response to concerns raised about the mosque and Copeton Gardens' housing of refugees. In her own mind, these were quite separate issues: one was to do with planning permissions for a building, the other was a private rental agreement; but she knew that for many of her colleagues, both were bundled under the one banner: 'The Muslim Problem'. She sighed.

People were beginning to arrive and the neat rows of stackable chairs were slowly being filled. She felt the familiar clenching feeling in her gut at the thought of addressing all of these people. Breathe. In through the nose, out through the mouth. She could see Ahmed and the other members of the mosque planning committee finding their seats. She read over her notes again, checked once more that the representatives from the nursing home and her elderly imam from the mosque were in their places, then closed her eyes for a quick prayer. When she opened them again, there was another feeling in her belly. A squirmy fluttering. For the first time that evening, Yasmin smiled. 'That's right, buddy,' she crooned, stroking her tummy. 'We can do this!'

It was around ten minutes into the meeting, as a representative of the mosque committee was giving a short presentation on the plans for car parking, that they arrived. There were five of them, four men and one hard-faced woman. Three of the men had beards; the other was a skinny youth, who glowered as if to make up for his deficiencies in facial hair. If Omar were there, he would already have thought up names for them. Perhaps, with all those beards, they could be the Kelly Gang? And the woman could be their mother? Yes, that would do. Ma Kelly, Old Kelly, Ned Kelly, Fat Kelly and Kelly the Kid. Of course Omar would have been able to think of something much funnier, but the Omar in her mind still had some good suggestions. She imagined how it would be when it was over and she was at home describing it all to her husband. It was a comforting thought. At some point, this night will be over. Breathe in. Breathe out.

The Kelly Gang remained quiet for most of the discussions about traffic flow and building regulations, but it was an ominous silence. She knew they were waiting for the Q and A part of the evening. As soon as the floor was opened for questions, Ned Kelly stood up. Just like that. She had hoped to choose from a selection of politely raised hands, perhaps start with a person she knew to be sympathetic, but no joy. Ned Kelly had already commanded everybody's attention and he was determined to speak. 'Will the mosque encourage more *Muslims*' – he spat out the word 'Muslims' the way another person might say 'rapists' or 'paedophiles' – 'to move to Copeton?'

Ahmed was a conscientious young man who understood numbers much better than he did people. Yasmin cringed a little as he eagerly started to reassure Ned Kelly that the building plans did indeed allow for future growth. Bless. Ahmed still thought the meeting was about approving a building permit.

Ned Kelly cut in, just as Ahmed began to elaborate on 'future projections'. 'What would you say to the residents who are worried about how this mosque will affect the demographics of Copeton?'

Ahmed cleared his throat and frowned slightly, as if he was only just beginning to realise how out of his depth he was. Yasmin stood up. 'This mosque is being built to cater to the current demographic of Copeton,' she announced in a smooth voice. 'As such, it will have a positive effect on demographics.' She placed a slight and delicate emphasis on that final word. *I know what game you're playing, Ned Kelly. And you don't scare me.*

Ned Kelly gave no acknowledgement of her response but ploughed on to his next question. 'Does the council acknowledge the conflict of interest in having a Muslim member on the committee when they're giving approval for the mosque?'

Yasmin drew a deep breath. The question, while unpleasant, was at least one she had prepared a response for. 'One of the realities of working for local council is the occasional overlap of interests and roles. For instance, when plans for the golf clubhouse were being reviewed, several councillors were also members of—'

She stopped. A blast of music had come from somewhere. Some AV issue. She cleared her throat to continue but Ma Kelly had already got up to talk.

'Why is the council using OUR RATES to house refugees while our elderly are being kicked out to house them? Shouldn't we look after our own first?'

One of the Kellys said, 'Hear, hear!' Another said, 'Shame!'

Yasmin felt a surge of confidence. She knew how to deal with this question. 'First of all, let me assure you that no council rates are—' She stopped. The loud music was blaring out again. It was some sort of traditional Middle Eastern dance music. It dawned on her that this music was no accident. The Kelly Gang sat with expressions of mock innocence and suppressed glee. They must have smuggled in some powerful bluetooth speakers. The music stopped.

That was it. She would take no more questions from the Kelly Gang. She called on one of the older men. Muhamed was a little hard of hearing and spoke with a booming voice. He enunciated his question loudly and deliberately, completely unaware of Ma Kelly's attempts to hold the floor.

'Would you SHARE with us the BENEFITS the NEW MOSQUE will bring to our COMMUNITY?'

Yasmin ignored the loud scoffing coming from the Kelly corner and nodded towards the imam. Imam Jamil smiled warmly, first at Muhamed and then at everyone in the room. 'Thank you, Muhamed.' Here, the scoffs turned to snorts of laughter at Muhamed's name. 'The new mosque will benefit the community in many ways. A mosque, you know, is not only a place of worship, it is a community hub that's—' Imam Jamil stopped. It was the music again.

Yasmin stared at the Kelly Gang in disbelief. Imam Jamil was a good and holy man. He had come through years of hardship and never allowed it to turn him bitter, but remained always prayerful, always kind. Imam Jamil deserved respect. She swallowed the lump that was growing in her throat. She must not cry here, she must not. The music stopped. Yasmin stood up. 'You need to leave now.' She was looking at Ned Kelly, but, really, she meant all five of them.

Ned Kelly stood up. 'I don't know what you're talking about. We've done nothing wrong. That's not our music. It sounds more like *your* music.' The others sniggered and elbowed each other.

She wanted to slap the lot of them, but she forced herself to be calm as she addressed the whole room. 'At any rate, the time is now nine o'clock: we have come to the end of our meeting. Thank you, everyone, for—' That damn music again. She gave a nod and a wave to signify the end of the meeting and quickly started packing up her papers as she strove to keep the hot tears from springing to her eyes. Ned Kelly was dancing like Barbara Eden in *I Dream of Jeannie* while the other bushrangers jeered.

Somehow, she managed to hold it all together while directing the packing up of chairs and tables. She avoided eye contact with all sympathetic allies. Sympathy at this point would bring her undone. As she was carrying her bags and folders to the car, she glimpsed one of the protest spiders tied to the fence. And the stupid thing made her jump in fright. With her free hand, Yasmin savagely ripped the spider off the fence and flung it in the bin. She repeated the exercise for the two other spiders further along and stomped through the carpark. As soon as she reached the cool sanctuary of her car, she burst into angry tears.

There were now at least eight different spider installations in Copeton. Yasmin had been counting. The council cleaning team had been destroying them, but as soon as they got rid of them, still more appeared. At lunch, she decided to take a walk around the neighbourhood to check if any more had sprung up.

There were two spiders on Brookes Avenue. The cleaning team might need a ladder to reach one of them. She stopped to take a few photos so they could assess it. Technically it wasn't her job to do this, but if she left it to someone else, it would take forever to be fixed. She'd already left multiple messages for the cleaners about the reinstallations. Anyway, she was a resident of Copeton, just like anyone else. She had every right to report these things to council.

There was something different about the spiders this time, she could see as she approached them. Something colourful was caught in the fence next to the installation. When she got close enough to see what it was, she gasped and smiled.

After she'd taken photos of these spiders, she went to find the other ones. The same, wonderful thing had happened to almost all of the spiders. Yasmin couldn't keep the smile from her face. Her phone rang. It was Julian from the council.

'Jan said you wanted to talk to me about an urgent clean-up job?' he said.

She grinned. 'No worries, Julian. The problem fixed itself.'

As she walked, she flipped through the photos she had taken. She couldn't wait to get out her crochet bag. All of a sudden, she knew exactly what she wanted to do with her leftover yarn.

Claire's children had started counting the spiders they encountered as they walked to school. Some had been taken down, but more had been put up, in more difficult-to-reach places. As she rounded the Churchill Street corner, with the twins in the double stroller, Piper and Ben in their school uniforms and Harry stopping to inspect every bug and every blade of grass, she came across an intriguing scene.

There was a police car parked on the side of the road. Alongside it was the noisy protest van. It had been playing some Middle Eastern music through its speakers all week. The police looked like they were having an argument with the van's driver, an overweight bearded man.

'Mummy, what are the police doing?' Harry asked in a loud voice.

'Shh!' Claire said sharply. She wanted to hear what was going on. She oh-so-casually slowed her pace. She pretended she hadn't noticed the scene unfolding as she watched from the corner of her eye.

'There have been many complaints from residents. You've made your point. Don't you think it's time to give it a rest?' That was the male officer. He spoke in a slow and measured way.

'I am not breaking the law. It is after seven a.m.' This was the van driver. He stared straight ahead as he spoke, his voice a dull monotone.

'We just think it's time to stop with the early-morning wake-up calls. They're really annoying. And some people even find it distressing.' The female officer. She had a chirpy 'let's all be reasonable' tone.

Just as the van driver was responding to this, another car pulled up, and two people got out and walked over to join the conversation. *The plot thickens!* Claire would soon be out of earshot, even walking at her slowest pace. She decided Ben's shoelaces needed retying and put the brakes on the pusher.

The two newcomers, a man and a woman, were a lot more confident and outspoken than the van man. 'Is there a problem here?' demanded the man, with the air of someone who is in charge of things.

'Has anyone actually broken the law?' asked the woman in an accusing tone. Then she kept asking variations of this question loudly over the top of the police as they tried to respond. ('Has he broken the law?' 'Has he broken the law?' 'Yes or no?' 'Yes or no?')

Claire had spent as long as she possibly could tying shoelaces and pretending to adjust the pusher. As she wandered slowly out of earshot, she could see everybody getting back in their cars. The police looked frustrated, the newcomers triumphant. She guessed the van wasn't going to stop its noisy wake-up calls anytime soon. Still, she had a fun bit of gossip to share at the school gate.

She was mentally rehearsing the bearded man's part using a robot voice, when Piper pulled on her sleeve.

'Mum! Look!' They had reached the next spider installation on their path. Claire blinked in surprise. Why, that was *wonderful*. That was *perfect.* The same thing had happened to the next site. Claire burned with sudden inspiration.

After she had safely deposited Ben and Piper at school, she raced home. She searched through the house, gathering up balls of acrylic yarn in red, green, yellow, black. Then she set to work.

CHAPTER FOURTEEN

Holy Cross Abbey was a large stone building on the east side of Copeton. It was owned by an order of religious sisters, who now lived in a small house on the property. A hundred years ago, the building was filled to capacity with classrooms of novices: young women who would dedicate their lives to celibacy and service – the nurses and social workers of their time. Now, only a handful of sisters remained. There hadn't been a novice in thirty years. Today, the abbey functioned mostly as a retreat centre and a popular wedding venue. Many of the old rooms were converted to office spaces let out to various Catholic agencies.

The beautiful old building attracted a good many tourists: comfortable, middle-aged folks who enjoyed drinking flat whites and buying antiques. But the bluestone archways and gothic spires were wasted on Harper as she stood outside the door of St Maximilian Kolbe Ministries, chewing the ends of her dark, greasy hair.

'This is bullshit,' she muttered. She was just turning to leave when the door opened.

'Can that be Harper? I just spotted you out the window and was saying to Marian how much you look like someone I know. But it turns out you look *exactly* like someone I know! Come in! Come in!'

Harper gave a half-shrug and followed Sister Pat's slightly wobbly gait into the cramped office. A small, unexpected lump had formed in her throat. She swallowed. Sister Pat always acted so happy to see her. It had been so long since somebody had looked happy to see Harper. Of course, she reminded herself, it was Sister Pat's job to be nice to her. Still, Pat's warmth caught her off guard.

Now the dread came creeping back. The first thing Sister Pat would ask her was if she had a job. That's all anybody wanted to know. Then Harper would say that she didn't have one, even though it had been months since she got out – and then she would become less of a person. This was bullshit. She didn't want to be here. She sat on the proffered armchair and glanced fitfully at the door.

'So,' began Sister Pat, 'how's the crochet coming along? The last time I saw you, you were in the middle of that extraordinary shoulder bag. Did you ever see the end of it?'

Harper nodded and reached behind her chair to pull out a crocheted satchel bag. It was simple and elegant, worked mostly in brown jute, with subtle detailing of cream lace at the sides. Two brown leather buckles ran parallel at either side down the front, clasping it shut. Sister Pat gasped in admiration.

'When you first started working with that *garden twine*, I had no idea you would turn out something so lovely. You truly have a gift, Harper.'

She shrugged. Sister Pat wanted to know more details. Where did she find the pattern? Was that front-post treble crochet? What was the jute like to work with?

They sat there for a while holding the shoulder bag between them and talking over the stitches. Harper told Sister Pat how she had found an old leather handbag with holes in it at an op shop for $1.50 and had pulled it apart for its buckles and strap ('Genius!' said Sister Pat). She was surprised to find herself talking so easily. It had been a while since she'd had a conversation like this. Sister Pat was saying how she had given up on the tea-cosy she had been working on when they last met.

'I just can't manage the popcorn stitch,' she lamented. 'Are you supposed to take the hook out completely? And what do you do in the next row? Where do you work your stitches? I kept getting it all tangled about and I gave up.' Sister Pat was treating Harper like she was some sort of expert, like she *respected* her.

But it was bullshit.

'I don't have a job,' Harper announced suddenly. 'I'm not that clever. I'm unemployed.'

Sister Pat gently handed the shoulder bag back to Harper and pulled a folder off the desk next to her. 'Well, of course you don't,' she said. 'You're intelligent, creative, hardworking and full to the brim with initiative. What on earth would employers want with you?'

Harper flared up. 'Are you saying I haven't tried hard enough? I've applied for fucking heaps of jobs. They don't want me.'

'I'm not saying you haven't tried hard,' Sister Pat replied, in her calm, unruffled manner. 'I'm just saying that these employers don't know a good thing when they see it. But don't worry, we'll find a way to muddle through.' She opened the folder on her lap.

'Things are always tricky at the beginning,' Pat continued, as she turned pages of sheet protectors, fat with brochures, documents and handwritten notes. 'You might find yourself having to work lots of little jobs, none of which seem to amount to much. But it won't be forever. The good news is, you are smart, you are literate and you can speak English. That opens up a lot for you that many of my other girls can't access. Now, I seem to remember you were particularly good with computers. I have some data entry and research jobs here. Do you have a computer at home?' Harper shook her head. 'Well, we have an office here with computer, printer, phone and internet that you can rent for five dollars a day if you need it. I've also got a pamphlet route not far from where you live. I know none of this is career-building stuff, but you never know where you'll get a foothold. Actually ...' She paused to think. 'I might have a word with Andrew next door. He could do with a research assistant at Loyola Press. Lord knows they're understaffed.'

Pat continued to chatter as she flipped through her book of contacts. Harper had spoken to other, court-appointed careers counsellors when she first got out. Actually, it would be more correct to say Harper had remained silent in the presence of these careers counsellors while they talked at her. But Sister Pat was different somehow.

Sister Pat moved the folder onto Harper's lap and stood up. 'You keep looking. I need to get something.'

Pat emerged from the other room holding something black and woollen. 'I hope you don't mind: I made you a hat.' Pat placed the beanie in Harper's hands. 'I worked out that this pattern is perfect for praying to. I'm not trying to convert you, I know you're not religious,' she added, somewhat apologetically, 'but I am – I can't help it. I prayed a full rosary for you into this hat. Each round works out to be one decade of the Glorious Mysteries, more or less. I prayed that you would find work and I prayed that you would find peace. And I prayed that you'd come back to visit so I could give it to you. Not everybody does, you know.'

Harper held the hat carefully in her hands. Sister Pat was right – she wasn't religious. She hated God and, what's more, she didn't believe in him. But the thought of somebody putting so much care and so many kind thoughts into a present for her made the lump come back to her throat. She stood up.

'I have to go now,' she said abruptly.

Pat stood up too. 'Come back any time. I mean it. You don't need an excuse to come here.'

Later, as she sat in the bus, Harper shifted the hat around in her hands. *You're an idiot to fall for that shit*, a voice in her head muttered. *She probably has a whole box of them in a back room to hand out to randoms like you. She probably imported them in bulk from China.* She flipped the hat inside out and stopped. She felt tears spring to her eyes. There. Near the edge, in purple embroidery floss, the word *Harper* was neatly stitched.

Sister Pat Baker watched the pale, poorly clad figure stalk off down the path. She hoped the Holy Spirit was guiding her words when she spoke with Harper. She said a quick, fervent prayer for the brooding, closed-up girl. She felt like such a dull instrument sometimes. How was Pat, with her clumsy ministry, ever going to help? 'God's in charge, not me,' she said out loud to herself as she packed her notebook and breviary into her bag. She planned to walk to the inter-church council meeting at the Baptist hall. She hadn't been home that morning to pray the Daily Office with her community, so a prayerful walk was just what she needed to get back on track.

Almighty Father, we thank Thee for the job of this day.
May we find gladness in all its toil and difficulty,
its pleasure and success,
and even in its failure and sorrow.

It was a pretty walk along North Abbey Road. The trees had lost all of their leaves, but their slender branches and twigs looked like lace against the chill blue sky. Today at the meeting, she would see Ruth, the reverend from St Thomas's; Father Iain; Pastor David from the Baptist church; and Imam Jamil from the Muslim community. They really needed to find some more non-Christian faith leaders for their group, but Pat was glad they at least had Imam Jamil. He was such a holy man, with his prayerful aspect and ready smile. Pat could see the light of the Holy Spirit alive in him, even if that was perhaps not the right thing to say. Pat believed it was all the same Light, given different names, but it would not be right to use Catholic terms to describe Islamic spirituality. That might be a good topic for conversation when they next caught up. But now she was getting distracted.

We would look always away from ourselves,
and behold the glory and the need of the world.

And the need of the world was so great at the moment. Today, they would coordinate efforts to help settle the refugees into their new rentals. Many were starting from scratch. So many people wanted to help, but they needed to be careful not to duplicate services, to consider the actual needs of the people they would be assisting and not just the desires of the volunteers.

That we may have the will and the strength to bring
the gift of gladness to others;
that with them we stand to bear
the burden and heat of the day.

Of course, not everyone was rushing to donate their spare refrigerator. There was some shameful sentiment growing in this town. Pat had seen the spiders that were fast taking over every fence, bench and traffic island. There was one coming up around the corner, Pat knew. It was up high. She kept meaning to bring a broom along with her to knock it down, but she'd forgotten again. It just made her so mad. She knew so many people in Copeton who were excited to welcome the refugees, who weren't at all bothered by the building of a

132

mosque. Why were these noisy bigots getting all of the attention? But she was supposed to be praying.

Lord, I'm getting distracted. Please help me to pray.

She could see the spider up ahead, but there was something different about it. What was it? There was something else up there. As Pat got closer, it became clear. Next to the spider, in fluorescent pink, was a crocheted spiderweb. Worked into the centre of the web was a single word: 'WELCOME'. Across the street, the second spider had received similar treatment. This time the spiderweb was bright orange. The website sign that had accompanied the spider had been replaced. Pat took out her notebook and wrote down the new URL. It looked like it was named Welcome to Copeton.

Around the corner was a new spider. A large pink web stretched beside it, making the spider look no longer sinister, but sweet. The next three spiders all had neon webs, often with words stitched into them. Welcome. Together. Community. Diversity.

As Pat continued on her journey, she saw that all of the spiders had been transformed. Most had neon webs containing embroidered messages, but a couple of the installations looked like they might have been the work of other artists. There was a spider on Alford Street that had been placed in its own little woodland scene, with crocheted ladybirds, flowers, toadstools and butterflies surrounding it. It was beautiful. On the pillar of the gate to the town hall, a soft yellow duckling perched innocently, eating a spider. Pat laughed out loud.

There was now one block to go before she reached the Baptist hall. Just enough time to finish her prayers and thank God for this small miracle.

My soul proclaims the greatness of the Lord.
My spirit rejoices in God my Saviour.

CHAPTER FIFTEEN

After work, Yasmin planned to drop in on her dad. Something Meesha had said the last time they spoke had been bothering her. Meesha seemed to think Yasmin was in a fight with her dad. They weren't in a fight, not at all. But when it came down to it, it seemed a long time since they'd had a proper conversation. Ramadan was starting in a few days. It seemed like the perfect excuse to drop by.

Khalid smiled broadly at the sight of his daughter. Yasmin pushed her way into the house and started unloading her shopping bags. 'I got you some oats for suhoor. They are already prepared with all you need in the jar. All you have to do is add milk the night before and they're ready to go in the morning. It's really important that you don't skip the pre-dawn meal, Dad. Even if you go back to bed and get up later, you need to eat. And I want you to drink this whole bottle too. This much water. The whole bottle before the sun comes up.' Yasmin pulled a drink bottle out of another bag.

'How are you, Yasmin?' Khalid looked like he was amused at his daughter's fervour.

'Yup. I'm good, Dad. I've marked the oat jars so you can see how much milk to put in. Or you can just use water, but milk tastes better and you need the calcium.'

'Will you be having this fridge porridge for suhoor as well?'

'Yes. I made heaps, even though I'm not fasting this year. I'm still going to get up early and eat with Omar. It will help me feel like I'm still part of things.'

Khalid took both of Yasmin's hands in his, so that she had to stop unpacking. 'It's good to see you, Yasmin. And you could never not be part of things. It must be hard for you to be doing things differently this year.'

Yasmin made a little shrug. 'It is a bit. I'm not sure if it will even feel like Ramadan if I'm not fasting. But I'm going to make some small sacrifices. I won't eat treats and I'm going to give up social media during fasting hours.'

Khalid gave Yasmin's hands a squeeze and released them. 'I think you are doing just fine.'

Yasmin nodded briefly, then stepped into the kitchen. She opened up the fridge, then stopped. She looked for a moment and then closed the door. Then she opened up the pantry and stopped again. 'You – you have so much food. Dad, there's fruit and salad in here. And it's *still fresh.*' There was already a large box of oats in the pantry. There were leftovers in the fridge. This was not the usual emptiness, sparsely populated with ready-meals and packets of sweet biscuits. These were the supplies of a fully operational kitchen. There was even a large bag of medjool dates, all ready for Ramadan. What was going on?

'Well, yes. I suppose …'

'Why is it – what is this?'

'I'm getting better at looking after myself, and, well, Noor …' He said the name like it came with a small apology.

'Did Noor buy you all this stuff?'

'Of course not! She hasn't been here. We only meet in public. But … we have been watching cooking shows together on the YouTube. I mean, not *together*, but we watch the same shows and talk about them. And sometimes I ask her advice about what groceries I should buy. She wrote me a list.'

Yasmin nodded. 'Okay. That's nice,' she said, and tried to make her voice sound like she meant it.

She began loading the jars of oats and other groceries into the fridge and pantry. Then she busied herself folding up one of the carry bags. 'Meesha says she's met Noor already.'

'Yes. Her exhibition is going very well. Did you know her hair is blue now? Like Marge Simpson. Blue.' His tone was light and chatty. He was choosing to ignore the hurt in her voice.

Yasmin continued to fold. She said nothing.

Khalid lapsed into thought. When he spoke again, his voice was subdued. 'I know …' he paused. 'I know. When your mother died. I know that my "mental health" …' he said the two words like they were foreign, swallowed, then tried again. 'I know that my mental health was …' he scrunched up his face, frowning, pushing his lips out. His hands stretched in front of him, one waving back and forth. It looked like he was describing an overcooked biryani or a sub-par coffee. He ended in a shrug. 'I let you look after me too much. Far too much. And I drove Meesha away.' Yasmin tried to protest, but he held up his hand. 'I did. I did. It took me a long time to get better. I let you be my mother for too long, instead of my daughter.' He shook his head.

Yasmin pushed the folded shopping bag aside. 'No, that's not fair, Dad. I took that role on. I wanted to keep busy. And Meesha was always going to run away to chase her dreams. That's who she is. It didn't have anything to do with you, really.'

Yasmin pulled the folded shopping bag back towards her. She rotated the neat square on the bench in front of her, tapping the corners against the surface. Eventually, she spoke. 'I think one of the reasons I've been so scared to have this baby is because I didn't want to neglect you. How could I care for a newborn without abandoning you? And now you're so much better, so I should feel good, but I don't. Because if you're better, then where is Mum?' Khalid gazed back at Yasmin, but before he could answer, Yasmin spoke again. 'It's weird seeing you with someone else. It hurts.'

Khalid nodded gently. 'I know.'

Yasmin briskly put the folded bag under a coffee cup to weigh it down, then reached for another bag. 'What's Noor like? Does she have any children?'

Khalid watched as Yasmin folded the second bag. 'She divorced five years ago. She has a son who is grown up. She would have liked more children, but … it was hard for her. She is Muslim, of course, and she usually attends the mosque in Clayton.'

Yasmin placed the second folded square under the cup and began folding the last bag. 'And how is she as a person?'

'She is clever. She is smart like a knife.' Khalid had always preferred to invent his own idioms rather than employ existing ones. 'And she is so very thoughtful and so very kind. Every day she thinks, "What can I do to make Khalid's day better?" And then she does that thing.'

Yasmin peered at her father.

Khalid cleared his throat. 'I know that she would love to meet you, inshallah. When you are ready, of course.'

Yasmin nodded slowly. 'I'll think about it.'

Khalid watched as Yasmin finished folding the shopping bag. She stacked all three up together and fastened them with a bulldog clip. Khalid smiled. 'Perhaps you could come to my house for iftar next week?'

Yasmin hesitated. Khalid had always come to *her* house for iftar. This is how it had been ever since she moved out. 'I'll think about it,' she said.

It's remarkable the effect a warm bath can have on a child's mood. 'When the kids are ratty,' Claire's mum would say, 'just add water!' Harry, sweet-smelling and, for a wonder, dressed in his pyjamas, was demurely piecing together a train track. Ben and Piper were in the backyard, and the twins were still napping. Claire could steal five minutes for herself before she started dinner.

Beautiful World had a new post up! And it wasn't even Thursday!

'Racism Under Repair' was the title. There were no words in this post, only pictures. But the pictures were enough to make Claire almost drop her phone.

Two pictures of the vivid pink crocheted spiderweb on High Street. The big one, that said WELCOME. This was followed by more artistically framed pictures of the Copeton spiderwebs, definitely Copeton, and then ...

'My minibeasts!' gasped Claire.

The photos showed the woodland scene Claire had hastily installed on Alford Street. The ladybird and the butterflies, the frog and the flowers, the caterpillar and the toadstool. The detail on the photos was extraordinary. You could see every stitch.

She was distracted as she prepared dinner that night. She forgot to preheat the oven and added minced ginger instead of minced garlic to the meatloaf mix. Did this mean that Siobhan lived in Copeton? There was nothing in the previous posts that suggested she *didn't* live in Copeton. She had to live *somewhere*. But what were the odds? She knew what Peter would say. He would say that given Siobhan had a lot of followers, the chances of her living in the same town as one of them were quite high. But still! This was extraordinary!

She moulded the mince into a loaf shape on the tray. What if she'd seen her before at the shops and she didn't even know it? After all, she didn't know what Siobhan actually looked like. She never posted photos of herself or her family. What if she went to the same dentist or chemist or supermarket as Claire?

She stared out the window at Ben and Piper playing as she washed the mincemeat off her hands. Were there any mums at the school named Siobhan? Not that she knew of. But what if Siobhan was a pseudonym? Of course it was a pseudonym. Siobhan could be anyone!

She thought about Lynette, the uber-capable mother who ran all the school fundraisers. But then Claire thought of the homewares Lynette had bought to stock the school Mother's Day stall. Wooden signs emblazoned with swirling white font: 'This house is powered by love, laughter and PROSECCO', 'Life is the art of drawing without an ERASER', glass bowls of potpourri, oversized mugs shouting 'GIRLBOSS' and 'MOMMY NEEDS COFFEE'. Siobhan could never endure such frippery.

Claire's brain scrolled through more and more possibilities. Every elegant lady she knew or knew about. She squirted tomato sauce, barbecue sauce and chilli sauce across the meatloaf as a kind of makeshift glaze. She needn't have bothered. Dinner was destined to be burnt.

Jim Thompson sat in the short-term rental they called the Frat House at the kitchen table they called Mission Control. Spread out in front of him were all the plans they needed for Saturday: map, running sheet, speeches, list of supplies. The bushy Ned Kelly beard was now gone. Jim Thompson was clean-shaven and ready for action.

For now, it was just him. Gideon was off doing his Islamic wake-up calls in the van. Travis and Justin were lifting weights together in the garage, and Dylan was still asleep. Melinda would probably drop in after the school run. This was like the calm before the storm, and Jim was like a general before battle. He studied the map. His breathing slowed and he felt the rush that came with having a sense of purpose, a place in the world. This. This was worth taking annual leave for. Jim didn't like holidays. You're either sitting on your arse all day doing nothing or you're getting bossed about by some shrill tour guide telling you to get back on the bus. He didn't see the point. He didn't want a holiday; but a mission – that was another story. This was his real work: standing up for Australians, being a patriot, having his say. Working in the bank – that was his day job, but that wasn't who he was.

The march. Straight down Main Street, under the train bridge and then to the oval. That's where they would give the speeches. They had gone through the council, contacted the police, got all the permissions. This was how they would get more locals on board. But it was more than that. It was important for them to have a big event to work towards. It helped morale. Plus, that was the way to get new people involved. You gave them jobs. He'd given Katy a job already. She was putting the spiders up. Of course, Travis and Justin had been pissed off when Jim reassigned their job to the new girl. But Travis and Justin were massive hulking blokes. They couldn't get the job done as well as Katy, who was a nimble little thing and a great climber. Plus, Katy would know how to respond if she were confronted while doing it. She looked tough with all her tattoos, but she was smart.

Travis and Justin came in and went to the kitchen counter and fridge and started using up the last of the milk with their bloody protein shakes. Jim observed them. It would not do to have those two out putting spiders up and confronting people. It was obvious they were just itching to punch someone, and an assault charge was the last thing the group needed.

Travis and Justin: they had no subtlety. That's why it was better that they stayed away from the council meeting: they didn't know how to deal with normies. There was an art to it. You needed to go slowly. Sound people out. A meme here. A one-liner there. See how they reacted before you went any further. Know when to back off: 'Nah, mate, I'm not racist. I just think …' Maybe he could teach Katy that. She was smart.

These days you had to watch your words. It was exhausting. Sometimes you just wanted to relax and be yourself without people calling you out, without the PC police getting on your case. That's the thing about customer service: all day long having to watch your words. All day long having to smile and curtsey and grovel to people who thought they were better than you, even though they were fresh off the fucking boat. That's what Jim liked about the forums. He could say what he wanted and let off steam in a safe place without being called out by the Groupthink Sheeple all just itching to be outraged.

Still, there was a danger in being too comfortable. The others were far too happy to stay in their little group. There was no thought for the future. There was no concept of growth.

And growth was what they needed. They couldn't accomplish what needed to be accomplished with just the likes of Travis and Justin. Jim smirked at them, now sitting at the table after their weights session, heads bent in conversation over their protein shakes. Gay as fuck, and they didn't even know it.

CHAPTER SIXTEEN

The scout hall was cold and the ancient heater made it smell like baked cobwebs. Edith had sent through her apologies, but Yasmin, Claire and Harper sat on the plastic chairs, and, apart from Harper's standard glower, all looked more or less content. Meredith took a sip of water and continued. 'Crocheted baskets may be constructed from a variety of materials, including old T-shirts and plastic bags.'

The door was opening. The hall door always opened with a loud thump-and-screech. Meredith blinked. She'd assumed Lottie wasn't coming because she was usually on time.

It was Luke. Which made no sense. Edith wasn't coming tonight. Or was she? Meredith peered into the darkness behind Luke, but then he closed the door. It was only Luke.

Luke nodded wordlessly at her and moved into the room. He hovered awkwardly, standing behind the circle of chairs. She took another sip of water and continued.

'There are – ahem! – several methods you can use to create the ridge at the base of the basket. My favourite method involves half-treble crochet stitches.' Her heart was racing. That stupid door must have given her a fright. Loud noises did that to her. Luke was still standing at the back of the group, watching intently. He really should sit down. What was he even doing here? Hadn't he quit the group? 'Once you have constructed the base, you can build up the sides for as long as you like until you have the size you need. Then you can finish with an invisible join.' She concentrated on keeping her voice level, her breathing regulated. Luke watched her steadily.

Yasmin gave Claire a poke. Claire looked at her. Yasmin continued to watch the presentation as if nothing had happened. Claire grinned. She wasn't going to get the giggles this time. When Meredith said 'a method for more experienced hookers', Yasmin turned to look directly at Claire with a quirked eyebrow. Claire made a sound like a smothered cough.

Before the meeting started, Yasmin had sat down next to Claire and got her workbag out. She was starting a new ball of yarn. It was soft and buttery yellow. As she reached into the centre of the yarn to find the end, she inadvertently pulled out a large tangle from the middle of the ball.

'Ugh! Yarn barf!' Yasmin exclaimed. 'And I still can't find the end!' Claire giggled. She hadn't heard that expression before. Yarn barf. She giggled again.

Claire gestured to Yasmin's workbag. 'What are you making?'

Yasmin held up something delicate and soft. 'It's a matinee jacket. I'm making a set for the baby. I don't know if I'm having a boy or a girl. You?'

She shrugged as she pulled out her work. It was chunky and textured, worked in a rich rust-orange yarn. 'I'm a bit over this. I'm making fingerless gloves. But I'm bored. Once you make the first glove, there's no mystery! And it looks like I'm going to run out of yarn before I'm finished.'

'They call that "second sock syndrome". The second sock is never as exciting to make as the first.' Yasmin inspected the glove. 'Maybe you could put a stripe in it? Or a different colour for the cuffs? It would be a pity not to finish it. They would be such lovely gloves.'

Claire shrugged again. 'I've thought of that. But what goes with orange? I've gone through every colour in my head and nothing works. Even cream, which goes with everything, doesn't go with orange.'

Yasmin frowned for a moment. 'You're right … but what about grey? Like charcoal grey? You'd have to rework some of the first glove so they'd match, but it would stretch your supply of orange yarn just enough to finish both.'

Claire squinted at her work. 'I never thought of using grey. Well, I did, but I never thought of using dark grey. I think it could work!' She paused and looked around the room. 'It feels funny to be talking about crochet to other people who actually understand what I'm talking about. Talking in real life, I mean, not talking online.' It was also funny to be having a perfectly ordinary conversation with a Muslim person, Claire thought, but she didn't say this out loud. She felt ashamed that she hadn't considered Yasmin to be 'friendship material' before now.

Claire stuffed the glove back into the bag. 'Hey, have you seen those crochet spiderwebs? Do you know who's behind them?'

Yasmin grinned broadly. 'How good are they? I have no idea who is making them, but—'

'All right, let's come to order everybody. It's time to start,' Meredith was calling out over the top of them.

'Somebody should crochet Meredith a gavel,' Yasmin muttered in an undertone to Claire. A bark of laughter that was far too loud escaped

Claire's mouth and she blushed again as Meredith gave her a quizzical look. Yasmin was *funny*.

Meredith, meanwhile, was in presenter mode. She didn't waver even when Luke came in late and stood behind them, casually waiting for a break in the presentation before he sat down. 'So you can see, without the invisible join, the final round has an uneven look. It's obvious where the end of the round is. But when using the invisible join method, you create something that looks just like another stitch, but which lies flat. Here is the step-by-step method. You will need a darning needle for this …'

Claire groaned inwardly. She was forever losing her darning needles. Sometimes she could get away with using a bobby pin instead, but they weren't really pointy enough.

The door opened noisily again. Everyone was late tonight! It was Lottie, with another lady Claire hadn't met before. They clattered inside.

Meredith paused for a fraction of a second before continuing with her presentation. 'Firstly, cut the yarn, leaving a long tail, and remove your hook from the work—'

'Sorry we're late!' Lottie trilled. 'Hi, Meredith! Hi, Luke! Yasmin, Claire, Harper: this is Nina.'

The lady beside Lottie grinned broadly and waved. She looked energetic. Slim with olive skin, her hair was stylishly short. Claire waved back. Yasmin smiled warmly.

Meredith lowered her hook and tapped her foot impatiently.

Lottie beamed around the room. 'Nina works at St Maximilian Kolbe Ministries and is here to talk to us about our welcome project. We've collected a lot of squares already. Everybody here has contributed at least one, and we've had plenty sent in from around Australia as well. Luke, I was very impressed with your Bluey and Bingo squares. They will do well for a children's blanket.'

'How do you know about Bluey and Bingo?' Claire asked, intrigued.

'My nieces are obsessed,' said Luke.

Meredith raised her hook in the air pointedly. 'If you don't mind,' she pronounced with ice in her tone, 'we are talking about invisible joins. Kindly sit down so we can continue.'

'This is great,' said Luke, sitting down next to Harper. 'Do we just sew all the squares together at the end, or can they be crocheted together?'

Harper blinked, and then said, 'Well, you could do either. It depends how you want it to look.' Claire looked up. This was the most she'd heard Harper say to anyone. Harper shrugged at Luke and continued, 'But you would need to be careful not to mix yarns. If you sew a wool square to an acrylic square, the wool square might, like, shrink, and that would pull—'

'HARPER! Please would you stop talking so that we can continue with the meeting. We have a lot to get through and have no time for chitchat.' Meredith's nostrils flared. Her tone had become scathing.

Harper uncrossed her legs and shifted in her seat. 'Look out, here comes the Crochet Police,' she muttered darkly to nobody in particular.

'What did you say?' Meredith snapped.

Harper lifted one shoulder and dropped it. She did not look up.

Meredith tugged her blazer straight and resumed her talk. 'There are several methods you can use if you want to introduce a new colour to your work …'

'I just don't see why you have to be such a fucking bitch about everything all the time.' Harper wasn't muttering anymore. Her voice carried clearly, resonating off the walls of the scout hall.

Meredith gave Harper a cold stare, and Claire said, 'Harper!' but Harper wasn't finished. 'You control everything. It's like this is some kind of yarn dictatorship. Who made you the boss, anyway? I don't remember having an election.'

Meredith sniffed primly. 'I established this group, so I get to say how things are run. We run meetings according to the agenda. We are not controlled by the loudest or the most outspoken.'

She means Lottie, thought Claire. Her skin prickled. She hated conflict. She cleared her throat. 'Let's hear more about invisible joins!' she squeaked lamely.

Harper continued as if she hadn't heard her. 'And what's with the membership fees? Where does all that money go? Are you making a profit off this? Is this your little side hustle?'

Yasmin cleared her throat. 'Great idea, Claire! I'd like to hear about those invisible joins too.' Claire shot her a grateful look.

'What are you even talking about? It's three dollars. And you never pay it anyway!'

Lottie deposited herself onto one of the chairs with a huff. 'Well, I must say, if this is the sort of welcome we give to newcomers, our membership will be in dire straits!'

'It's fine!' said Nina, smiling nervously as she too sat down, then, to herself, she added, 'You obviously have some issues you need to sort out.'

'Answer the question. Where does the money go?'

Yasmin leaned towards Claire. 'There would be some major overheads in whiteboard marker ink,' she muttered in an undertone. Claire choked on an unexpected giggle.

'The money covers hire of the scout hall,' said Meredith, and turned to Claire. 'Are you okay? Do you need a glass of water?'

Claire had descended into a coughing fit. Water streamed from her eyes. 'I'm fine!' she croaked. Yasmin smiled innocently.

Luke spoke up. 'I think we just need to calm down a bit …'

Meredith eyed Luke with distaste. 'I would be a lot more calm if you were to stop interrupting. None of this is on the agenda. We have a lot to get through and we need to stick to the agenda.'

Luke tried a disarming smile. 'Surely we don't need to be so strict with the agendas. I don't think it's important that—'

Meredith snorted. 'Well, there's a great surprise.'

Luke raised his eyebrows. 'What do you mean?'

Meredith glared at Luke. 'Extroverts never think agendas are important. They'd rather just talk over everybody because that's what works for them. Just like how people who don't wash their cups are more than happy to get by without a cleaning roster.'

'But this is a crochet group! Not some high-powered board meeting!'

'Excuse me? I always wash my cups, thank you very much.' Lottie was looking highly offended.

'I would have been more than happy to include Lottie's suggestion on the agenda, had she emailed me in advance …'

'You wouldn't fucking stop going on about us getting a group project last month and now that somebody has one, you don't want it because it's not your idea!' Harper, having found her voice, seemed keen to continue exercising it.

'You can ask anyone, I'm constantly at the sink …'

'Meeting protocols exist for a reason …'

'Look, I can come back at another time. You can find my details on the Maximillian Kolbe website …'

'What's more, we are a crochet group. We are not a social action group …'

'Feel free to call my mobile. Or you can email me. You can always email me if you prefer …'

'Just because I'm an extrovert doesn't mean I don't get to have an opinion too. This is important. Racists are taking over our town. We need people to know they don't speak for us. We need …'

'I even wash other people's cups. I do more than my fair share of cup-washing, I'll have you know …'

'I have a proposal.' Yasmin's voice rang across the hall. Everyone stopped. 'Item 4.3 on the agenda is Crochet and Chat. Meredith, I propose that we utilise this agenda item to discuss this project.'

'I second the motion!' said Claire. She wasn't sure if that was the right thing to say, but it sounded official enough.

Meredith nodded and expelled a long breath. 'Agreed. Now please can we get on with things?'

Meredith was glad when the presentation part of the evening was over. She managed to deliver it, but couldn't help clicking her pen with a rhythmic click-click, click-click as she spoke. If she went along with every idea Lottie had, pretty soon it would be Lottie's group, not hers. As soon as it became Lottie's group, they wouldn't need her any more. They might even start a new group without her in it. That is how it had always gone at school. Meredith would put all of the effort into thinking up a fun game or club. Then other girls would be charmed by her idea and ask to join. Then they would whisper. Then they would go off and make their own group without her, taking her intellectual property with them. Every, every time.

Right now, more than anything, she wanted a nice dark room with no people in it. Crochet time was the next best thing. She pulled her ripple blanket out of its bag and set herself up with the hook and yarn. The feel of the soft, springy yarn under her fingers, the sight of the rich interplay of colours and the anticipation of the predictable repetition of stitches soothed her.

And then Luke sat down next to her and spoiled everything.

She didn't want to talk to Luke. She didn't even want him to be there. He wasn't a real member anyway. He was just there to transport Edith, who was a real member. Without Edith present, Luke was …

'Extraneous,' said Meredith to her stitches.

'What did you say?' said Luke.

'What?' said Meredith.

'I said, "Hello, Meredith,"' said Luke. He was grinning. What was he so happy about?

'Oh,' said Meredith. 'Hello, Luke.' She made a point of turning away and picking up her crochet. This would signify the end of the conversational exchange and the beginning of silent work. She thought she'd telegraphed her intentions clearly, but Luke was still talking.

'Are you okay? Things got a little hairy there before.'

'Hairy?' What was Luke talking about? Her eyes darted to his sandy-brown waves of hair.

'Before. When everyone was arguing. Things got kind of intense.'

Of course. She'd forgotten that 'hairy' was an expression. Why couldn't people just be clear and say what they meant? 'It was fine. It was merely a useful illustration of the need to follow a strict agenda at all times.'

Luke wrinkled his brow. 'What do you mean?'

'We stopped following the agenda and chaos ensued. Arguments and shouting. It was impossible to navigate. This clearly shows why it's imperative to follow the agenda at all times.'

Luke smiled. 'I don't know about that. We're a social group.'

Meredith nodded. 'Yes, but don't you see? I've scheduled opportunities for spontaneity throughout the agenda in deference to that.'

Luke laughed. Meredith frowned. 'What's so funny? When you have an agenda, everything is clear. Everyone knows what to say and when they can say it. Everybody gets a turn, even if they're shy and don't know how to interject. Without an agenda, everything is just a confusing mess.'

Luke's laughter subsided. 'Okay, you might just have a point. Gran sends her apologies, by the way. It was just too cold for her tonight.'

'I know. She emailed me.' *So why are YOU here?* Meredith gave her yarn an impatient tug. 'That's what people do when they can't make it to a meeting. They email through an apology.'

'Oh! So that's why you're cross with me!' said Luke.

'What? I never said I was cross.'

'You didn't need to. I'm sorry I missed the last meeting. I had to go back to work to sort something out for a few weeks. Was I supposed to email an apology? I'm a bit hopeless at that sort of admin stuff.'

'It's not enough to say you're hopeless at something. If you're hopeless at something, you learn to do better. There's nothing difficult or confusing about writing an email.' Meredith shook the blanket smooth across her lap.

Luke unzipped his backpack. 'Well then, let me apologise for not providing an apology to apologise for my absence at the meeting. Later, can we go to a lecture on apologetics? A well-known apologist is speaking about Apology Day.'

Meredith looked at Luke levelly. 'Meeting protocols exist for a reason. When they are in place, things remain fair and respectful' – she paused in her stitching – 'and why is Apology Day the theme for discussion at an apologetics lecture? Apologetics is the discipline of defending religious doctrines through systematic argumentation and discourse. Apology Day is a secular event marking the National Apology to Indigenous Peoples. There is nothing theological about Apology Day. You make no sense.'

Luke groaned. 'Shot down! You're right, I was talking nonsense. And I am sorry for not letting you know I couldn't come. I'll try to do better next time. Now. Can I please tell you what I've been up to?' He produced a beanie from his bag. It was charcoal black with a red stripe. 'This is for you. I wanted to thank you for helping me with my beanie kit idea.'

Meredith took the beanie. It was made from thick, good-quality yarn, probably merino, and felt solid and heavy in her hands. 'You didn't need to do this. I barely helped at all.'

'Yes, you did,' said Luke firmly. He was pulling something else out of his bag now. It was a small metal box, sturdy and industrial-looking. On the lid was stencilled a silhouette of a burly fisherman in a beanie pulling his fishing line above his head, where a large tuna thrashed. Below this were the words 'REAL MEN HOOK THEIR OWN'. Luke flipped the two large, square clasps at the side of the box and opened it. Neatly assembled inside were two balls of thick yarn, a large crochet hook, a fabric tag to attach to the finished product and a booklet of instructions. 'I took a whole bunch of these up to work with me and they sold out in a week. Look here.' Luke fiddled with his phone, then held it out for Meredith to see. It was a group of photos on a social media site, grouped under the hashtag #RealMenHookTheirOwn. Young people, mostly men, sitting on couches around a fireplace crocheting. Men skiing and snowboarding while wearing crocheted beanies. Selfies of people on the slopes with their beanies crusted in snow. Meredith clicked on one of the video posts. It was a crochet tutorial. A close-up of Luke's hands as they worked the stitches, while Luke's voice, with its deep, broad Australian accent, explained the process.

Meredith was suddenly conscious that looking at Luke's phone had brought her much too close to him. She politely handed it back and shifted in her seat. Then she picked up the kit and inspected it. 'Where did you source the yarn?'

'Bendigo,' Luke said. 'I know somebody at the mill there, and we worked out a good deal. The hooks I bought on the internet. They sell them in boxes of five thousand.'

'And where did you say you sold them?'

'At work. I own and manage a bar up in the alpine village at Falls Creek. It's called Powder Keg. That's where I was last month.'

'Meredith! Okay if we talk about the group project now?' It was Yasmin. Meredith nodded, pulling the beanie down over her ears. It was very comfortable.

Yasmin looked around the room as Lottie and Nina stood up and began talking to the group about the work of Welcome to Copeton. When they began discussing blanket dimensions, Meredith, who for some reason was now wearing a beanie, handed Nina the whiteboard marker so that she could demonstrate what she meant.

'We have put a shout-out on the website for people to send in squares as well. It would be great if we could get enough together so that each unit could have its own welcome blanket.'

It was a pity, Yasmin mused. Here was a group of committed residents who were all working hard to make the refugees feel welcome. But you would never hear about their efforts on the news. There was going to be a protest against the mosque and the refugee resettlement in a week. The protesters had applied for a permit to march down Main Street and then congregate at the sports oval opposite the nursing home. Yasmin was certain the news programs would be all over that story. But what about them? How could they let people know there were plenty of people who disagreed with the protesters?

Everyone was listening to Lottie and Nina. Everyone wanted to help. Some of them were crocheting at the same time. Yasmin stood up.

'I'm sorry to interrupt,' she said breathlessly.

'It's the fashion,' said Meredith crisply.

'It's just that I've had an idea of something we can do. About the protest, I mean. I've thought of a way we can fight back!'

CHAPTER SEVENTEEN

There was something exciting about getting up really early in the morning. Not 6am – 6am was boring. But to get up before five? Getting up before five meant travel or concerts or watching Grandpa march in the city or Christmas morning. Claire woke with a start several times in the night and checked the glowing digital display before the alarm finally chirped at 4.40am. She shut it off quickly as Peter stirred beside her, and slipped out of bed.

When she arrived at the site, she could see somebody had already been at work. Neon spiderwebs, some with 'WELCOME' worked into them, were strung up against the fence and in the branches of a nearby tree.

Meredith and Yasmin were setting up. Yasmin was examining the display, shivering a little from excitement and cold. Meredith had a clipboard, because of course she did.

'Hello, Claire,' Meredith called. 'No Harper?'

'Not today,' she replied. 'I don't think Harper does mornings. Hey, I love those fluoro spiderwebs! Was that you or Yasmin?'

Meredith was crossing something out on her clipboard and adding a note. 'No. Those spiderwebs were already here.'

'Hello, everyone!' Lottie's voice cut through the darkness. Claire could just make out her face under her colourful scarf and beanie. Lottie set her big shoulder bag down on a nearby bench and started unloading equipment, decorations and two large thermoses.

Yasmin was unfolding garden chairs. 'Here comes trouble!' she said. Claire looked across as two dark figures approached, a large man and a small lady.

'Luke and Edith!' she called.

Luke waved and pulled off his backpack. Edith gave an excited little skip as she approached them. 'I'm so excited, I almost forgot my false teeth!' she exclaimed.

Lottie had already started working. Wearing reading glasses with bright red frames, she shone a pen torch at a design scrawled on a piece of graph paper. Yasmin, meanwhile, had set up on the footpath with a box of artist's sidewalk chalk.

Luke and Edith were talking with Meredith in a huddle. Claire took her bag to the chain-link fence and began tying flowers to it. Crocheted daffodils, roses, tulips and poppies. Purple pansies and blue forget-me-nots. She had already worked out the design and balance of colour, so now it was just a matter of putting it together.

The fence shook. With a run-up and two big upwards strides, Luke had scaled the wire mesh. He now sat atop the crossbar and took the items Edith passed up him to tie to the top part of the fence. Lottie had finished weaving a 'W' and an 'E' into the chain links with rainbow ribbon. She paused in her work to bring a shopping bag to Edith. 'Can you get Luke to string these up as well?' she asked. 'Some of the children from the Muslim community made them last week.'

'Thanks, Lottie!' Yasmin called from the pavement.

'Right-o,' said Edith, pulling out a colourful spiderweb fashioned out of icy pole sticks and string. 'These look terrific.'

Yasmin stood up, dusting chalk from her hands. She peered up at Luke. 'I wonder if I should get up on the fence too, to make things go quicker?'

'Don't you dare!' called Edith, without looking up.

'Don't you have morning sickness or something?' asked Claire.

'Second trimester, baby!' grinned Yasmin. 'No more morning sickness and heaps of energy. I could climb a fence twice as high and then tap dance along it!'

After an hour and a half, the bags and thermoses were empty and their work was done. Claire, Lottie, Meredith, Luke, Edith and Yasmin stood shoulder to shoulder to admire the display. There was nothing left to do now but to go home and wait.

'Are you sure we're doing the right thing, just leaving all this here?' Edith asked. 'Shouldn't we stay and have our own protest?'

'No,' said Yasmin firmly, 'that's not what we're about. We need to speak our truth quietly and clearly in a way that is peaceful. If we were to have a counter-protest and a fight broke out, then that becomes the headline.'

'It's like we're the secret resistance!' said Claire. 'The Copeton Craft Resistance.'

Yasmin grinned. 'I like that.'

'Vive la résistance!' cried Lottie. 'VIVE LA RÉSISTANCE!'

Claire and Luke shushed her. Yasmin got an attack of the giggles. 'Claire said *secret* resistance!' said Meredith.

'Are you absolutely sure we shouldn't stay?' Edith looked unconvinced. 'I don't like leaving all this unattended.'

'C'mon, Gran, you know if you were to stay, you'd only start a punch-on with one of those tattooed body-builders,' Luke quipped. 'Let's go home, I'm hungry!'

Claire spent the rest of the morning looking at news websites on her phone. Would they report on the protest? Would they mention their display? She refreshed and refreshed again, but there was nothing. The prime minister had sacked a member of cabinet and this had completely taken over the newsfeed. When Claire drove past the protest site later that day, the scene made her heart sink. All traces of their handiwork had been stripped from the fence. Yasmin's chalk art had been smudged into dusty pools of colour. Apart from a good amount of litter, there was no evidence of what went on there that day. Claire sighed. Even though she had suspected this would happen, she was sad to say goodbye to her little flowers.

When she got home, she consoled herself with some screen time. *Beautiful World* had something new up. She sat straighter on the couch. There were pictures of the crocheted webs again. But, more specifically, there were pictures of the webs that had been on the fence that morning! There was the large one in lime green, the one that said 'ALL ARE WELCOME', except it wasn't tied to the fence, it was pinned to a base board in a light box. Another one, in fluorescent orange, was shown half-made, with the hook still attached. The final photo, taken at night, showed the webs affixed to the fence, before the others had come to decorate things further. Siobhan wasn't just photographing the spiderwebs. She was the creator!

That night, Yasmin and Omar went to Khalid's house for iftar. Meesha had already told Yasmin to watch Noor closely and report back to her. 'I've only met her once and that was on a tiny screen. There's heaps you can't tell about a person when you meet them on a screen. Like how tall is she? What are her mannerisms when she's not paying attention to anything? How does she *smell*? That's important. I need information on how Noor smells.'

'Gross, Meesh. You want me to go up and sniff her? You want me to check if she has bad fasting breath? I'm sure she smells fine.'

'No. I want to know if she's one of those women who wears so much perfume you can smell her coming before you see her. Because that might be a dealbreaker for me. I want to know if she skunks things. Like, she's in a room and then she leaves but the room still smells like Chanel No. 5 for an hour. She could skunk your baby! She could skunk your poor innocent baby, Yasmin.'

Khalid opened the door and ushered them inside. Noor arrived soon after, laden with dishes and shopping bags. There was no way Yasmin was going to provide a comprehensive air-quality report on Noor for Meesha. But as she greeted her, she couldn't help noticing, just the same. Meesha would be happy to discover that Noor did not really have a 'smell'. She was fresh and bright and there was a barely discernible fragrance about her, which might have been perfume, but could just as easily be soap or shampoo. As far as the smell test went, Noor passed. But smell was Meesha's test, not Yasmin's.

They broke their fast in the traditional way, with dates and water. Noor was around the same height as Khalid, who wasn't particularly tall. She seemed a little self-conscious under Yasmin's scrutiny, but she wasn't nervy.

After the sunset prayer, Yasmin forgot to look at Noor and found herself looking at her dad instead. He had seemed worried when she had first arrived, but now she could see how happy and relaxed he became in Noor's presence. He smiled a lot more and laughed often.

Noor was teasing Khalid about his relationship with his new air fryer.

'I'm wondering if I should be jealous. He takes it places with him. He talks about it all of the time!'

Yasmin grinned. 'You do realise they're just glorified ovens, don't you Dad?'

Khalid's mouth was full, but he shook his head and held up a finger. He swallowed. 'No. No. They are so much more than that. Have you tried the samosas? I made them in the air fryer. So crispy!'

Omar looked up with interest. 'Did you make the samosas, Khalid? What recipe did you use?'

Noor laughed. 'I'm pretty sure the samosas were made by the Woolworths frozen food section.'

'Yes, but I cooked them. I can cook anything you want in the air fryer. Twenty minutes. Anything you want.'

Yasmin shook her head. 'It's like he's joined a cult.'

Noor nodded. 'I'm thinking of staging an intervention.'

Yasmin smiled, then everything felt suddenly cold. She stood up, shaking her head. 'I can't do this!' she said, and rushed from the room.

It wasn't her bedroom any more. It was the guest room. The single bed with the bookcase built into the frame and the pink-and-white quilt had given way to a modern queen-sized bed with an upholstered bedhead. There were boxes of clutter in the corner, a green armchair and a bookcase filled with the books that weren't good enough to go on the living room shelves. Yasmin sat on the edge of the bed and gazed at the window. It was almost too dark to see much more than her own reflection, but she could just make out the shadows of the front garden. The fountain. The flowering gum. The leaves of the agapanthus that had always grown outside her window.

There was a knock at the door. Probably Omar. She said a reluctant 'Yeah,' and the door opened. Noor quietly walked into the room, turned the armchair to face Yasmin and sat down. Yasmin eyed her and said nothing.

For a while, they both sat there, gazing at the window. Then Noor spoke. 'It's hard, isn't it?' Yasmin glanced at Noor, then looked back out of the window. A crescent moon was just visible above the silver wattle tree, half-hidden by ragged cloud.

A moment lapsed. Noor drew a breath. 'I want you to know I'm not here to fix things. I'm never going to try to be like your mother. She has already done an excellent job raising you and Meesha.' Noor left a pause, which Yasmin did not fill.

A shadow moved along the telephone wire outside. A ringtail possum was speeding along the tightrope thoroughfare. Yasmin watched its progress.

Noor continued. 'I know things will be difficult. I am ready for things to be difficult. Because I love your father. I love him deeply. He is worth the struggle.'

Until now, Yasmin had been striving to keep her expression blank. At this, when Noor said 'love', she could not help flinching.

Noor continued, slowly, undeterred. 'Grief is a mixed-up thing. I lost my own mother nineteen months ago. She was old, she had been sick, and still I don't think I will ever recover. For you to lose your mother so young, for you to have to bear your first child without your mother here to support you, that's …' Noor trailed off, wincing.

Yasmin did not want to cry in front of Noor. She definitely did not. But she could feel it coming. She could feel her body being taken over by a surge of helpless despair. The tears. The choking sobs. There was no hiding it. She felt humiliated.

Noor did not rush to comfort her, but neither did she pretend that it wasn't happening. She simply watched and waited.

Yasmin covered her face with her hands. When the worst of it had passed, her breathing slowed. She looked at Noor and drew a breath. A calm had descended over her. She was going to apologise for walking out on dinner, for her silence. She wanted to explain that the reason she was struggling was because of how *good* things were. How happy and relaxed and natural. Instead, she found herself saying something else. 'Do you remember much about what it was like when you gave birth to your son?'

Noor nodded. 'Yes. I remember it clearly.'

'How much does it hurt?'

Noor smiled. 'It hurts a lot. It will probably be the most pain you ever have to deal with. But you'll get through it. It won't be more than you can manage. I've never run a marathon, but I always think that must be a bit like labour. That last part of the race, there is so much pain and effort, but, inshallah, you will cross the finish line and know nothing but exhilaration and joy.'

Yasmin gulped and nodded. 'And what about when the baby is born? When that happens, can I ask your advice about things? Would that be okay?'

Noor ran her hand along the smooth arm of her chair. 'The first thing you'll find when your baby is born is that everybody everywhere will have advice for you. And lots of it. But the only experts on your baby will be you and Omar. Remember that. On the other hand, I do love giving advice. I especially like to give advice about the things I am bad at doing myself. That is my specialty, I think.' There was a definite twinkle in Noor's eye. She stood up. 'I made sweet kunafa if you still have room,' she said. 'And your dad has cooked some sweet pastries,' she paused for a fraction, a droll beat, 'in the air fryer.'

Yasmin stood up. She looked at Noor and nodded. Together, they went back to the table.

On Monday morning, as Claire was flipping out the double stroller in the school carpark, her phone pinged with a text from Lottie. *Can you drop by my place after the school run? I've something to show you.*

Lottie's house was gorgeous. The decor was warm and colourful, and the smell of warm scones seemed to pervade the air. The kitchen table was in a spacious, light-filled room. Yasmin and Edith were already sitting at it.

'Why do you always have delicious things baking?' Claire asked as she gradually unburdened herself of nappy bags and offspring. A patchwork rug was set out on the floor next to the table with toys for the twins. On the other side of the room, a small wooden train set waited for Harry.

'I've found that not being a superstar mum to five children gives me more time to bake.' Lottie was setting out a tray with cream, butter, honey and a jar of homemade jam. 'Tea or coffee?'

Lottie poured out the tea. 'I'm going to need you to take down the request for blankets off our website, Claire,' she said. 'We have more than enough now. I had four parcels arrive in the post yesterday!' When everyone was settled with their drinks and scones, Lottie produced a broadsheet newspaper. 'So, have you seen this yet?' she asked.

It was the front page of the 'Analysis' section. A full-page colour picture accompanied by a headline: 'The Battle for Copeton'.

It truly was a remarkable photo. On one side of the picture were the protesters, armed with Australian flags and black-and-white print-out A3 signs with slogans like 'PROTECT OUR ELDERLY' and 'AUSTRALIA FIRST' in bold Times New Roman font.

On the other side of the picture was the fence with their display. Claire didn't know much about photography, but something about the way the light hit the fence showed the madly colourful mural at its most resplendent. It was the focus point of the photograph, and a distinct colour contrast to the black, white and navy tones of the approaching crowd. You could clearly see Yasmin's chalk art; it was almost glowing off the pavement. Siobhan's bright spiderwebs were everywhere. Claire's flowers, Edith's doilies and Meredith's butterflies. And across the length of the fence, the word 'WELCOME' with a spiderweb on either side, woven in rainbow ribbon.

The photographer had managed to capture the moment of bewildered surprise on the face of the protester in the foreground. Beside him, a woman's lip curled in fury.

'That's amazing,' Claire breathed.

Lottie flipped over to the article inside. Claire skimmed the text: 'Police, expecting a violent clash, were pleased with the outcome. The pro-refugee advocates were nowhere to be seen, but their presence was clearly felt.' There were smaller photos alongside the article: a shot of the protesters marching down Main Street, a picture of a chalk spiderweb, and …

'My flowers!' Claire exclaimed. A close-up of the fence, taken from a side angle, showed the crocheted blooms and their fragile bows securing them to the fence. The morning light caught the detail of every stitch. Claire smiled and sipped her tea. This was a good morning.

CHAPTER EIGHTEEN

Meredith squinted in the bathroom's fluorescent light. Her running gear was laid out neatly in a line: sports bra, T-shirt, shorts, socks, runners, phone, keys, headphones, hair tie. She dressed automatically and went outside. It was only when she was walking in the pre-dawn twilight towards the park, the air fresh on her face, that she really started to wake up.

At the second lamppost in the park, she began to run. She didn't put her headphones on. Not yet. It was enough to listen to the thump-thump-thump of her feet on the pavement, the blood pounding to her muscles, the cold air rushing into her lungs. It was enough to just be Meredith. Soon, she would have to talk to people, have to carefully monitor her words and behaviour to conceal her lack of social ability. She closed her eyes briefly and thumped on.

She maintained a steady pace for two-and-a-half kilometres. She made a point of saying 'Good morning' to the few people she passed. This way, if she ended up being murdered and left in a ditch, there would be witnesses to point the police in the direction of her bloated corpse.

She owed her mother that at least. She was also careful to assess each passer-by while they were still a good distance away, to determine their threat level. Was the stranger male or female? Were they behaving erratically? Could she out-run them if needed?

The picnic table by the creek was her halfway point. Meredith stopped here and checked her shoelaces. Then she took her headphones out of their little pouch. She slipped one earbud into her left ear and tucked the other one under the shoulder strap of her sports bra. As she was setting up the podcast, a sound made her look up. A man was running down the path towards her. She immediately rated his threat level as 'high'. Tall, powerfully built, a fast runner. And it looked like he wasn't wearing a shirt. That was a definite warning sign. Shirtlessness was not normal behaviour. She arranged her house keys in her fist so that the metal parts poked out between her fingers, like knuckle dusters. As she was taking note of potential exit routes and replaying her taekwondo training in her head, she got her first good look at the man. It was … Luke.

She felt a wave of relief, quickly followed by a fresh surge of panic. Luke! She couldn't see Luke now! She was in her silly little running shorts. She was *covered* in sweat. Her hair was a mess. And it looked like he had already recognised her. No! This was all wrong!

At least Luke had enough decency to look self-conscious also. Running along with his shirt off like that. His chest was broad, his stomach firm, dusted with a patch of sandy-brown hair leading … down, leading under the waistband of his …

Look somewhere else!

'Good morning, Meredith!' Luke said.

'Good morning,' Meredith said to a small clump of nasturtiums.

Luke's T-shirt had been hanging out of the back of his shorts. He put it back on now, in one swift movement. It was too late. The image had been burned onto Meredith's brain. She could not unsee it.

'What are you listening to?' Luke asked, smiling with his hand out.

It took her a moment to realise he was beckoning for her earbud. She passed it to him, a little dazedly. 'It's a TED talk,' she offered. It was a TED talk about making new friends. She would pretend she was only listening because she found the topic interesting, not because she was deficient in this area. People could say 'I'm terrible at maths!' or 'I hate parallel parking!' and everybody just accepted it. But you couldn't say 'I'm no good at friendship' or 'I hate making friends'.

Luke placed the bud in his ear and listened for what felt like forever, though it was probably only thirty-five seconds. His face was close to hers. Meredith realised she should have given him both earbuds so he wasn't tethered to her in this way. 'I love TED talks,' he said with a grin.

She nodded mutely. When Luke handed her back the earbud, she swiftly tucked it back under her shoulder strap. Then she nodded again and started running. She accelerated to her fastest pace, confident that she was leaving Luke far behind, congratulating herself on the natural and straightforward way she had terminated the conversation. It was with a jolt of dismay, mixed with another feeling she couldn't identify, that she realised that Luke had fallen into step beside her. Luke ran with long, loping strides and didn't seem at all put out by the pace Meredith was setting. 'You're fast!' he said with another grin. She didn't answer. She had to focus on breathing.

He ran beside her the whole way back. It wasn't so bad, after a while. They fell into a comfortable rhythm, thumping along the path. Luke didn't insist on conversation, and the silence between them did not feel awkward. He pointed out a group of rainbow lorikeets, their feathers flashing orange and green as they flew out of a nearby flame tree, and nodded towards a mob of eastern grey kangaroos. It was different. It was nice.

When they reached the second lamppost, Luke slowed to a walk beside her. 'So was the talk any good?' he said.

She shrugged, pulling out her earbud. 'It's okay, I guess. They always talk the same way about how to make friends: smile, find a hobby, join a group. But it's never that simple in real life.'

Luke began his stretches. 'Is that why you started the crochet group? To make new friends?'

She frowned. 'No,' she snapped. *Yes*. Did Luke really think she was some pathetic loser who couldn't make friends? Could he see through all of her carefully constructed gloss to the strange eight-year-old, quietly making tiny gardens out of twigs and gumnuts, while the other children raced and laughed around her? She straightened her T-shirt and glowered. 'This is me,' she said briefly, as they reached one of the park's exits. She successfully executed a goodbye ritual and left.

She thought again about Luke's words later, as she was massaging shampoo into her hair. On Saturdays, she allowed herself a longer shower than her usual two-and-a-half minutes, so that she could wash her hair. Her mind would often drift. She didn't really want friends, but she did want to be social. It was important to be social. She remembered her mother's questions when she came home from school.

'With whom did you play today, Meredith?'

Meredith would pause to finish chewing her carrot. Zelda, their housekeeper, used to make her plates of sliced carrot, celery and cheese, in equisized sticks, with none of the food touching the other food. It was her favourite snack. She swallowed. 'Myself,' she'd say, feigning nonchalance. She knew that this was not an acceptable answer. She used to say 'nobody', and it made her mum cross. She thought that if she changed her answer to 'myself', it might be more acceptable. It wasn't.

Mrs James would sigh. 'We've talked about this, Meredith. It's important to make friends. It's important to be social.' Meredith's mum was on the parents' committee, the school board and the fundraising team. She knew how to be social. But she wasn't good friends with Dad. They argued a lot. And she wasn't good friends with Zelda. Sometimes she shouted at Zelda, but that wasn't arguing, because Zelda didn't shout back, she just nodded and said, 'Yes, Mrs James.'

Meredith would select another piece of celery, take a bite, chew and swallow. 'It isn't easy,' she would venture. It wasn't easy. First, you had to find somebody to play with. The playground was huge, and sometimes, Meredith thought, the girls ran away when they saw you coming. And then, when you did find someone, you had to work out all of the rules to their game and try to join in. Sometimes a girl would stand with one hand on her hip, looking at you appraisingly. 'We've already got enough people for our game,' she would say.

And so Meredith would sit on the edge of the playground, using a twig to smooth the dirt for her tiny garden. She felt her breathing slow down as she gradually added sticks and leaves, gumnuts and flowers, bringing order and beauty to the small space. One time, she dug a small impression, lined it with sandwich wrap and trickled water into it to form a pond. One of the older girls stopped to admire her creation. 'That's pretty!' she exclaimed.

Meredith had blinked, startled from her task. She looked up at the girl. 'Can I tell my mum I played with you?'

The girl made a strange face and ran away.

In the shower, she massaged the Lustrous Shine Conditioner onto her head, dragging it out to the tips of her hair. Luke was probably right. The crochet group meant she could be doing something social, but in a structured way, and on her terms. She didn't mind being social, so long as she could be the boss.

Meredith glared at the papers. Focus. She needed to focus. Strategically splayed across an otherwise neat desk were site maps, glossy photos, mock-ups from graphic design and various brochures from competitors' estates in Doreen, Melton, Wyndham Vale. She needed to convince homebuyers to visit Copeton first, to fall in love with the estate. What would make Copeton different? What would give Copeton the edge?

They were running out of time. Everything needed to be fully formed by the twenty-fifth. That was presentation day. That was when Meredith would prove that she was not too young, or too female, or too socially awkward to carry this off.

At least they had the cafe sorted. It had taken a lot to convince people to retain the existing structure, but it would be worth it. 'Farmhouse cafe' would appear on all of their promotional materials. But what else?

The concept needed to be crisp and classic. Unique, but not a gimmick. Unusual, yet reassuringly familiar. Meredith's scowl deepened. It felt like the idea was just tantalisingly out of reach. What? *What?*

There was a knock. On her desk, not her door. Steph was standing right in front of her and gave a little jump when Meredith looked up.

'Sorry to disturb you!' Steph shouted. 'I did knock on your door, but I couldn't knock loudly enough.'

Meredith looked at her mouse-like subordinate, with her pale skin, messy ponytail and ears that stuck out, just a little bit. She waited for her to continue.

Steph swallowed. 'That white noise sound is really loud!' she shouted.

'Pink,' said Meredith. She spoke loudly, but did not shout.

'Sorry?' Steph shouted. Why was she sorry?

'It's pink noise, not white. White noise uses all audible frequencies across the spectrum. Pink noise uses reduced higher frequencies.'

Meredith turned the volume down with a sigh. 'My bluetooth headphones were refusing to pair, so I had to play it out of my computer speakers.'

Steph cleared her throat. She opened her mouth, shifted her jaw and then clamped her mouth shut again. She tried again: 'I ...' Steph looked at the door, as if assessing her escape route. Then she looked back at Meredith. 'I have bad news.'

Meredith studied Steph's face. She couldn't decide whether she looked frightened or miserable. Maybe it was a little of both? It would be nice to have some staff who weren't terrified of her. It really got in the way of things sometimes.

Meredith waited, gazing steadily at Steph. When Steph realised she wasn't going to say anything in response, she continued, 'I just heard from Ashley Bleeker, the tenant I found for our cafe. She said she's pulling out, she's not going ahead with it. She's going to London instead. London! I had no idea she would be such a flake! I'm furious! I mean, who does that? I mean, I guess lots of people go to London, but I mean ... I mean, like ...'

Meredith continued to watch Steph, unblinking. 'You mean – what? What is the upshot?'

Steph swallowed. 'It means we are stuck without a tenant for the cafe unless we can find a new one, like, really quickly. It means we are pretty much stuffed.'

This was bad news. This was really bad. Meredith needed to figure out a way to end this conversation. If she could bring it to an end, this wide-eyed employee would leave her office. If the wide-eyed employee left, she could put her pink noise back on, perhaps turn the lights down. If she could put her pink noise on, if she could turn her lights down, she could finally, finally think.

Meredith stood up. 'Get out,' she said.

CHAPTER NINETEEN

Yasmin straightened papers on her already immaculate desk. Her bullet journal was open in front of her, to a page headed 'Talking Points'. Time to read over it for the ninth time.

- Most of the residents I have spoken to have been overwhelmingly positive about these developments. The protesters represent a vocal minority.
- The building of a mosque will benefit Copeton in many ways. A mosque is not merely a church, but a community hub and a centre for charity work.
- Neither of these issues, neither the building of the mosque nor the renting program for refugees, is related to council rates.
- Many charities and community groups have mobilised to assist the refugees in settling into their new homes. Make sure to name their websites in the interview.

She felt her breathing slow down as she continued to read the rest of the notes. She could do this. It wasn't about her. It was about getting the message out.

She heard the camera team arriving before she saw them. A man with a beard and a large camera, a younger man with a boom mic, and a woman with a clipboard came striding in, barking to each other about light sources and acoustics.

Crossfire Report was a popular current affairs program on a commercial network. Although Yasmin didn't usually watch it, she knew it had a large audience. She took a few more deep breaths.

Yasmin's desk, which she had carefully tidied, was not to be the place for the interview. Clipboard Lady bustled her over to another desk with better light. Yasmin smiled apologetically as Doris from Facilities gave up her space.

The woman with the clipboard turned out to be Rachel, whom Yasmin had spoken to on the phone to set this up. Rachel had seemed nice on the phone, but now she had a look of guarded distaste on her face, as if she did not want to be there. Did she have something against Yasmin? But no. When Rachel spoke to her, it was, again, with warmth and courtesy. The reporter arrived. The guarded look returned to Rachel's face.

The reporter sat opposite Yasmin with a strong whiff of expensive aftershave. He was a blandly handsome man, with hair carefully styled to look casually ruffled and a complexion that hinted at long holidays in the south of France, or at least regular visits to the tanning salon. But it was his teeth that Yasmin found unnerving. They were too white, too straight. She was so mesmerised by their militant uniformity that she almost missed his first question.

'Mrs Yasmin Malak.' The way he tasted every syllable of her name, the little breath he took before saying it, the careful, studied air he gave to the pronunciation he hadn't even bothered to check with her before the interview started – it all had the effect of making her name sound more foreign, more exotic. Yasmin blinked.

'Tell me, as a Muslim woman, do you feel targeted by these protests? Do you ever find yourself fearing for your safety?'

She cleared her throat slightly and then stopped when she saw the boom operator wince. 'Well, here at Three Rivers Shire Council, we believe everybody has the right to feel safe and we also believe in the right to free speech. But, as my father likes to say, "You can have the right to your own opinion, but you can't have the right to your own facts!" So I would like to clear up a few misconceptions that seem to have gained traction of late.'

'Certainly, Yasmin, but tell me: have members of your community been suffering as a result of this targeted campaign?'

Yasmin frowned. 'I suppose there have been some members of the Copeton community who have been put off by the misinformation that has been circulating. The secretary of the Copeton Kindergarten Association was telling me …'

'Excuse me, Yasmin, I was not asking about the Copeton community, but *your* community. The Muslim community. How do the Muslims feel about these protests?'

'That's an interesting question. You are asking me, as the representative of *all the Muslims*, to let you know how all the Muslims feel? Should I tap into our collective consciousness and get you a quotable quote?' Yasmin cut the tension with a disarming smile. 'I guess it doesn't work like that. I can answer for myself personally, though. As a Muslim, I do feel threatened sometimes. I do feel unwelcome and "other". But now, let's get on to the council's response to this.'

'Yasmin, do you think some Muslims might be provoked to respond in a violent way to these protests?' A mental image coalesced in Yasmin's head. Her Wednesday night Qur'an group forming an all-woman, middle-aged militia in khaki uniforms, brandishing weapons-grade baklava and Turkish delight. Imam Jamil painting his eighty-three-year-old face in war paint before gently lecturing his victims to death. She smothered a smile.

'Now let me think about that for a minute, Darren. May I call you Darren?'

'Actually, my name is Damien—'

'Darren, do you know a lot of the people who are making trouble for us come from a particular social group? They are predominantly white men. Tell me, as a white man, how does this make you feel?'

'I—'

'Do you think these troublemakers are representative of white men in general?'

'Well—'

'Do you think you are being unfairly targeted for being a white man because of the actions of these people?'

'That's—'

'And when is a representative of the white men going to come out to condemn their actions? We're still waiting!'

'What—'

'What I need from you, Darren, is a response on behalf of all white men. When will this behaviour stop? And now, let me outline the council's response to these protests.'

Yasmin smoothly, and without pausing for interruption, covered all of her talking points. She even managed to work in some commentary about the nature of bigotry and how it was everybody's problem. She was rather proud of herself.

The reporter, no longer smiling with those massive teeth, looked far less intimidating. He had a weak chin.

At lunchtime, Yasmin and Claire ambled through row after row of jumpsuits, singlets, bottle sterilisers, baths, little hats, bunny rugs and some electronic contraption for warming disposable wipes. Claire pushed the double stroller, where Lily and Hope dozed peacefully. Yasmin clutched a list of baby clothes sent out by the hospital. 'Five bunny rugs,' Yasmin read aloud.

'Here.' Claire steered the stroller into the next aisle. 'You want to get these bigger ones. They have a bit more stretch in them and are easier to use.'

'I don't understand why I need so many of these. Are they to put on the cot?'

'No. That's cot sheets. They're different. You need bunny rugs to make baby burritos. And they're good for cleaning up spew.'

Yasmin wrinkled her nose. This just raised more questions. But, before she could ask them, she was interrupted by another shopper.

'Are you getting ready for a new baby?' the lady crooned. Yasmin nodded. She had the uncomfortable feeling that the woman had been watching them for a while before she decided to start a conversation.

'Are you a Muslim?' the lady pointed at Yasmin's headscarf. She nodded again and swallowed the sigh that was threatening to escape. 'Do you have to eat lots of special foods, like halal pork and everything? Is that hard?'

She gave a small shrug. 'I'm used to it.' It was the easiest answer. Now was not the time for an in-depth discussion on the benefits of only eating the meat of certain animals that have been healthy and well-treated in life, humanely and prayerfully slaughtered, and drained of all toxins. She could tell the woman wasn't really that interested. She had already moved on in the conversation.

'I've noticed: there's a lot of you around these days. Not that I think that's a bad thing!' The woman gave her most winning smile.

'A lot of me?' Yasmin had a ridiculous mental image of the shopping centre being full of Yasmins: Yasmins browsing the shelves, Yasmins stopping for coffee, Yasmins running the registers.

'I just think it's wonderful that you've made friends with – you know – a regular Aussie.' The lady gestured towards Claire, who was standing awkwardly to the side.

'A normal person?' said Yasmin brightly.

The lady hesitated and nodded.

Yasmin leaned in, her eyes wide. '*That's not a normal person,*' she said in a stage whisper. Claire snorted.

'Oh, you know what I mean. Too many of these Muslims only hang around with their own kind. But you're not like that. You're one of the good ones.'

'I can't imagine why Muslims don't feel welcome enough to make friends.' Yasmin spoke innocently, the trace of irony almost imperceptible.

'Exactly. Well, I must go now.' The woman leaned in and clutched Yasmin's arm. 'That's a lovely headscarf!' she pronounced triumphantly. Yasmin gave a tight smile and thanked the lady, who was nodding impressively. Yasmin was only wearing a plain brown hijab today, but she'd learnt that complimenting a Muslim woman on her headscarf was a shorthand way to broadcast your tolerance to all around you. Yasmin imagined the woman boasting to her friends later that day. 'I met a Muslim lady at the shops today. And I told her she had a *lovely headscarf—*' She stopped herself. She was being nasty. She mentally said a quick prayer for the woman and her family and turned back to Claire.

Claire raised her eyebrows. 'Well, that was awkward,' she deadpanned.

Yasmin grinned. 'I have that same conversation every day of the week: Are you Muslim? Do you always wear that headscarf? Do you miss bacon? Do you think my tank top is a sin?' She rolled her eyes. 'I don't mind talking about my faith, but it gets boring. Always the same questions. Always the same answers: Yes, I'm Muslim. No, I don't always wear the headscarf. No, I've never tasted bacon. No, I don't think your tank top is a sin. But the fashion police might have other ideas. I wish sometimes people would just ask me if I've read any good books lately or who I think is going to win *MasterChef*.' She frowned at the shelf in front of her. 'Do you think I need to buy a pacifier?'

Claire shook her head. 'You'll get some samples in your hospital show bag. Your baby might not even like them, so try the freebies out first. Just don't let the midwives see you.' She picked up a value-pack of singlets and studied it. 'My daily conversation is "twins". Especially when they were newborns: Are they twins? Are they identical? Are they naturally conceived? Double trouble! Is your husband getting a vasectomy now?'

Yasmin broke into a peal of laughter. 'No way! You made that last one up!'

Claire chuckled. 'I swear it's true. I've been asked that one more than once by randoms in the supermarket. People are strange. But my favourite is "Are they twins?" I used to have fun thinking of different responses to that question, just to mix things up.'

'Like what?'

'Let me see. Are they twins? No. They were having a buy one, get one free sale at Babies R Us. Are they twins? Nope. That one's a decoy.'

Yasmin giggled. 'Are they twins? No. This is what the new baby bonus looks like. You get a bonus baby now.'

'I think you might need glasses. That's *one baby*.'

'No! Triplets! Good Lord! Where'd the other one go?'

'No, just the one – but she has the ability to bilocate: isn't she advanced?'

Claire and Yasmin collapsed into laughter. Then Claire grew thoughtful. 'I just realised something,' she said. 'I mean, this is stupid, but, I only just realised how different it is for me and for you, like with the protests and everything. I'm worried about the protests, of course I am. But I have the luxury of not having it always in the back of my mind. It must be so much harder for you.' Claire frowned, looking for the words. 'Like, for me, racism is like litter in the local park and I want to do something about it, but for you, it's like someone has dumped a whole bunch of rubbish in your front yard and you can't escape it.' It seemed that once she found the words, they all came out together in a nervous rush. 'Wait – is it still racism when they do it to you? Or is it, like, religion-ism?' Claire's face was bright red.

'It's both,' Yasmin said simply. 'People use religion as the excuse, but most of the time it comes down to what we look like. Having brown skin and wearing a headscarf is not what an Australian looks like, apparently.'

'I've always been paranoid about saying the wrong thing to you. I feel like I need to issue a blanket apology in advance for all of the times I'm going to put my foot in my mouth.'

Yasmin shook her head. 'You already put your foot in your mouth wherever you go, to people of all creeds and cultures. You are an equal-opportunity offender. Why should I miss out?'

Claire made a face and pelted Yasmin with a baby sock. Then she smiled. 'So, who *do* you think will win *MasterChef*?'

Later, in the food court, Claire showed Yasmin the *Beautiful World* posts on her phone. 'She's from Copeton!' Claire exclaimed. 'I wish I knew who she was. Wait – it's not you, is it?'

Yasmin grinned. 'I wish it was me! Those spiderwebs make my day! But I did make one contribution, only it was taken down within a few days – and not by the council.' Yasmin fiddled with her phone and passed it to Claire. 'I put it at the entrance to the town hall.'

The picture showed an adorable amigurumi duckling, made from the same soft yellow yarn Yasmin had used to make the baby clothes. It was standing on the fence pillar, next to the gate. Poking from the duck's orange bill was the spider that had previously been tied to that fence.

Claire laughed out loud. 'That is priceless! The expression on the duck's face! I'm so sad it got taken down – what a waste!'

Yasmin smiled as she took her phone back from Claire. 'Yes, it was sad. But at least I got the photos.' She put her phone back in her handbag. 'I'm still trying to think if I know anyone who could be Siobhan,' she said. 'It would be so great to meet her. She should join the CCC!'

Claire's phone chimed with a message from Lottie. *Are you sure you took down all of the call-outs for blankets off our socials? I got SEVEN new blankets in the mail today. HELP!!!!!!!!!*

Claire laughed and showed the message to Yasmin. Then she paused. 'Hey, Yasmin, what if it's Lottie?'

Yasmin frowned. 'What?'

Claire nodded emphatically. 'I think it could be Lottie. Charlotte's webs!'

Yasmin paused for a moment. 'I don't know,' she said. 'I can see Lottie doing something like this, sure. But I definitely can't see her keeping it a *secret*.'

Claire looked about to argue the point and then stopped. An elderly man had approached their table. He pointed at the stroller. 'Are they *twins?*' he asked.

Yasmin watched *Crossfire Report* carefully that night, but her interview wasn't there. Instead, there was a special event that took up most of the episode. An exclusive interview with one of the survivors of a disaster that had occurred in Tasmania over a decade ago. This particular survivor was now going through a marriage breakdown. The current affairs show had managed to secure rights to interview this man and his soon-to-be-ex-wife. This also gave them the opportunity to get more mileage out of the exclusive interviews with the survivors that they had purchased eleven years ago.

On Tuesday night, there was an exposé, entitled 'Butter Price SCANDAL'. 'SCANDAL' was in red letters, stamped diagonally across the screen. But, still, no Copeton story.

Wednesday and Thursday were also bereft of Yasmin's interview, but all was not lost. She did find out that one of the supporting actors from a hospital drama in the 90s was going to jail. Half the segment was spent explaining who exactly this man was, which Yasmin found very helpful.

At last, on Friday, the segment screened. The host frowned thoughtfully at the camera. Beside her there was a graphic of shouting, flag-draped protesters and an Islamic crescent alongside the words 'Battle Lines'. 'And now: A Suburb in Turmoil. Racial tensions threaten to overflow in Melbourne's outer fringe as concerned residents protest what they see as an invasion of Muslim ideology. Damien Cook goes to the epicentre of this simmering suburban pressure-cooker to find out more.'

The segment opened with shots of the racist ice-cream truck, the ugly spider installations and a small, staged protest with members of the Kelly Gang. This led into an interview with these members in the same outdoor location.

Yasmin felt her stomach clench as Ma Kelly and Ned Kelly repeated their rhetoric ('Our old people deserve better', 'We pay our rates, and for what?'), while the others put on a good show of background nodding. She quietly reassured herself that they would screen her interview next, dispelling their claims. And here she was. Ugh. She hated watching videos of herself. Still. She looked calm and poised. Off screen, the reporter asked, 'What do you see as your biggest concern, living in Copeton?' TV Yasmin responded immediately. 'As a Muslim, I do feel threatened sometimes. I do feel unwelcome and "other".' The scene switched to a final long shot of the Kelly Gang standing behind a banner chanting 'JUSTICE FOR COPETON' while the voiceover said, 'Challenging times, indeed. Damien Cook reporting.'

Yasmin continued to stare at the screen, mouth agape, as if hoping the commercial for roof sealant might somehow morph into something resembling journalistic integrity. It didn't happen.

CHAPTER TWENTY

The last round increased on every second stitch, but it was making it too floppy. Perhaps she should pull it apart and increase on every third stitch instead? Harper was frowning at her work, pondering, when her phone pinged with a message.

Hi Harper, this is Claire from the crochet group. I had an idea and it's ok if you say no, but I noticed how beautifully you cleaned the kitchen for me when you came over. Thank you! I mean, I didn't realise until I got home later but it's just beautiful and I really need that in my life so I was thinking I'd really like it if I could give you a job. Like, a couple of hours a week? Or a fortnight? Whatever you can do, really. What I need is somebody to help me deal with all the clutter. Regular cleaners don't do that. I don't need a cleaner. I need a tidier! And I'll pay you, of course. I hope you don't think this is weird. You can definitely say no. I'm only asking because you're so good at it.

There followed a long string of cleaning-themed emojis interspersed with flowers and, for some reason, a dancing lady. Harper read the text over a couple of times to try to work out what it was about. A cleaning job. So she could have a cleaning job along with the pamphlet round and research work. Would this count as 'gainful employment'? And how much would the cleaning job pay? Harper did some quick research, then sent Claire a text suggesting a generous rate. It was worth a try. Claire texted back, almost immediately: *DONE! Thank you so much, Harper!* followed by two lines of emojis featuring many flowers, a rabbit, unicorn, superhero, and again with the dancing lady.

It had rained last night. It might still rain this morning. Meredith ran through the park in silence, neatly dodging the puddles at the edge of the trail. When she got to the picnic table, she could see Luke loping towards her from the other direction. He raised his arm in a lazy hello. Meredith nodded in acknowledgement.

'Let's do the Mick's Creek loop today,' Luke said when he got close enough. 'What do you reckon?'

'Mick's Creek sounds good,' said Meredith. 'We're due for a long one.'

They set off. This had somehow become their routine on Saturday. They never made arrangements or put appointments in their diaries. It just happened in an easy rhythm, like the thumping of their feet. Running with Luke wasn't so bad. Meredith worked harder when she ran with him, so she felt better afterwards. Luke was an undemanding conversationalist, happy to chatter or be silent without expecting input from her. And when Meredith did say something, he didn't squint at her the way other people did. If he thought her odd, it didn't bother him. If he thought her odd, he never let it show.

He was talking now. She was only half listening. Luke was like a gentle podcast that accompanied the crunching of their feet on the trail. What was he talking about? His business at Falls Creek.

'And, to be honest, it's getting a little much. I dunno. I'm getting old. I'm thinking I might move back here somewhere, closer to Gran. The High Country's so far away. I could open a cafe or something and stay in the same place all year round. I reckon I'd like that. What? Meredith? Are you okay?'

She had stopped running suddenly. Luke had to double back to meet her. She looked at him. 'Did you say you were thinking of opening a cafe?' she asked.

They ran past the series of billboards announcing the new housing estate. They climbed over the gate with the 'Display Village Coming Soon!' sign. A detour from the Mick's Creek loop. The straight driveway, lined with trees, led them up a gentle slope.

'Here it is,' said Meredith.

It was an attractive brick building. A spacious, renovated post-war clinker with large windows. A broad shed dormer window peeked out of the tiled roof, suggesting an upstairs room.

Meredith didn't have the keys with her, so they wandered the perimeter of the house peering into windows. 'At the moment, the plan is to use the front room on this side as the site office,' she said. 'But after a few years, this can be incorporated into the cafe or else leased to another tenant. You can see there's work that still needs to be done,' she added, trying to hide a note of defensiveness in her voice, 'but it definitely has potential.'

Luke was looking in at the main room through a large window at the side. 'Good natural light,' he said. 'You can't tell that from looking at the facade. And this is a decent-sized room,' he added. 'What's the kitchen like?'

The kitchen was visible from a high window further along. Luke stood on his toes and craned his neck around to take it in. It was recently renovated, with a broad bench capable of hosting a coffee machine dividing it from the main room.

'So what's your background in hospitality?' Meredith asked.

'Well, I own the ski bar in the alpine village, and have managed it for eight years.'

'Why aren't you there now?'

Luke smiled. 'I'm not the manager anymore. I don't need to be there twenty-four seven. It still feels weird, though. I got really into snowboarding when I was at uni. I joined the Melbourne Uni Snowboarding Club and spent whole winters snowboarding all day, then working in the bar at night. I didn't like uni. I've never been much of a student, and my grandpa had just died, so everything was pretty messed up. After a while, my boss put me in charge of the evening shift, and I started to learn how to run things.

'It had been such a long time since I felt interested in learning anything. But I found everything about running a bar fascinating. The inventory. The staff roster. I read everything I could get my hands on about it. Then my boss said he was thinking of selling the business, so I bought it.'

Meredith looked up. 'Just like that?'

Luke stopped stretching and smiled down at her. 'Actually, I think it was a little more complicated than that at the time,' he said. 'Gran was having kittens over the whole idea. Shelly, that's my sister, was really against it too. At the start, my older brother Charles was the only one who took me seriously.'

Luke walked to the rear of the house and surveyed the untidy back garden. 'Charles knew I hadn't been going to classes, so he wasn't as shocked at the idea of me dropping out of uni. In the end, he helped me to convince Gran and Shelly. He made me promise to have financial counselling with him once a month and he's always looked after my investments and all that.'

Meredith peered at Luke. 'How old were you? Twenty-something? How could you afford to buy a business at that age?' Rude question. Money questions were rude. But Meredith found herself so interested in the conversation, she'd forgotten to be careful with her words.

Luke shrugged. 'I had an inheritance that was being held in a trust for me,' he said. 'From my mum and dad,' he added, in a quieter voice. 'I made a lot of mistakes that first year of running the bar, but luckily I'm a quick learner.'

'What was the best thing you learned?' Meredith asked.

Luke frowned. 'When I first got the bar, I felt like it had to keep its old personality, like I couldn't change anything,' he said. 'Things got better when I stopped second-guessing myself and just made things the way I would like them. The old place was all about "artisan" and "bespoke". The wedges were supposed to be made from a special sort of potato and served up in this tiny gold basket, like a miniature deep-fry basket with handles. It looked very fancy, but it just wasn't me. Eventually, I worked up the confidence to do things my way. Simple food, and decent portions. Sure, it's nice to be stylish and cutting edge, but people are hungry when they're on the slopes.'

'People in the suburbs are different to people on the slopes. How do you know what they'll want down here?'

'Well, that's the fun of it,' said Luke with a smile. 'It probably will be different. But, I dunno …' he paused, thinking, 'it's like making a friend. You have to be confident in what you have to offer – nobody is better at being you than you – but you also have to listen to your customers. That's it. Be yourself and listen.'

'Surely it's more complicated than that?' Meredith tilted her head the way she'd seen other women do when they used 'surely'. 'Surely' was a strange device. On the surface, it made the sentence sound more didactic. But for some reason, when you added this word, it made the words softer, less pedantic. It made no sense, really. Perhaps it wasn't the word. Perhaps it was the questioning tone, the slight uplift of the chin. She had practised this technique in the mirror at home and she had almost mastered it. But it was important not to use it too often, or it would become strange again. She had used it with Luke today; she would need to wait a few more days before she used it with him again.

She only knew a handful of these tricks. She always hoped that eventually she would master enough of them to be socially acceptable. Yet here was Luke talking about making friends like it was a simple two-step process.

Luke shrugged. 'I reckon it is that simple. Customers will tell you what they want and don't want. You just have to take the time to listen and adjust. No point keeping the best vanilla slice if it just stays in the cake fridge day after day.'

Meredith frowned. 'You are talking about business. But surely friendship isn't as simple as that?' This 'surely' was okay, she decided. It was merely a repeat of the last one. It was not a new 'surely'.

'Friendship is definitely as simple as that. I don't know why everyone overthinks it so much. Be yourself and listen. That's it.'

'That's not it. Friendship is not easy. You are just doing a lot of invisible things unconsciously and you don't even realise you can do them. People who don't know this secret language stand out, because there's no way to learn it. And anyway' – Meredith was trying not to raise her voice – 'I've tried that! I've tried everything! It doesn't work for me!'

Luke was inspecting a pile of flagstones beside the house. He paused to look at Meredith. 'I said it was simple. I didn't say it was easy. Are you saying you're a good listener?'

'Of course,' Meredith snapped. How could he even ask that after she'd let him talk on uninterrupted for the past twenty minutes?

'My sister's name.'

'What?'

'My sister's name. What is it?'

'Um. Sarah? No, Sharon? That doesn't count. I was still waking up.'

'Well, then: Lottie's job.'

'What?'

'What's Lottie's job?'

'How should I know?'

'That's my point. You ask her. Except, with Lottie, you don't have to ask anything, she will just tell you. What's Yasmin's husband's name? How many children does Claire have?'

'I didn't even know Claire had kids.'

'She has five.'

'You are making that up.'

'I'm not. The youngest are twins.'

'How do you know that?'

'She was talking about them at the last meeting. You were there.'

'I don't remember.'

'Because you weren't listening.'

Meredith glared at Luke's teasing grin. 'Easy for you to say,' she snapped. 'You're a natural at all this.'

Luke gave an easy shrug. 'True. I am good with people. But my brother's not. Gran used to give us all lessons in how to have a conversation. We'd have pretend dinner parties and practise saying "hello" and "thank you". And when we met new people, she'd test us when we got home on their names and interesting facts about them. She said it was for all of us, but looking back, I can see she was doing it for my brother. Gran used to say to Charles, "People won't care about

191

your quirks once they know you care about them."'

Meredith looked at Luke, thinking. Then she stepped down from the retaining wall. 'We should get back on course before our heart rates drop too much.' She yanked her ponytail straight and ran back to the driveway.

Stage one was nearing completion. Meredith and her team would deliver their presentation on the twenty-fifth. This project had seemed plagued with problems from the start. First, there was the whole debacle sourcing a cafe tenant, then there were the issues with the computers. None of her team had been able to access their work. It was something to do with the files being overwritten by an older version of the software. Even now, when everything had been recovered, Meredith was yet to see the details of their contribution to the project. Their last few meetings had been cancelled and all of Meredith's queries on Slack had been left unread. Of course, Steph had reassured her that all three of them were on track and that their work was high-quality. It had just been a long time since Meredith had been given an update of anything concrete. In the past, Meredith had been criticised for being too overbearing. She was trying to improve in this area, but she really needed to know what her team had put together. Today, they would finally get it all out on the table, iron out the creases and prepare the presentation.

She could see Steph and Stuart standing outside her office having a conversation. Jared wasn't in the office today. He had called in sick. They hesitated, then came inside. Stuart, tall and gangly, stood a little behind the more compact Steph.

Meredith used her professional smile. 'Right. Let's get started.'

Steph cleared her throat. 'The first thing we need to say,' she said, 'is that we got a job with Norris Grand. We're leaving Rivergum.'

Meredith stared back at Steph. Norris Grand was Rivergum's main competitor. Meredith had received a phone call from them herself a couple of months ago. They were offering her a job. Meredith had explained to them that they were mistaken, reassured them that she already had a job and hung up. Was Steph leaving the team? And Stuart, standing behind her, making small nods, was he leaving too?

'Oh,' said Meredith, 'Oh.' She pressed her hands on the desk, fingers splayed out. She looked at her fingers, took a breath, looked up. 'In that case, we will need to go over everything you've done for the presentation so that I can get it ready to go. I've already blocked out a few hours to go over everything in detail, and we can order lunch.'

Steph swallowed. 'That's the second thing we need to say,' she said. She looked at Stuart, then back at Meredith. 'We haven't done as much work as we said we did.'

Meredith frowned. 'I don't understand. You told me you've prepared everything we need for the presentation. You told me it was almost done. You said it was really impressive.'

Steph nodded. 'We had planned to work it out. We were going to get on top of it. And it would have been impressive when we, like, did it.' One arm crossed her body as she scratched her elbow. 'I mean, I can't get anything done unless it's the last minute, you know? And part of it was that I wasn't really sure what I was supposed to be doing, but I was too scared to, like, ask? But now I've got a job at Norris Grand which means I actually don't have to do it, which is *such* a relief.' Stuart, beside her, exhaled a long breath and nodded. Steph looked back at him. 'Right?'

'Right.' Stuart's voice was emphatic, though barely more than a croak.

Meredith was finding it hard to follow exactly what was going on.

Stuart's breathing was *audible*. 'You said "finishing touches",' she said. 'You said you were putting on the finishing touches. I don't understand.'

'Well, yeah. I just said that because I didn't want to upset you. I didn't want you to worry.'

'You lied to me?'

Steph shook her head. 'I didn't lie. It was *going* to be true. Like, it hadn't happened yet, but it was going to be true.'

Meredith gazed bleakly back at Steph and Stuart, willing them to say something that made sense to her. 'I still don't understand.'

'So, in summary, you know, it's unfortunate that we didn't get the work done, but we're sure you'll be able to work it out.' Steph's face spread into a smile. 'We have faith in you, Meredith.' Behind her, Stuart was nodding again, eyes bulging.

Meredith sighed and shook her head. 'So, now the only person I have left on my team is Jared. And he's off sick!'

Steph grimaced. 'Oh. Actually, Jared is leaving too. He asked me to tell you. He's probably going to be off sick until it's time for him to leave. Actually I might be sick for a few days too.' Stuart nodded in agreement and gave a tiny cough. Together, they backed out of the office.

Meredith shook her head. She had lost her team. She had nothing prepared for the presentation. And now everyone was getting sick, on top of everything! Meredith reached into her drawer for her vitamin C with echinacea tablets. This was a disaster.

Taking Harper on to clean her house was the best decision Claire had made in a long time. And it seemed to be working out well for Harper as well. There was something incongruous about Harper when she was at work cleaning. It almost seemed like the tough, outspoken young woman became a little girl playing house. It was miraculous the way Harper would gently bring order out of chaos, setting up little systems and places to keep things. It was becoming normal to find neat labels taped to shelves and boxes in Harper's rounded handwriting. But it was more than that.

'You don't just tidy the house, Harper. You style it.' Claire had said, after coming through the door with the twins to find fresh, clear floors and surfaces, flowers and decorative vignettes brightening the corners and shelves.

'Not really.' Harper filled the kettle and flipped it on. 'It's all your stuff. Like, that's your blanket.' She gestured to an attractive throw draped over the couch.

'I disagree. You have a skill. I can see it. Like, what have you done to my coffee mug shelf to make it look so good? It didn't used to look like that.'

Harper gave a small laugh. 'I didn't do anything. You had too many mugs to fit there. I just took the ugly ones away and hid them in a shoebox. You could probably chuck them if you wanted to.'

'See. You have ideas that other people just wouldn't have. I think this is your spark, Harper.'

Harper's face clouded over at this unexpected compliment. She looked away. When she looked back, the unusually happy and relaxed Harper was gone. In her place was the closed-up and sullen girl Claire was used to.

Lily and Hope were tottering around on the rug, solemnly exchanging toys and chattering in what Claire liked to think was their 'twin language'.

Harper sat at the table with the two mugs of tea. Her face was supposed to look indifferent, but it was hard to believe there wasn't more happening under the surface. What was going on with her?

Harper took a quick sip of her tea and looked away. Then she looked back at Claire. 'I've been meaning to tell you something,' she said. 'I should have told you at the start, but I …' She looked away, looked down, picked up her tea, put it back on the table. 'I'm not – I – I'm on parole.' The last words came out in a rush. 'I was in prison for eight months and I'm on parole now.'

Claire took a slow breath. It was important that she didn't show any shock or surprise on her face. It was good that Harper was confiding in her at last. 'Okay. I'm glad you told me, Harper,' she said, in what she hoped was a natural tone of voice. 'It must be hard to keep all that a secret.'

Harper shrugged. 'Not really. It's harder to tell people.' She looked around the room slowly. 'I don't really like for people to know. It usually means the end of things.' She looked at Claire. 'Please don't tell the others.'

Claire tried an encouraging smile. 'I won't if you don't want me to.' She tried sipping her tea, but it wasn't cool enough yet. 'Are you in a good place now? Do you have supports in place?' Her old youth worker role. She slipped into it so easily.

Harper scowled and shrugged. 'It's fine.'

'And what about your family. Are they in the picture?'

Harper shot her a wounded look and shook her head. There was a slight twitch. She seemed to be suppressing a shudder. Claire realised that Harper would have already run this gamut of questions with countless social workers and parole officers. She decided to give it a rest.

Lily had had enough of the toy-exchange program and was preparing to embark on an adventure beyond the living room. She did not notice Hope's small fist clasped firmly on the waistband of her striped leggings.

She stood up, then toppled back to the floor with a *plop*. She looked bewildered.

'Will you still come and clean for me?'

Harper looked up. 'I'd like to. I mean, if it doesn't, like, bother you.' A ghost of a smile flickered across her face, then was gone.

Claire nodded. 'You're still Harper, aren't you?' She took a breath, hesitated, then spoke. 'I think things are going to change for you, Harper. I think good things are going to come your way.'

Harper's face, closed and hard, looked away.

CHAPTER TWENTY-ONE

Edith frowned at the dratted contraption in the corner of her kitchen and poured herself a strong cup of tea. She really should look at it today. Luke would be home later and he would ask if she'd looked at it this week, the dear child. Might as well get it done now.

She approached the machine gingerly and pressed the button. She sipped her tea as it whirred to life and went through its bleep routine.

Of course, she knew what Charles and Shelly would say about this. Charles, after all, was the one who bought the computer and set it up. Michelle had signed Edith up to the internet and the face book and whatever else was supposed to be essential these days. One couldn't possibly live without a computer – oh no! Not even if one had got along perfectly well without one for eighty-odd years. The computer had remained untouched for months. It was only when Luke took Edith through the basics that she began to venture onto the cipher space. She could just hear Charles and Shelly's amused groans. 'Of course, Gran does it when *Luke* suggests it. She would do anything for the Golden

Child!'; 'He-who-can-do-no-wrong has suggested something! Quick! Let's all listen!'

It was all nonsense, of course. Edith had always insisted that she loved her three grandchildren equally. Though 'equally' was a silly word, really. She had always loved Charles, Shelly and Luke the same *amount*, but it was impossible to treat three such different children *equally*. And perhaps she had been a little softer on Luke, the youngest, but that was just the way it was. He'd been such a little fellow when his parents died. But, there: she was rising to the bait again. She knew they only said this 'Golden Child' claptrap to get her goat.

The screen displayed a picture of Michelle's two little girls. Now she was supposed to move the arrow to the picture of the colourful circle and click two times. It could get rather fiddly if you didn't click just right. She consulted the exercise book she kept next to the computer. There was a list of things to do, written in Luke's square handwriting. So far, she was on track.

The computer hummed. Charles and Luke were especially different. She couldn't imagine two boys more opposite in personality. It was a wonder they were such firm friends. Perhaps it was their parents' death that made them so close? But then, they did fight like animals when they were younger.

The next screen showed the different places on the internet she could visit. One picture was Michelle's Instant Grams, where she could see photos of Shelly's family and their trip. Another was the newspaper. She couldn't remember what the third one was for. She clicked on the Instant Grams.

There were some new photos to look at. One of them showed Shelly with her husband and daughters at what looked like some sort of Lego exhibition. There was a Statue of Liberty, a Golden Gate Bridge and a huge Mount Rushmore, all made completely of Lego.

Edith smiled as she cast her mind back twenty-five years. Charles had simply adored his Lego sets. And he would get so angry when little Luke got into them. Luke would mix up the pieces to make all sorts of incredible creations. She remembered Charles screaming in frustration. Luke shouting, 'You're not the boss of me!' Charles smashing Luke's Lego sculpture (Edith honestly never knew what they were supposed to be. A spaceship? A houseboat?) into tiny pieces. Luke punching and kicking his brother, bursting into impassioned tears. She'd been at her wit's end wondering how to deal with them. 'Naughty boys! You wait until your grandfather gets home from work!' The truth was, her heart had gone out to both her boys. Charles's world had been turned upside down and, as the eldest, he was expected to step up and be responsible. He craved order. Luke, on the other hand, desperately wanted to be included in his big brother's world. And Luke had a creativity that couldn't be suppressed. She could see them now: Charles's stormy brow and Luke's tear-stained face. Both of their little chests heaving as she tried to sort them out. And then she remembered what happened next the day of that fight.

Shelly had put a bookmark in her copy of *Five Go Adventuring Again* and approached the mess of Lego bricks. She'd retrieved the three instruction booklets and turned each to the inventory page. Then she had sat down at the table and got to work.

Luke was the first to become mesmerised by the neat rows of matching bricks. 'I want to help!' he exclaimed.

Shelly handed Luke a red brick. 'Find me another one just like this,' she instructed. Luke crawled all over the floor in search of a matching brick. Shelly continued her sorting, lining up the bricks to match the lists in the booklet.

Charles stood still for a while, watching silently. Edith could see Shelly's methodical system was soothing the boy's fractured nerves.

Eventually, Charles summoned all of the dignity his ten years could muster and sat at the table next to Shelly. He picked up the 497 Galaxy Explorer instructions. 'I'm sorting this one,' he said in a tone of authority. Shelly gave a brief nod. Edith watched them for a moment, Shelly and Charles working silently side by side, Luke crawling happily among the coloured bricks at their feet. Edith left the room. When she returned, she was carrying three biscuit tins. As she placed a tin alongside each carefully gathered collection, Shelly beamed up at her. Edith gave Shelly a wink.

Oh dear. She hadn't been paying attention and now the computer was playing up. *Learn to Lose Weight FAST Using This One Weird Little Trick!* 'No. I don't want you.' she said aloud to the screen. How did she get back to where she was before? She was afraid to try anything in case it hurt the computer. She stared at the flashing red letters in bemusement. Perhaps, if she waited, they might go away of their own accord.

Now that she thought of it, she could see that the real reason that Charles and Luke had such a good relationship was Shelly. There was nothing obvious about it, but Shelly was the invisible glue for their odd little family.

Edith turned to a page in the exercise book filled with her own swirling copperplate. She took up her pen. *'Weird trick' weight loss – how to get rid of it?* Perhaps Luke could talk her through that later.

'Where does it say to do that? I didn't see anything about a rubber band in the instructions.'

Meredith and Luke were standing in the backyard of the farmhouse cafe. It had been a good morning's work. They had cleared the yard of overgrowth and bundled and stacked the green waste. They had replaced the broken pavers with the spare flagstones they had discovered around the side of the house. Now they were going to paint the side gate.

Luke was stirring the open can of paint. 'It's not in the instructions. It's another one of my Pa's tricks.' He took the rubber band Meredith passed him and fitted it around the can lengthwise, creating a rubber tightrope across the opening. 'Now watch this.' He dipped the brush into the paint and used the rubber tightrope to wipe the paint off the brush. The excess paint dropped straight back into the can. No waste.

'Where did your grandfather learn to do that?' Meredith asked.

Luke began painting the first vertical wooden slat. 'He was full of stuff like that. How to lay pavers. How to build a retaining wall. He wouldn't let any of us go for our licence until we showed him we knew how to check the oil levels and change a flat.' He dipped his brush back into the can. 'Pa wasn't the sort of person to say "I love you",' he said, 'but every Saturday, he'd teach us a new skill.'

'Why did you live with your grandparents?' Meredith asked. It was the wrong thing to say, she remembered as soon as she said it. She hadn't been concentrating and had forgotten that being too curious was rude sometimes. She watched Luke carefully. He didn't seem to mind the question or notice that she'd been maybe rude.

'Mum and Dad died when I was four,' he said, 'so I was brought up by Gran and Pa. You've met Gran,' he said, passing the other paintbrush to Meredith, 'and Pa died five years ago.'

'I'm sorry for your loss,' said Meredith. This, at least, was the correct response. She knew this much.

Luke smiled and shrugged. 'It's not your fault,' he said. 'We all found it hard when Pa died. I still miss him every day. I miss Mum and Dad too, but I think it was a lot harder on the others when they died. I reckon I was too young to really understand what was happening.

For almost as long as I remember, my idea of a normal family has been two grandparents and a brother and sister. Mum and Dad are like the characters in a nice story of long-ago.'

Meredith unwrapped the paintbrush and folded the packaging neatly. 'I never had any grandparents,' she said. 'Mum and Dad were pretty old when they had me, especially Dad. I sometimes wonder what it would have been like to have brothers and sisters.' She dipped the brush carefully in the tin. 'When I was younger, I would pretend to have a little sister. I'd teach her things, and she'd follow me everywhere.'

Luke grinned. 'That's the best thing about imaginary sisters. They always agree with you. What was her name?'

Meredith smiled. 'Alice. And she didn't always agree with me. We had pretend fights sometimes.'

'Who won?'

'Well, me. I'm older – I know better,' said Meredith.

Luke hooted with laughter.

She began painting the gate, starting from the other end. She watched as the dull grey turned to glossy white. For a while, they worked in silence.

It wasn't her role, of course, to do maintenance work on the cafe. By rights, she shouldn't be doing this at all. But it wasn't like they were doing anything wrong. She was just helping her friend and ensuring the cafe project got off the ground. Still, she would keep this to herself.

It was a good feeling to be helping a friend. Meredith's experience of friendship was limited and had always involved another girl taking her on as a compassion project. She was expected to respond with gratitude, but this always turned to resentment, and then the girl would leave. With Luke it was different. She never felt like Luke was doing her a favour just by having a conversation with her. He treated her like she had something to offer, and then she discovered she did have something to offer. She decided she wouldn't mind having friends, if they could be a friend like Luke.

She reached the middle of the gate and stepped back as Luke finished painting the slat. 'I do sometimes wonder what it would have been like if I'd had an older brother or sister. A real one, I mean. Siblings *have* to like you. They don't get a choice.'

'Oh, I don't know about that. My siblings chose not to like me plenty of times when I was growing up. They were constantly telling me to pull my head in.'

'See, but I think that's a good thing,' said Meredith shortly. Luke looked at her. 'Oh I don't mean you,' she added, and then paused. 'Well, I don't mean *just* you. It would be so useful to have somebody around who told you when you were getting it wrong, but who wouldn't go away.'

Luke stepped back from the gate and put his paintbrush down. He looked at her. 'Uh-oh. Hold still.' He grabbed the old T-shirt he was using as a rag. He came and stood in front of her, close, and brought his hand to the side of her face. 'There's paint.' he said. 'It's about to go everywhere.'

Her skin prickled as Luke caught and wiped the paint out of her hair with the T-shirt. She looked at him. 'Sometimes I think if I'd had an older sibling, I wouldn't be so much the way I am.'

Luke looked back at her. His eyes darkened somehow. 'I'm glad you're so much the way you are,' he said. He was looking at her.

Meredith blinked and stepped back. She pulled out her phone to check her reflection. 'Did you get it all?' Her voice a squeak.

Luke began cleaning the paintbrushes. When he spoke again, his tone was casual. 'Usually when a mate helps me with a working bee, I buy him a slab,' he said, 'but you don't strike me as a beer drinker. Maybe I could buy you dinner instead?'

'No.' Meredith shook her head firmly. She did not want Luke to pay her back. She wanted to keep things as they were. With him being grateful. With her being the valued friend.

'Oh. Okay.' Luke pressed the lid firmly onto the paint can. He was quiet for a minute. Meredith wondered if she'd said something wrong. She'd said there was no need to repay her. Surely she had done the right thing? But when Luke spoke again, it was with that same, easygoing tone. 'There must be something I can do?'

You can keep being my friend. 'No. There's nothing.'

Charles Mullaney's restored and extended Federation home in Middle Brighton was a haven of style and simplicity. White. Sunlit. Tasteful. The professionally decorated interior felt like a luxury hotel. And Charles should know: he spent half his life on five-star business trips. Scrupulously tidy and fully appointed, the only thing that was not graceful and understated in Charles's house was his downstairs room.

'The Cavern' – its name announced by a novelty car numberplate affixed over the door – was a garish tribute to Billy Joel, circa 1983. It was set up like an American bar, or, more specifically, like the set of a bar in an American TV show. A bookshelf beside the air hockey table was crammed with piles of battered board games. The bar itself boasted three beer taps, two humidity-controlled wine fridges and a full complement of spirits and mixers.

When she first visited, Shelly, his sister, had looked askance at the leather bar stools, the neon-strip lighting and the life-size cut-out of Christie Brinkley. 'Charles, you must never bring a girl down here,' she said. 'You'd scare her off completely. You don't even drink that much. What do you need a bar for?'

'I don't expect you to understand, Michelle,' Charles had responded. Then Shelly had started talking about how Charles had to get 'out there', how he wasn't going to 'meet someone' if he spent all his time at home in this lurid cave. Charles had busied himself with the cocktail garnishes and tuned her out completely.

Tonight, it was just Luke and Charles. They were meeting for Budget Beers. Every couple of months, the brothers got together to drink beer and talk finance. In the past, Luke had provided the beer and Charles the financial advice, but lately they had been meeting in Charles's cavern. Luke had protested at first. 'You are giving me the benefit of all your financial experience, and I can't even shout you a pint?'

Charles didn't see it that way. 'This is fun for me,' he reassured his brother, 'and I'd much rather meet here than some pub. Even your pub.'

He rubbed his hands together in anticipation as Luke pulled out a green binder. 'It's been a good season,' Luke said. 'Plenty of snow, but not so much that people feel they have to make the most of it and can't take a break. And Flic, the new manager, is fantastic.'

'Excellent. So, do I get to take my cut?'

Luke groaned. 'You do realise that me giving you money to invest on my behalf is not the same as you "taking a cut". You should *actually* take a cut. You have earned me so much money over the years.'

Charles pursed his lips. 'Family doesn't pay,' he said firmly. 'I have fun playing with your money. And you always supply me with free beer and wedges when I go skiing. Besides,' he gestured around the room, 'look what happens when I get spending money. It's not a pretty sight.'

They lapsed into companionable silence as he cast his eye over the figures. 'These are excellent,' he said. 'You've got things down to a fine art now you've sorted out your suppliers. Have you thought about expanding?'

Luke took a sip of his beer. 'It's funny you should mention that. I was just thinking about it this week.'

Charles raised his eyebrows. 'Is that right? Well, I think the timing's spot on. We should start looking at Buller and Hotham to see if there are any likely places. You could even consider franchising.'

Luke nodded. 'I was actually thinking about Copeton.'

Charles placed his beer firmly down in front of him and peered at his brother. 'Copeton. You're thinking of opening a ski bar in Copeton?'

Luke grinned. 'Not a ski bar, a cafe. Breakfasts and lunches. And good coffee, of course.'

'But a cafe in the outer suburbs is a completely different business model to a bar on the slopes. You can't just replicate Powder Keg in Copeton.'

'I don't want to replicate Powder Keg,' said Luke. 'I want to try something new. I'm getting too old to be traipsing to Japan and Canada in the off-season. The bar is running fine without me being there all the time. It's time for a new challenge.'

Charles raised his eyebrows. 'It would make better business sense to stick with what's working,' he said.

'It would make better lifestyle sense for me to stay in the same place for more than a few months at a time.' Luke took a sip of his beer. 'Think of it as me broadening my skill set.'

They sat quietly for a moment, the weight of unsaid words between them. Charles knew what Shelly would want him to say. Shelly would want Charles to ask Luke about Olivia. Shelly would want Charles to ask Luke if he was okay since the break-up. She'd been in his ear about it only a week ago.

'He's running away.' His sister gazed at him earnestly through the tablet screen, her eyes cartoonishly large, her face a delicate shade of lavender, two perky rabbit ears blooming from her forehead. Madeleine, his niece, squirmed in her lap, tapping at the animation filter settings.

'He's fine,' Charles had said. He had made his own face morph into a walrus. Madeleine giggled.

'So you don't think it's odd that he just moves back home weeks after he breaks up with his girlfriend of two years? Just ups and leaves right before the ski season starts? And he's taken up crochet! Don't you think it's weird that he's taken up crochet?'

'When are you going to trust that Luke can manage his business? It's very successful. He knows what he's doing.'

'Charles! I'm not talking about his business. I'm talking about his emotions. Is he okay? Has he moved on? You need to talk to him!'

He shifted in his chair. 'I thought that was your job.'

'Luke never talks to me about his love life. Anyway, it's not the same when you're talking through a screen.' Small rainbows began showering from Shelly's ears. A unicorn horn appeared on her head. 'Just ask him if he's okay. Ask him if his heart is broken.'

He looked at his brother sipping his beer. Luke looked like a person with a perfectly intact heart. 'Where are you thinking of putting this cafe?'

'I've been offered a good deal in the new housing estate. Very cheap rent, and the building is perfect. An old farmhouse, and the landlord is paying for modifications. It already has a commercial kitchen. The previous owners used to run a pie business from home. You could fit tables enough to serve fifty people and still have room for wheelchairs and strollers.'

Charles watched Luke as he spoke. His brother always became so animated when he had an idea for a new venture, but this was something else. He cut him off. 'Luke, a cafe is one thing, but haven't you thought of putting it on Main Street or next to the station? There's no point having cheap rent and nice premises if you're miles away from all of the customers!'

Luke beamed. 'But there will be customers. I've been talking it over with Meredith—'

'Who is Meredith?' Charles interrupted.

'She's my contact at Rivergum Estate.' Luke smiled. 'We were talking about how, once it's a display village, there will—'

'So she's from the building place,' Charles interrupted again. 'Not exactly a disinterested party. I'm surprised she didn't tell you how the streets will be paved with gold.'

Luke sighed. 'It's not like that. We're actually friends. This whole venture just came up in conversation naturally.'

'I'm sure it did. I don't want to see you taken for a ride.' He looked at Luke carefully. 'Who is this "Meredith" person, anyway? If I were Shelly, I'd say you're in love.'

Luke picked up his beer and took a long draught. He placed the glass squarely down on its 'Uptown Girl' beer mat. 'I told you. She's just a friend,' he answered at last. 'Anyway, it's still just an idea. I can do some more research before we catch up again. Let's look at the forecast for this month.'

Charles raised his eyebrows. Luke was bringing the conversation back to finance. There was a first time for everything.

CHAPTER TWENTY-TWO

Meredith was having a difficult time of it. Her life was always a perfect model of order and routine. That is what made her great. That is what made her such a success. She was a master of her thoughts and the queen of logic and reason.

Until now.

She knew that having a friend was a bad idea. She'd known it from the start. She'd got by without friends just fine before now. Luke had messed everything up. Meredith was becoming forgetful, scattered even. The idea of Luke was taking up too much space in her brain. Conversations with him played on a loop as her mind sifted through a gallery of his smiles. Of course, there was a voice in her head that suggested to her that these were not normal 'friendship' feelings she was experiencing, but she never paid any attention to that voice. It was not possible that she had those feelings for Luke, because that would simply be unacceptable. She was just not a sexual person, that's all.

More likely it was because Luke was such an anomaly. He didn't fit into any of the categories she had developed to classify the men she encountered. He wasn't middle-aged, sweat-stained and power-hungry, with a belly that tested the tensile strength of his expensive suit. He was good-looking, but he wasn't an arrogant young man with a shark-eyed smirk and a fervent adherence to the Church of Armani. Nor was he the type to hang out of a car window with his hyena-pack friends, shouting obscenities at girls on the street. He wasn't a weak-chinned sycophant, wasn't an absent workaholic. Luke was an enigma. But Meredith was smart and good at puzzles. She'd work him out eventually.

Yasmin shifted in her swivel chair. It was difficult to get comfortable at her desk (or in her car, or on the couch, or in bed, or anywhere for that matter). She felt so unwieldy. She wished, not for the first time, that she could take her belly off for ten minutes, just to have a rest from its relentless bulk. The relentless bulk nudged her ribs, then kicked her in the bladder. As no one in the office was looking her way, she gave her belly a furtive hug. Then she got to work on her emails.

Ugh. Thirty-seven unread. Oooh! But two were from Meesha! She'd save them till last, as a reward for working through the boring ones.

Reply. Flag. Delete. She was so absorbed in the task that she didn't realise a person had walked into her office until the woman was standing right in front of her desk. Yasmin's heart sank. It was Ma Kelly. How did she get in here? 'Can I help you?' Her voice was smooth. *Show no fear. Deep breaths.*

Ma Kelly did not shout. Instead, she spoke in a threatening whisper, spitting her words out with vitriol. 'I know all about it. Don't you bother hiding from me. I know your *plans*. I know you did a deal with the papists at the old folks' home to funnel more Muslims into here. I know how you want to build a mosque to attract more and more of your kind. And once you have *majority*, once you have *taken over*, you're gonna declare a caliphate. The Muslim State of Copeton, with sharia law for everybody whether they like it or not. Do you think I don't know?'

Usually, in a situation like this, Yasmin would stand up, to remove the height difference and gain an equal footing with her opponent. But, these days, there was just no dignified way to do that. She sighed. 'Of course. You've got me. Sharia law. But, like you said, we're in league with the Catholics, so it will have to be a mix of sharia law and canon law. That is the deal those pesky Catholics made. Not just mosque, but mass as well! And rosary beads will be compulsory for everybody.'

Ma Kelly narrowed her eyes. 'This isn't over,' she hissed, then turned on her heel and marched out of the room. Yasmin saluted her retreating form with a single finger.

Yasmin pulled out her letter opener and grabbed a large envelope from her in-tray. She ripped it open savagely and pulled out its contents. Just some brochures. She fed them, along with the envelope, into the shredder on her desk. So satisfying! Next!

If she had been paying attention, she might have noticed that the next envelope was strangely crumpled and that it had no stamp. Indeed, she might have noticed that this envelope had not been in her in-tray ten minutes ago. But Yasmin was not paying attention. She just wanted to rip something.

In one swift movement, she slit the envelope wide open. It was only then that she realised that the envelope was moving.

As if in a frenzy, spider after huntsman spider came clambering out of the envelope, running up Yasmin's arm, dropping onto Yasmin's belly. As she shrieked and struggled to stand, more spiders, these ones dead, fell from the envelope to the floor. Steve from Accounting and Jan from Facilities rushed over to her desk. Steve recoiled at the sight of the spiders, but Jan reached purposefully over, hoisted Yasmin out of her chair and brushed the spiders off her with firm, broad sweeps.

'No Copeton caliphate!'

They looked around, startled. A young man – *was he the same one as from the meeting?* – was standing near the door. He was filming them on his phone. How long had he been there? Then he was gone.

Yasmin kept trying to shake spiders off herself long after they were all dead. Steve from Accounts tried to compensate for his initial cowardice by stomping on every spider he could find. The floor was strewn with their mangled brown and grey corpses. Yasmin couldn't bear to look at them.

Within ten minutes, a grainy video of Yasmin, shrieking and covered in spiders, had been uploaded to the UCR website. It was shared and reposted many times. Within an hour, the video had made it onto the mainstream news websites.

'I need to ask you something,' said Meredith.

It was Tuesday evening, a week before the next meeting. Luke stood at the counter of the farmhouse cafe, pouring raw sugar into rinsed-out jam jars. Meredith liked to watch the way he worked. He had a deft and practised air about him. The opening of the paper sack was folded into a sharp point, creating a spout. So far, none of the golden-brown granules had gone anywhere except inside the small clean jars where they belonged. She smiled, in spite of herself.

Meredith had debated whether she should come tonight. She was running out of time to put the presentation together for work. There was still so much to do. By rights, she should be locked in her office right now, spending the night powering through the work of four people. But she *liked* spending time with Luke. It was maybe her favourite thing to do. This was important. She was finally developing her interpersonal skill set. She had made a real friend, somebody whose company she enjoyed, somebody who was happy to spend time with her. She was finally making progress on her social goals.

Luke eased the sack upright as the jar filled. 'What's on your mind?'

She took the full jar from Luke, screwed on its gold lid and set it on the tray. 'Why did you decide to lease this cafe?'

It was Malcolm who had planted the anxious seed of doubt in her mind. Stopping by her office on his way to lunch, he had loudly commiserated with her on the loss of her team. 'Poor little Meredith – a manager with nobody to manage! Chin up, you'll get through it. And I heard you lost your tenant. I suppose you won't get that cafe you wanted after all. It was probably a little ambitious to think you could convince somebody to open a business in an old farmhouse. Now, if you'd listened to me in the first place ...'

'It's okay. I've got a new tenant.' Meredith didn't look up from her screen. She had little time for unscheduled work conversations.

Malcolm paused. 'What are you talking about?'

'I've got a new tenant. I emailed you about this two weeks ago.'

He dropped his phone. 'What? When? There's been nothing from head office.'

She switched her monitor off and reached for her handbag. 'It didn't come from head office. I arranged for it informally. But the paperwork's been done.'

'Who's the tenant? Where did he come from?'

She sighed impatiently. 'Luke Mullaney. He runs the Powder Keg ski bar at Falls Creek. He plans to name the new cafe Beanie. If you want to check the email, it was sent on the twenty-sixth.'

'Ah. So you made an informal last-minute arrangement with a man who runs a ski bar. I think I understand everything now.' Malcolm was doing something with the tone of his voice. She didn't have the patience to decipher what it meant.

Malcolm placed his hand on her desk and leaned forward. 'I doubt it took a simple conversation to convince him. I bet you went above and beyond. I bet you crossed a few boundaries to get him on board.'

Meredith remembered the unofficial working bees she'd spent getting the cafe fixed up. 'I don't see how that's any of your business,' she said.

'Ha! So you're not denying it. You are unbelievable.'

A key ring jangled on the buckle of Malcolm's laptop case. Meredith watched it idly. How much longer would this conversation take?

'People always talk about discrimination against women. You never hear people talk about the unfair advantages a sexy woman has in the workplace.'

The key ring was gold, and had the crest of one of Melbourne's elite private boys' schools on it.

'Men like me, we have to use our brains, our wits. It's not like I can lift my skirt and show a bit of leg to get what I want.'

Meredith blinked and looked up. 'Pardon? Are you talking about me?'

Malcolm rolled his eyes. 'No. I'm talking about some other girl who batted her eyelashes and scored herself a man willing to beg, roll over, shake hands and sign a contract.'

She paused to process. That was sarcasm. He *was* talking about her. 'There was nothing inappropriate in the arrangement. It's true that Luke is a friend, but he applied through all the proper channels …'

Malcolm interrupted with a scoffing sound. 'A friend! Oh, that's rich! Yeah, I'm sure this Luke is all about the friendship and nothing else. He is definitely not your friend. Don't act like you don't know exactly what you're doing. The only way you managed to get yourself out of a desperate situation is because you managed to get yourself somebody desperate to – bone – you.' Malcolm tasted the last three words lasciviously, then hitched his laptop bag up his shoulder as he prepared to lumber off. 'If you want to use your feminine wiles to get ahead in this game, fine. Just don't play innocent when somebody calls you out on it.'

Meredith stood up and stared levelly at Malcolm as he attempted to raise his eyebrows impressively. She held his gaze long enough to allow the silence to grow distinctly uncomfortable. 'You know nothing,' she pronounced, and swept from the room.

Luke was opening another sack of sugar. 'Why did I take up this lease? Because it was a good business opportunity and I wanted to help you out.'

Meredith watched the granules tumble into the jar. 'You wanted to help me out. Because you're my friend?'

Luke grinned. 'Because I'm your friend, yes.'

They worked in silence for a little while. When the tray was packed with full glass jars, Meredith picked it up. 'Are you attracted to me?' she said.

A spill. Some of the granules landed outside the jar Luke was filling. He put the sack carefully back on the table and adjusted the paper spout. 'Am I attracted to you?' He was being careful. He worked on the paper spout for a long time before he spoke again. 'Am I really that obvious?'

Meredith frowned. A rhetorical question. Which meant …

Luke sighed, and gave a frank smile. 'I guess I was waiting for the right time to talk about it. I didn't think you felt the same way.'

She narrowed her eyes. 'Do you want to bone me?'

Luke gave a start of surprise, knocking the sugar so that it poured across the table. 'What? What is this about?'

'Do you want to bone me? Yes or no?'

'Meredith …'

'Yes or no? Do you want to bone me?'

He gave a small bark of laughter. 'Well, I mean, I don't *not* want to bone you …' he quipped, then his smile evaporated. 'Meredith, are you okay?'

Meredith was not okay. She was definitely not okay. Everything was a mess. The sugar. It was all over the table. Some of it was even on the floor. They would get ants. They would definitely get ants now. And her feelings. Her feelings were everywhere. Panic, and shame, and despair, and sadness, and guilt and a whole bunch of other ones, too complicated to process right now. There were hot tears in her eyes. Her throat felt like it might burst. She never cried. What was this?

She slammed the tray down on the table. 'No!' she shouted. 'This is wrong! This is *all wrong!*'

Luke's voice was quiet. 'Why?' he said. 'I mean, "bone" isn't the word I would use. We're not teenagers in an American high school movie, but apart from that, it's just how I feel. Do you not feel the same way?'

She reached over and yanked the sack upright with a jolt. 'What I feel is irrelevant! What I feel is *none of your business!*'

She started to fold the bag closed, but Luke placed his hands over hers. 'I'm not done yet,' he said, and firmly removed the bag from her grip. 'I want to know why you are so upset.'

Meredith said nothing. Her head felt like it was going to explode with heat and emotion.

Luke unfolded the bag of sugar. 'Meredith,' he said, 'what is this about?'

She backed to the door with shaky steps. When she spoke, it was in a strangled sob. 'You were never my friend!' she said. Then she stumbled blindly out of the room.

One of the parents had offered to throw the after-party to celebrate the closing night of the school production. It had not been an official school event, but every member of the cast and crew had received an invitation. It would be Meredith's first real party. Although she went to an all-girls school, the production itself was co-ed, with boys from the neighbouring private school invited to fill the male roles.

Boys were still exotic creatures to the Year 10 class of Bridgewood Girls Academy, but to Meredith, who had no brothers or boy cousins, who had attended an all-girls school since kindergarten, these rowdy, grunting specimens seemed almost an alien race. She liked to study them.

Some were smelly and bad-mannered. She didn't bother too much with this set. Some were full of jokes, and it was a different kind of humour from the usual homeroom antics of the more boisterous girls in her class. Many were boastful and full of their own importance. A few were rather good-looking. But there was only one who was divinely beautiful.

Sebastian Gordon had bright blue eyes and carefully tousled blond hair. And his teeth were so straight and white. Meredith spent a lot of her time in the lighting department at the back of the school hall casting furtive glances at Sebastian's lazy smile, the way Sebastian's hair would flop over his perfect forehead. The way Sebastian would casually flick his perfect hair away from his perfect eyes.

The best time of her day was approximately 4.05pm. The school day over, Meredith would walk into the school hall for rehearsal; she'd walk past the group of main actors waiting to talk to the drama teacher/director, and into the lighting box. When she was about halfway across the hall, Sebastian would call out 'Hello, Meredith James!' from amid his guffawing cast-mates. She would blush and nod and quicken her step. Only once she was safely hidden behind the mixing board would she permit herself to smile.

On the inside back cover of her binder, where the others couldn't see, she practised signing her name: 'Meredith Gordon', 'Mrs M. Gordon'. She finally had a name to play love-match formula with. 'MEREDITH LOVES SEBASTIAN' only got 32 per cent, but 'MEREDITH JAMES LOVES SEBASTIAN GORDON' got 67 per cent. She'd fiddled around with middle names and initials, but couldn't get a score higher than that. It was a silly game anyway.

She sometimes wondered what it would be like to chat to him. By himself, away from all his hangers-on. She just knew he would be sweet and intelligent and articulate and witty. What would it be like to hold his hand? Would he have warm hands? He looked like he would have warm hands. What would it be like to *kiss* him? She held her breath and started to calculate the minutes until the next 4.05pm.

As the after-party drew nearer Meredith's thoughts about Sebastian acquired a new focus. Would he talk to her? Would she be able to think of anything to say back? She was in a wonderful agony for days.

And now here she was, standing in Portia Fulham's five-star, industrial-grade kitchen awkwardly sipping some sort of mango and mint punch. It had too many *bits* floating in it. It was hard to manage.

And then, all of a sudden, Sebastian was *there*. Right in front of her. Seemingly brought in on the tide of all his mates.

'Hello, Meredith James.'

She almost choked on a piece of mango. She said, 'Hello, Sebastian Gordon.' Her voice came out all wrong.

One of Sebastian's mates was nudging another of Sebastian's mates. It felt like everyone was tuned in to their conversation.

'Listen, Meredith.' Sebastian dropped his voice to a confidential tone. 'This party's really noisy and there are people everywhere. Do you want to go somewhere quiet where we can just talk?'

That was *exactly* what she wanted. How did he know? She nodded mutely and Sebastian took the cup of punch from her hand and set it on the table. Then he put his arm around her and led her out of the room. His crew made hooting noises.

'Ignore them. They're dickheads.'

She smiled and still couldn't think of anything to say. She walked away as if on a cloud.

He led her to a quiet room and closed the door. For a minute or two it was lovely. It was exciting. Sebastian started kissing her the minute the door was closed. Meredith felt surprised and *honoured*. All the girls liked Sebastian. But then – well, she didn't like to think about the details. Suffice it to say, Sebastian seemed to understand 'No' and 'No, really, stop' and 'Stop it now!' to mean 'Please, persist in what you are doing until I am compelled to punch you hard in the face.'

To this day, she could still see the horrified look in Sebastian's eyes as his nose bled through his fingers. 'I'm sorry ...' she'd faltered in a small voice.

'What is *wrong* with you?' he spat and stormed out of the room.

Carly Matthews walked up to her locker after homeroom a few days later.

'I just thought you should know,' she simpered, with faux concern, 'all the Barkley Grammar boys are talking about you. They all know that you tried to have sex with Sebastian, but that you couldn't because you've got teeth … down there …' She giggled and ran away.

The story of Meredith James's monster vagina was soon all over the school. It had been important to Sebastian that he reclaim some dignity after returning to his group of friends with a blood nose and a split lip. He had been as creative as he could. In some versions the monstrous beast had sharp teeth; other stories told of broken glass or barbed wire. The girls repeated the joke gleefully. They loved any urban legend that involved sex in some way and this one was especially delicious because it cut Meredith James down to size. Carly Matthews and her friends had been particularly insulted when Sebastian singled out this perfect little princess with the clear skin and swingy ponytail as his trophy. Meredith was not even in their *group*. She was *nobody*.

Whenever Meredith walked past Sebastian's friends on her way to the train station after school, they would clutch their crotches protectively in mock fear. One time, they ran wailing out of the platform's waiting room the minute she stepped in. 'And stay out!' she muttered aloud to herself. The lady in the ticket booth overheard and gave her a complicit smile.

CHAPTER TWENTY-THREE

'So,' said Peter.

Claire looked up. Peter's voice had that careful edge it got when he knew they were about to have an argument.

'So,' said Peter, 'tell me more about Harper.'

She put the wet plate in the drainer, stiffening slightly. 'I told you: Harper goes to my crochet group. She doesn't drive so I give her a lift there. She helps me out with cleaning sometimes, and I let her use our computer and internet when she needs to.' She tried to infuse a sense of finality in her tone and reached nonchalantly for the next plate. Peter raised an eyebrow at her. She sighed. 'And I think she might be at risk. She doesn't seem to have anyone around her.'

Peter picked up a pile of clean cutlery and took it to the drawer to sort. 'It's not your job to fix her, you know,' he said shortly. It sounded like he wanted to say a lot more, but instead focused his energy on clashing the knives and forks into their spots.

She grimly scrubbed at the plate. Peter could be so condescending! Did he even know what he sounded like? She huffed out a sigh. 'I

223

don't want to fix anybody.' *That's more YOUR style!* 'But she's come from a difficult situation. I'm just being helpful. And she helps me too.'

She handed him the dish. He accepted it warily. 'What do you mean? What situation has she come from?'

Claire reached for another plate. 'Well, there's been a few things, like the way she overreacted to you when you first met, that makes me think she might be dealing with trauma. Plus, I think she's served time in prison.'

'Prison? What? That's not nothing, Claire.'

'Yeah, well. It happens. Not everyone has had it as easy as us.'

'I hope you don't leave valuables lying around.'

'What are you implying? Harper's not like that! And it's not like we have anything worth stealing. What? You think she might make off with my rainbow plastic Kmart jewellery?'

'I just think it's an unfair situation to put somebody who has just got out of prison into. For all you know, she might have a problem with stealing. Maybe that's why she went to prison.'

Claire jabbed a squirt of Morning Fresh at the sink, as it refilled with fresh hot water. 'Don't you think you're being just a touch judgemental? Just because somebody looks different and dresses differently, they can't be trusted? Harper's not a thief. That's not the sense I got. There's something else going on there.'

'Sense? Sense? Claire had a sense. Well, I guess I should rest easy. I can't argue with that.' He shook the tea towel dry with a snap. 'You know nothing about this woman! People don't just go to jail for no reason. Have you ever left her alone with the children?'

She paused mid-scrub. She'd really thought she'd gained some moral high ground with the 'don't judge people because they're different' line, but he'd seen right through it. They'd been having arguments for so long, they were becoming experts on each other's tactics. He peered at her. 'Well? Have you?'

She placed the scourer carefully on the side of the sink and turned to face him. 'Last Thursday afternoon, Harper was over. The twins were asleep and I just had to zip up to the shops. Harper said she didn't mind watching them. I was gone for ten minutes and they were still asleep when I got back. I *trust her.*'

Peter shook his head. 'So you didn't feel the need to consult me before letting a *convicted criminal* near our kids. Good to know I'm important to you. Good to know you respect my opinion.' He slapped the tea towel onto the bench. 'I can't do this right now,' he said abruptly, and strode out of the kitchen.

Claire banged the pot down on the sink and followed him out of the kitchen, dripping dishwater as she went. Peter stalked into the study and closed the door firmly. Slamming the door would be undignified. Peter didn't slam. Peter merely shut the door with enough force to provide a loud full stop to their conversation.

'Oh, so I'll just finish these dishes myself, then, will I? That's *convenient,*' she shouted after him, a little lamely. She had an uneasy feeling he might have made a good point somewhere along the line.

The sound of the printer grumbled out from the study as Claire put the last dishes away and wiped down the sink. Peter returned to the kitchen holding a piece of paper. 'Great timing,' she said, hanging up the tea towel to dry. But a lot of the snark had gone from her voice.

He handed her the piece of paper. 'You said Harper's been using the computer. Have a look at the browser history.'

Claire took the piece of paper. There was a list of URLs and dates. Peter had made asterisks next to some of them in scratchy pen. She recognised the UCR website among them.

'These are all extremist anti-Islam and anti-refugee sites,' said Peter.

'Looks like your friend Harper has been busy. What if prison turned her into a white supremacist?'

Claire shook her head. 'You watch too many movies. This means nothing. I've been down a rabbit hole of these sites myself. It was probably my browser history. Just because you visit a website, doesn't mean you agree with it.'

'No, but look.' He took his pen and underlined a section of text on one of the URLs. 'This is a members-only section of the website. It looks like an administrator platform.' He passed the paper back to her. 'Has Harper ever told you what she's working on when she uses the computer in the study?'

'It's nothing,' said Claire. But in her mind, something had quietly clicked into place: last Friday.

She had been walking the kids to school. The racist ice-cream truck had driven past. Ben had waved to it and said 'Harper!' Claire looked up to see that there was a passenger in the van, but couldn't see her face. Ben said it was Harper, but Claire assumed he was mistaken. But what if he'd been right? Why was Harper getting a lift with the racist loudspeaker man?

Later that evening, when the next day's lunches were all packed, Claire pulled out the newspaper covering the Copeton protest. She had bought it after meeting at Lottie's that day, so she had a copy of the double-page spread where her crocheted flowers were featured. Now, however, she was looking for more information about the UCR. She turned to the first page of the article, which was accompanied by a large photo of the march. Claire gasped. The protester was further back in the crowd, but still, she was unmistakeable.

It was Harper.

High Score! Are you enjoying playing Word Smash? Please leave us a rating and review!

Meredith dismissed the notification box and began a new game. She felt her brain slide into comfortable numbness as she solved the puzzles. It was her second day home from work. Tomorrow she would have to go in. She couldn't be sick for three days without a doctor's certificate. She nestled further under the doona and allowed herself to become absorbed by the colourful game.

Usually, the game would be interrupted every few minutes with an ad. Meredith had found she could bypass this by switching her phone to aeroplane mode. This had the added benefit of blocking all of her phone calls. A few had come in before she'd discovered this hack. One had been from work and two from Luke. She'd ignored all three.

There was a knock at the door. A delivery? A parcel? Her breathing quickened as she burrowed further under the covers. *Go away. Please go away. I am invisible. I do not exist.* A minute passed. There were no more knocks. She felt her heart rate slow as she turned her attention back to Word Smash.

She forced herself to go to work the next day. Her brain was buzzing as she pulled into her allocated car space. She did not feel like she was in work mode. She was still processing her failure to achieve her social goals, the loss of her one friend. She passed one of the directors on the way to the lift.

'All set for the Ironbark Room at nine?' Meredith had no idea what he was talking about, but she nodded smoothly and stepped into the lift. As the automatic doors rolled shut, she felt a jolt of horror. The twenty-fifth! *Today* was the twenty-fifth! She was supposed to give a groundbreaking presentation today! How could this have happened? She had no time and nothing prepared.

The CEO's personal assistant met her as she stepped out of the lift.

'Meredith! Oh thank goodness! I've been trying to call you. Did you get my emails? Are you okay? We should probably go in now. Almost everyone's there already.'

They stepped into the boardroom. Sitting around the large, central table were the CEO and the board of directors. Meredith introduced herself to the thirteen men and tried to keep the note of panic out of her voice. She had no plan. She had no plan.

The door opened and the director she had met on her way to the lift strode in. 'Sorry I'm late, everybody!' he announced. 'What did I miss?'

'Nothing at all,' she said. 'We were just getting started.'

Stalling for time, she placed her bags on the side table near the front and looked through them for inspiration. She had nothing to hand out, nothing to display on the screen, no visual aids whatsoever. Her designer handbag was small and contained only the essentials. Perhaps she could bribe the directors with breath mints? Her laptop was no use – she had nothing prepared, electronic or otherwise. Meredith's eye caught the blue and gold ripples peeking out of her crochet workbag. Her brain worked very fast. Then she took a deep breath and turned to face the directors.

'For years now, our approach to our display homes has been much the same as our competitors'. We dress to impress. Our homes are sleek, sophisticated, on-trend. We aim to stir up feelings of admiration in our clientele. But what if we could evoke a feeling more powerful than admiration? What if our display units could make you feel, well, *homesick*?'

She turned to her bag on the side table. In one swift, fluid movement, she swept the ripple blanket from its bag and shook it out across the boardroom table. The effect was dramatic. The richness of colour and texture against the blank white tabletop, the steel conference chairs, the black and grey suits: a couple of the directors almost gasped.

'We don't want the visitors to our village to feel impressed. We want them to feel like they have come home. We need to tap into that deep yearning that they already have – it's why they came to visit in the first place.'

'Well, that all sounds very interesting, but how do you expect to achieve it?' rumbled the finance director.

Meredith leaned forward confidentially. 'Let me talk to you about the "handmade edge". In the past, we've bought all of our furnishings in bulk to use across all of our display villages. It's efficient and makes good economic sense, but it also makes for bland displays, lacking in warmth. What I propose for Copeton is a new approach. We source local makers to provide bespoke soft furnishings for each display home in the village. We could even provide some of these decor items for purchase in the sales office. In fact' – Meredith was on a roll now, her pulse was racing, her brain bursting – 'we should host a monthly makers market, right there in the village, to inspire people to visit Copeton, to promote the nesting instinct. And all of our branding should move towards ideas of coming home.'

Now that Meredith had the idea, it was easy for her to spin out the details and projections. Several of the directors were nodding by the time she finished and a few of them even clapped.

She folded the blanket away as people filed out of the room. People were even suggesting she spearhead this bold new initiative. This was who she was. This was where she was supposed to be. This was what she was good at. The Friendship Experiment had failed. She could see that now. Friendship was a useless distraction.

Harper ran. She was blocks away now, but she didn't stop running. If she stopped running she would have to think and she couldn't manage all of her thoughts. So she ran and ran until her lungs burned and her limbs flailed. She had nowhere to go, and she was going there at top speed.

Yasmin heaved herself out of her car and lumbered to her front door. She was feeling so enormous. She was glad it was Tuesday. Omar would have dinner on, and Yasmin could pass out on the couch for a bit. Everything ached. Her face, her legs, her feet, the insides of her elbows, her neck and her back – oh, her back. Yasmin stifled a yawn as she unlocked the front door and waddled down the hallway.

Omar was checking the oven as Yasmin sank into an armchair and kicked off her shoes. She shifted her weight around. It was impossible to get comfortable. 'So I was talking to Jan today,' she said, with a grunt of frustration. Omar said nothing, but she continued anyway. 'She was going on about how she's scared for my safety and doesn't want me to get hurt. Her genius suggestion? Stop wearing hijab! "Oh Yasmin, it only needs to be for a bit. It's making you a target. What if you just wore a beanie instead?" Ugh! It's like, let's not expect them to behave like decent human beings. Oh no! Apparently it's my fault for looking like a target! "Oh Yasmin, would you just compromise your entire belief system for us? There's a dear. Some white men want to behave like dickheads."'

Yasmin glanced across at Omar. He hadn't responded. Usually her Jan impersonations set Omar off on a whole comedy routine, but there he was, quietly busying himself with the zucchini. Was he cross about something? Or just tired? 'Omar?'

He grunted and tipped the zucchini into the slow cooker. Then he slapped the oven mitts down on the bench. 'Well, it's not like she doesn't have a point!' he finally exclaimed.

She watched him carefully. 'It's not like she doesn't have a point. Oh wow, I can just see the headlines: "Oppressive Muslim Husband Forces Wife to *Not* Wear Hijab!"'

He didn't even crack a smile. 'That's not what I mean. Of course I'm not going to tell you to do that. But Jan has a point. Things are getting dangerous. And you are becoming a target.'

She shifted again in her seat. 'So what? So how is that my fault? Why is it *me* who has to change my behaviour? I am so sick of this! Here comes Yasmin the Muslim. The ambassador for all things brown. Want to say something offensive? It's her job to explain to you how to behave decently. What's that? You don't want to behave decently? Don't worry! It's her job to change her behaviour to accommodate that too!'

'Yasmin, it's not that simple. How do you think it feels for me to say goodbye to you every morning without knowing what's going to happen to you? What some hate-filled nutter might get it into his head to do?'

'I'm not some weak princess who needs to be protected or rescued!' she shot back. 'Maybe *you* need to respect *me*!' It was a cheap shot, really. Changing this argument into a feminist debate would bring Yasmin onto her home turf. But Omar was having none of it.

'It doesn't make me an oppressive member of the patriarchy if I don't like it when my wife receives daily death threats and rape threats from anonymous pricks.'

'But that's not my fault! That's just how the internet responds when it wants to silence an outspoken woman. It happens all the time. I shouldn't have to change who I am to please some trolls.'

'I'm not just talking about internet trolls.' He spoke slowly, through gritted teeth. 'That woman with the spiders – what if she'd been armed? What if the envelope had anthrax or something? What if all this stress is harming the baby? I just think it might be time to take maternity leave early. Keep a low profile.'

Yasmin stretched her legs out in front of her. 'Ugh! Keep a low profile. That's all I ever do! Every day, watching myself. Watching my behaviour so that I'm a good representation of my culture, because half the time I'm the only one. And when I do hang out with other Muslims, it's made out to be something sinister. I am sick of this low profile. I am tired. I am so tired.'

Omar's phone started ringing. He fished it out of his pocket. 'Ah, Imam Jamil,' he said, reading the screen, and answered it. Immediately his face turned white. Omar spoke quietly for a few minutes and then hung up. He turned to Yasmin.

'That was the police,' he said. 'They were calling from Imam Jamil's phone. Yasmin, he's in the hospital. They found him outside the units where the refugees are moving in. They think he was beaten up. He was unconscious and there was—' his voice broke, 'there was blood everywhere.'

CHAPTER TWENTY-FOUR

It was six-thirty when the doorbell rang. Harper was early. Claire hadn't talked to her since her conversation with Peter. Harper was fidgeting even more than usual, which was quite an achievement. Her eyes darted around the room as if she were conducting a panicked search.

Claire moved a basket of clean washing and some papers to make space at the kitchen table. Dinner tonight was nothing special. Oven pizza and fish fingers. A cleaning-out-the-freezer meal. But there was enough for Harper if she wanted some. Claire's mind was racing. Should she confront Harper? Should she just casually mention that she knew Harper had been associating with the Patriots League and had attended their protest? Or should she wait and see if Harper confided in her?

Piper lined breakfast bowls up along the kitchen table. A plastic rainbow. Ben carried a large box of cornflakes over. It tipped, spitting a few flakes across the table. Ben righted it. Piper stood on her chair and pulled the inner bag open with a rustle. Harry stood on the table beside her and peered into the box. Claire blinked. 'What are you doing?'

'We're hungry. We want cornflakes,' Piper announced.

Claire frowned. 'You can't have cornflakes. Dinner is in ten minutes.'

Piper made a tortured face. 'But we're *hungry*,' she said, somehow giving each word several more syllables.

Claire picked up the cereal box and took it back to the pantry. Of course, a bowl of cornflakes was probably more nutritious than the preservative-laden, high-sodium extravaganza she was about to serve them. She was mentally comparing the attributes of both meals (*cereal is mostly carbohydrates, but they're the good kind. Does pineapple on pizza count as fruit?*) when Harper stood up.

'Can I talk to you about something?' she asked quietly.

'Of course,' said Claire. Her heart sank. She didn't want to hear this. Claire knew she was supposed to suspend her own moral judgement. To listen with an attitude of neutrality and calm. But she couldn't. She just couldn't. Everything those Neo-Nazi thugs stood for made Claire so angry, she thought she might cry.

Harper sat back down and Claire sat across from her. 'You know the group that's been doing all the protests, the UCR?' Harper began.

'Yeah.' Claire struggled to keep her voice neutral. Images of racist and degrading slogans flashed through her head. Her stomach turned.

Harper's foot was tapping the floor in a persistent rhythm. She glanced out the window. 'Well, you know, the thing is. I mean. The thing is, I—'

CRASH. Piper stood, barefoot, in front of the fridge, eyes like saucers, in an island of splattered orange sauce and glass shards.

'Piper!' Claire shouted. 'What have I said about shoes in the kitchen? No. Don't move. You'll step on the glass. What were you doing with the chilli sauce bottle anyway?'

'I was trying to get to the milk!' Piper's lip wobbled as Claire gingerly picked her way towards her. Harry, always keen to get among the action, raced barefoot towards the scene of the crime. Harper quickly intercepted and scooped him up. 'Harry! My best bro! Will you help me find the mop?'

Claire lifted Piper across to a chair at the kitchen table. Luckily, the twins were still in their play penitentiary. Claire inspected Piper's foot. Was that blood?

By the time Claire had fetched the first-aid kit, cleaned Piper's foot (not blood, but a red flake from the chilli sauce), thanked Harper as she attacked the sticky, glass-strewn spill, put shoes on everyone and taken dinner out of the oven, it was almost time to go. Claire frowned as Harper finished mopping the floor.

Harper returned from the laundry and flopped down onto an armchair. There was a scrambling at the kitchen table. Ben sang, 'You're in the Story Chair. You have to read us a story!' and rushed to pull a book from the basket beside her chair. Harry ran across too, along with Piper, shouting, 'Harper's in the Story Chair! Harper's in the Story Chair!'

Claire gave Harper an apologetic smile. 'It's this whole new thing,' she said. 'If you get caught sitting in that particular armchair, you must read a story to whoever catches you sitting there.'

Piper pressed a book into Harper's hands. 'It's the rule. You have to. No excuses,' she said. 'Sometimes I sit here *on purpose*. Because I already *know* how to read. I can read *all these books*.'

When Peter clattered through the door five minutes later, Claire was clearing the table and Harper was sitting in the Story Chair, reading *Thelma the Unicorn*. Lily and Hope both sat in her lap. Piper perched on the arm of the chair and Harry sat cross-legged in front of them. Ben had climbed up to the head of the armchair and dangled over them like a brown-haired sword of Damocles. Peter raised an expressive eyebrow at Claire.

Claire smiled brightly. 'Okay, time to go! Be good for your dad! Byeee!'

Yasmin returned to the hospital waiting room. She had prayed Maghrib and made dua for Imam Jamil in the hospital prayer room with some other women from her community. She was glad of her faith at a time like this. Even when she felt completely helpless, completely useless, she could still pray. She could still do *something*. For now, she sat beside Omar in companionable silence, sharing a bag of chips from the vending machine.

'I know Jan was trying to be kind,' Yasmin said, inspecting a crisp that had folded over on itself perfectly. 'It seems so simple to her – just stop wearing hijab. Why wear a massive red target on your head?' Yasmin ate the chip and adjusted her veil. 'But it's not that simple. I mean, I've thought about giving it up. I know that Allah is merciful. I know He would understand. I know that dressing modestly doesn't mean I have to wear a headscarf. It's not like I think I'm going to hell or anything. It's just … It's hard to explain. Perhaps if I were a more spiritual person, I wouldn't need it. But going to the mosque, praying Salat, fasting for Ramadan, wearing these clothes – I need this. I can't explain it. It's not that I need it to feel close to Allah, although that has something to do with it, I guess. It's just …' She moved her hands as if trying to grasp at an idea just out of reach. 'It's so easy to drift from this path.' Tears sprang to her eyes. 'I'm always drifting away from Allah. I'm always failing. Always making mistakes. I guess I need these rituals. I need all the help I can get.'

Omar put his arm around her and they sat in silence for a few moments. Then Omar spoke. 'You're not failing at all. You're the best Muslim I know. You inspire me. And you're going to be an amazing mum. I've always been attracted to your spirituality.' His eyes twinkled. 'Well, that, and your smoking hot body, of course.'

236

Yasmin giggled and checked to make sure they weren't in earshot of anyone. 'Oh yes? This oversized novelty belly is really doing it for you?'

'Definitely. And your wrists. You have very sexy wrists. I'm not sure I should allow you to flaunt them in public.'

'Rump-pah-de-pah! Pah! Rump-pah-de-pah!' Yasmin sang her own parodic version of burlesque music under her breath as she inched her sleeve up, exposing her sexy, sexy wrists. Omar made an exaggerated expression of glee. Then he looked up and his smile suddenly disappeared. Jamil's doctor was in the waiting room. Yasmin took Omar's hand. News.

Harper stared out the car window. She did not see the neat houses flashing past or the streets she had run through only hours before. She was not actually in the car with Claire on her way to crochet group at all.

She was buying four bottles of kerosene from the twenty-four-hour supermarket, and a packet of Redheads extra-long safety matches.

She was watching the Jaguar burn. It hadn't exploded in a fireball like cars do in the movies, but she had managed to kindle a fierce enough blaze. The paint was blistering; the flames were consuming everything in a red-gold fury.

She was looking him dead in the eye as he came running out of the house. As his step faltered and his mouth opened and then closed again. As he turned around and went back inside.

She was standing beside the smoking black mess as the police arrived. She was calmly allowing herself to be taken in for questioning.

Harper blinked. And then she did it all over again.

CHAPTER TWENTY-FIVE

Meredith was behind the registration table again. When Lottie and Edith arrived – Edith, and not Luke – she had kept the conversation cursory and efficient. Now Edith and Lottie were absorbed in conversation. She straightened the registration sheet, aligned the pen and smoothed her skirt.

Going back should have been easy. She had survived without friends just fine before now. She was an expert at it. It was a simple matter of eliminating the 'Social' category from her goals list. It wasn't even like she had failed. Just readjusted. So why did she feel so … so unsettled? How could she miss something she'd never had in the first place?

She still had to stop herself, several times a day, from wondering what Luke would think about things, from filing interesting topics of conversation away in her brain for the next time they went running.

He wasn't interested in her as a friend. She knew that now. She just wasn't supposed to have friends. And that was okay.

Sometimes Claire felt annoyed by Meredith's sternness and rigidity, but today she found the sight of the agenda written neatly on the whiteboard oddly soothing. Her thoughts were everywhere. She welcomed the structure. She sat down. Edith was there, but no Luke. And Lottie was there too, but Yasmin was missing. Meredith started the meeting.

The door opened at least a full half-hour into the meeting. Claire smothered a grin. Yasmin was going to get into *trouble*. Claire would tease her and they would have fun giggling about it later. But her smile disappeared completely when she saw Yasmin's face.

Meredith paused the presentation. 'Yasmin,' she said, and walked over to meet her. 'I'm so glad you came. Please come in and sit down. Is there something I can get you?'

Yasmin, pale and drawn, gazed into Meredith's face with bewilderment. 'Omar texted me,' Meredith said quietly. 'I'm trying to be supportive. Is it working?'

Yasmin looked around at everyone in the group. She looked beleaguered. 'I've just come from the hospital. My imam was assaulted and suffered a big fall. They don't know yet if he's … if he's going to be okay.' Her eyes filled with tears.

The room erupted with concern. Lottie rushed forward to give Yasmin a hug; Edith led her to a chair; Meredith looked for a moment like she didn't know what to do, and then settled on carrying Yasmin's bag for her.

Claire looked at Harper. Harper's face had taken on a hard, closed-up expression. All of a sudden, Claire remembered how Harper had arrived at her house early. How she had seemed distressed and out of sorts.

Lottie was crying now too. She had linked arms with Yasmin and was sitting beside her. Edith pressed a cup of tea into Yasmin's hands. Meredith straightened her notes and watched Yasmin carefully. Claire watched Harper. She had seemed to go inside herself. She looked at nothing and her breathing seemed shallow.

Yasmin's eyes were closed and tears streamed out of them. It was like she was in physical pain. Lottie stroked her hand and said, 'There, now: let it all out.' Edith sat beside her, her expression fierce. Meredith began pacing.

What had Harper wanted to tell her before dinner? Why hadn't she pressed her?

Edith had begun a tirade: '… worrying about refugees settling in our community? It's not the refugees we have to worry about. Who are these thugs? Who are these *criminals*?'

'Harper,' Claire said quietly, with forced calm. 'What was it you were going to tell me before? At my house? There was something you wanted to tell me.'

Harper shook her head. 'It's nothing. It's not important.'

'… violent offenders out on parole. Does anybody care about the safety of the elderly? …'

'I think it's well past time we call this meeting back to order …'

'Harper,' said Claire, 'I think it is important. What was it?'

Harper did not look up. 'Forget it, Claire.'

'… need to be locked up. The blessed lot of them …'

'So, when it comes to correct yarn tension, the most important thing to know …'

'Harper, was it something to do with what happened to the imam?' Claire tried to keep her voice level, but she could feel the urgency creeping in.

Harper frowned. 'What do you mean? I was at your house.' There was definitely something evasive about the way she spoke. The room suddenly turned cold. Claire's heart sank.

'… lock them up and throw away the key …'

'… there are many benefits to creating a swatch before you start a large project …'

Yasmin's sobs were subsiding. She stared bleakly straight ahead.

'… prison system needs a complete overhaul …'

Claire swallowed. 'Before that,' she said. 'Harper, where were you before you came to my house?'

The room had lapsed into silence. Meredith had given up trying to call the meeting back, and Edith had stopped rehearsing her piece for talk-back radio. It seemed everyone was now listening to Claire's conversation with Harper.

Harper scratched her elbow. Her leg had started jiggling uncontrollably. She shook her head and looked away.

Claire looked at Harper steadily. 'Something went on before you came to my house this afternoon. I want to know what happened.'

Harper shook her head. There was a wild glint in her eyes. 'Why do you think it was me? Why would you think it was me? And why is she –' she jabbed a finger at Edith, 'going on about ex-prisoners? Did you tell them all about me?' She shot a look at Claire, but kept talking – ranting – without waiting for an answer. 'So what? I don't care. Hi everybody, I just got out of prison. So what? So an old man gets pushed down the stairs and you automatically assume it was me? Because all criminals need to stay in jail forever? I bet you couldn't wait to tell everyone the news.' Claire caught the scorching glare of Harper's eyes, as Harper began mimicking her. 'Hey everyone! Harper's been in prison! At last, something exciting is happening in my boring life! Spread the word!'

A shocked stillness descended on the room, punctured only by Harper's ragged breathing. Claire wanted to defend herself, but her throat had closed over.

Then: 'How did you know Imam Jamil fell down stairs?' Yasmin asked, pronouncing her words slowly and carefully.

Harper looked up in surprise. 'You said he did.'

'I said he fell down, yes. I never mentioned stairs.' Yasmin peered at Harper carefully.

'I must have heard it on the news, then.'

Yasmin shook her head slowly. 'None of the news reports have given those details. It's a police matter. They can't give out too much information.' She narrowed her eyes. 'Do you know something we don't, Harper?'

Claire swallowed. 'And what have you been doing with the UCR? I know you've been involved with them.'

Meredith cleared her throat. 'I think it goes without saying that if you are a racist extremist who beats up old men, you are no longer allowed to continue your membership of this group.'

Harper snatched up her bag, knocking her chair over with a clatter. 'As if I care about your stupid club!' she yelled, hoisting the bag onto her shoulder. 'What is the point of this, anyway? You've got all your agendas and plans but they mean nothing. You think you're making a difference? What's the point of getting together and crocheting like a bunch of sad losers? Do you honestly think bad stuff's not going to happen if you get your half-treble stitches just right?' Harper reached into her satchel and pulled out her crochet work. A tea-cosy, Claire remembered. She grabbed the end and yanked, unravelling it in curly purple handfuls. 'This is pathetic. You all are pathetic.' She glared around the room, flung her work onto the floor and marched out.

There was a moment of utter stillness and then everybody started talking at once, loudly and over the top of each other. Meredith was desperately trying to reinstate some sort of order, but nobody was listening. Then Lottie stood up. She spoke in a loud voice that echoed across the hall, cutting through the chaotic babble. 'I can't crochet!' Her face was pale and panicked.

'What are you talking about?' said Edith.

'I can't crochet!' said Lottie. 'I never learnt how. I'm a fraud!'

'Of course you can crochet. What are you talking about? You've been coming here all this time. You've been crocheting *all this time*,' Claire said helplessly. She kept looking at the tangle of purple yarn on the floor and at the door where Harper had left.

'No, I haven't!' Lottie was wringing her hands. 'I've been coming here. Yes. But have you actually ever seen me perform one stitch? I'm all talk, and untangling yarn, and offering food and showing off things I bought at the market.'

Yasmin winced. Edith shifted impatiently in her seat. 'Why on earth did you join a crochet group if you don't crochet? Did you want to learn? Any one of us would have been happy to teach you.'

Lottie nodded. 'I know. It's not that. The truth is, the truth is that I'm a knitter.'

Meredith stood up, her eyes flashing. 'I knew it! You had to be a knitter! I knew it!'

'Oh, sit down and let the woman talk,' Edith snapped. 'Is it any wonder she didn't want to own up with you running the show like it's a police state? Sit down, Meredith!'

Meredith sat.

Lottie drew a deep breath. 'I didn't get a chance to mention at the start, and things kept going and then I didn't want to say anything. I just loved being a part of this group. I wanted to be included and I thought if I said I was a knitter I'd be kicked out.'

'You thought right,' Meredith observed.

'Meredith!' Edith said sharply.

Meredith shrugged a *What?*

244

Yasmin frowned at the clock.

'I didn't want to deceive you all,' Lottie continued. 'I was going to tell you eventually. It's just …'

Lottie paused. Meredith opened her mouth to reply but Yasmin spoke first. 'I don't want to alarm anyone,' she said in a quavering voice, 'but I've gone into labour. I need to get to the hospital right now.'

CHAPTER TWENTY-SIX

The dishes were clean, the benches wiped, the boys in bed with their iPads. Now Melinda Keith could get some serious work done. She still had some finishing touches to do on her detailed report on Orania in South Africa before she got started on her presentation for the next meeting ('Why White Australians Are an Endangered Species'). She usually worked late into the night. Nobody worked as hard as her.

An hour in and it was time for a break. Melinda scrolled through photo after photo in the shared drive. She needed a good picture of the council woman to turn into a meme. None of the others had her skill at making memes. People thought that she was all harsh and grim but she actually had a really twisted sense of humour. She could be really clever with her jokes. But her skills were wasted on the other members. Half the time they were so dense they needed her to explain why the meme was funny.

She was carefully positioning the text box over the photo when her phone rang, making her jump. It was Jim.

'Are you listening to this shitstorm?' he barked.

'Language,' she chided. 'What are you talking about?'

'Turn on the news,' he said. 'Did you know Justin and Travis were trashing the flats?'

'I heard them saying something about it,' she said, grappling for the remote control. She turned the news on, but it was on another item. 'Something about getting pigs' blood from the abattoir? But they were supposed to raise the idea at the meeting, not just go ahead with it.'

'Well, they did go ahead with it. I found out at the last minute and sent Katy along to keep an eye on them.'

'Wait. You sent *the Temp* to keep an eye on them?'

'Don't call her that. I figured if she were there, it would be like I was there. They'd know she would report back to me and behave themselves. Fat lot of good that did.'

'What are you talking about?'

'Shh. Here it comes.'

The news was showing pictures of the refugee units with police cars parked outside.

'Grim scenes in Copeton today as a local religious leader fights for his life. Imam Jamil Khan was found here, at the scene of the controversial refugee housing project, after an anonymous call to triple zero. Police believe he was beaten by unknown assailants—'

'Let's hope they stay unknown,' Melinda muttered darkly. 'Though, if they do get caught it would serve them right.'

The news now showed the local hospital. Outside, a group of people stood with candles. 'A candlelit vigil. Muslims alongside people of all faiths gather to pray for the imam.'

Melinda shook her head. 'This is a nightmare.'

She indulged in a rant with Jim for twenty minutes ('steroid-munching idiots!', 'interfering old Muslim!') before she let him go to call the others. As she sat back at her desk, her brain was still buzzing.

This was what people didn't appreciate about her. She was smart. She was subtle. Her business with the spiders had finesse. It was on-brand. It was humiliating. It had a message. Most importantly, there was plausible deniability. Justin and Travis, the stupid thugs, were lucky no witnesses had stepped forward. What if somebody had seen what happened out of their window?

The plan with the spiders was approved by the group at a secret meeting with only the inner circle present. There was a process for these things. The group also approved Gideon's ice-cream truck. Gideon wasn't smart, but he knew how to doggedly follow orders. Jim wasn't a follower, but he was smart. The problem with Travis and Justin was that they weren't smart and they couldn't follow orders. So what was the point of them?

And the new girl. Melinda didn't trust her. To be fair, Melinda didn't tend to trust women in general. She had left Australia for Australians and Mums against Muslims because of feuds with other female members.

The new girl was the Admin Temp, that's all. Some Janey-come-lately who was handy with a computer and was a Young Person. Jim was obsessed with recruiting more young people into their group. 'Grooming the normies', he called it. And for what? They had a good operation going. Too many new people would just change the culture. Muddy the waters. Anyway, Jim never seemed to be as keen to invite any *male* young people.

But with the Temp, Jim acted like he'd taken on a protégée. Melinda was sure it was fantastic for his ego, having a pretty girl half his age following him around, asking questions and taking notes. She *was* pretty, despite all of her tattoos and piercings. As for Gideon, she didn't think it possible the weird beardy oaf could be more quiet and awkward, but in the presence of the Temp, he was reduced to a silent beetroot.

They were blind, as men always are. Melinda could see the Temp was hard at work worming her way in. She definitely had something to hide. But would anyone listen to her? Not likely. As for Melinda, she was perfectly capable of managing a computer without the help of conniving little tramps.

She should look up Twitter to see how this was playing out. She wondered if any of the others had the sense to do that. People didn't appreciate just how tech-savvy she was. They were all in raptures about the Temp and all of her skills but they forgot that Melinda was just as capable. Actually she was probably more capable. She just didn't make a big thing of it.

Idiots on the private forums were celebrating the imam's demise: *Serves him right!* and *Your playing with tha big boys now!* They couldn't see that this was a bad business. It's not like she wasn't pleased to see the filthy towel-head put in his place. But if the old man died, that could undo months of hard work. She sensed a definite shift in public sympathy.

She flipped over to Twitter.

The attack was definitely trending and not in a good way. '#PrayForJamil', '#EndIslamophobia' and '#WelcomeToCopeton' were high in the rankings. Many of these posts carried another hashtag, trending far above the rest. Melinda clicked on '#MalakForPM'.

And there it was, post after repost of the same video, apparently leaked from the offcuts of a television interview, alongside pithy comments: *Can we have an election now pls? I want this woman to be prime minister!*; *THIS*; *#DontBeADarren*; *Can we get an aMeN?!* The video showed the council woman, Yasmin Malak, as bold as you please, talking to a reporter about racism. *Look at her there in her headscarf, talking about 'casual bigotry' and 'hidden racism'. And why does she keep calling the reporter 'Darren'?*

CHAPTER TWENTY-SEVEN

Harper trudged up the road to the abbey. The cracks in the footpath seemed to pulse. Any minute they might gape open and she would fall down and down into an endless abyss. And maybe that wouldn't be so bad.

Everything was so hard, and she was so fucking tired. With each step the heavy file inside her satchel dug into her hip, again and again and again. She just had to dump it at Andrew's office and then she could … what? Disappear? Turn invisible? She kicked fiercely at a mangled pine cone.

She wouldn't be going back to the crochet group, she knew that much. And she wouldn't be going back to Claire's house. In a way, it was a relief. The past few months, she had lived in constant dread. Soon they would reject her. Soon they would find out about her past and kick her out and never trust her again. At least now it had finally happened.

Harper rapped on the door. The night was clear and cold. She hoped Andrew wasn't there. It would be easier to dump the file and run without having to talk or explain anything.

'Harper, is that you?' A door had opened, but not the one Harper had been knocking on. Further along the bluestone building, Sister Pat stepped out into the cloistered walk.

Harper glowered. She definitely did not want to talk to Sister Pat.

Sister Pat smiled broadly. 'Harper!'

Harper said nothing and turned her back on the old lady.

Sister Pat whisked along the paved walkway until she stood facing Harper again. 'Harper. I thought it was you. I just got back from a prayer vigil at the hospital and all the other sisters are out. I could really use some company right now. Would you like a cup of tea?'

Harper looked away. 'No.'

Pat moved herself into Harper's field of vision. 'Come on, Harper, do me a favour.'

Harper's eyes flashed. 'You were at the prayer vigil for the imam, yeah? What if I told you I was there? What if I told you that I saw him fall down the stairs? Would you be so keen to drink tea with me then?'

Pat gave her a level stare, but kept her tone light. 'If you were to tell me that, I'd want to drink several cups of tea with you. I think it might take that many to hear the whole story.'

Harper shook her head. 'It's pretty simple. Everyone else seems to have the whole story all worked out. I'm a violent, racist criminal. That's all I'll ever be.'

Pat cocked an eyebrow. 'If I know one thing about you, Harper, it's that you'll never be simple and uncomplicated. There's more to this story, and I want to hear it. Come on. It's cold out here, and I have biscuits.'

The sisters' residence was modest and homey. Clay vases, a cross painted by an Indigenous artist and photos of the five sisters graced the mantelpiece over a red incandescent heater. Harper perched nervously on the couch.

'What I want to know first,' Pat said as she arranged the tea and biscuits on the coffee table, 'is what you have in that big file.'

Harper sighed and ran her fingers along the spine of the binder. 'It's a long story,' she said.

Pat gave an exaggerated wiggle, settling into her armchair. 'I like long stories,' she said.

Harper rolled her eyes, but then she started to talk. 'Do you remember the job you got me next door?'

Pat nodded. 'The research job for Loyola?'

Harper picked up her cup and held it in both hands without drinking. 'It was a pity job really. It's not like journalists can't look up websites and chase up sources by themselves.'

Pat sniffed. 'You'd be surprised.'

Harper cast a look at the file on her lap. 'Anyway, Andrew was writing a long piece for *Faber* about the protests and wanted some information about the UCR.' *The Faber Review* was a small but highly regarded current affairs journal produced by Loyola Press, a Jesuit media group.

'I got really into it. It's not like I had much else to do. I couldn't find anything out without joining the private forums and closed Facebook groups, so I made up a fake profile for myself, Katy Kerouac, and they let me in. Then I kept getting invitations to their meetings, so I thought I could find out even more if I turned up.' The words were tumbling out, as if they had been waiting a long time to be said.

Sister Pat's brow darkened. 'Did Andrew know you were going undercover?'

Harper shook her head. 'Of course not. You don't need to get angry at him. Andrew didn't ask me to do any of this.' She paused and slowly rotated the cup in her hands. When she spoke again, her voice was subdued. 'I didn't know they were going to do that spider thing to Yasmin. I would have warned her. I – like, I mean – I wasn't invited to *all* the meetings. But, pretty soon they found out I was good at computers and they needed somebody to maintain their website and Facebook page. So I volunteered and they gave me access to their passwords and all of their files and then' – she passed the binder to Pat – 'I knew everything.'

Pat opened the file cautiously. 'There's a lot here,' she said, sifting through the papers. 'Are these financial records?'

Harper nodded. 'Andrew wanted to know how they were covering all their expenses. They've been renting that unit on Churchill Street for months now. It turns out they have a few generous donors who aren't public members of the group.'

Pat continued to flip through the papers. 'There are some powerful people named here. And are these addresses of the members?'

'Yes. Nobody actually lives in Copeton. Half of them live in a different state.'

Pat reached into a sheet protector and pulled out a memory stick. 'What's on this?'

Harper looked down, saying nothing.

Sister Pat placed the memory stick on the coffee table and leaned back in her seat. 'Harper?'

Harper stared at the cup in her hands.

Sister Pat sipped her tea. 'I'm guessing this is where we get to the part about Imam Jamil,' she observed quietly.

Harper shot her an anguished look. 'He wasn't supposed to be there! He just turned up! And then everything went out of control.' Harper took a deep breath and turned the cup slowly in her hands, as if manually rewinding to the beginning of the story. 'There are these two guys in the group, Travis and Justin, who are, like, really into body-building. They're always drinking shakes and eating protein bars and I reckon they've always wanted to get into a fight about all this.' She took a nervous sip of tea. 'They had this whole plan to chuck pigs' blood all over the units where the refugees were moving in. Jim asked me to go with them. I convinced them to let me film it on my phone so we could put it up on our private group. Like, to brag. They're not very smart. They got the blood from their mate at the abattoir and they were going to do it tonight, but then the blood started congealing, so they decided to go during the day instead. They dressed up as gardeners.' Harper set her cup down on the coffee table. 'Then the imam turned up. He was delivering welcome baskets or something. When he saw what they were doing, he confronted them and they' – Harper caught her breath – 'they started punching him. He's an old man and they started punching him. Then they pushed him down the stairs and ran off.'

Pat said nothing. She nodded at Harper to continue.

'So I called triple zero. And at the same time a bunch of Muslim women turned up. I think they were going to give out welcome baskets as well. But they found the imam there and were giving him first aid and stuff. So I left.' Harper's leg started jiggling and she looked away. 'But now the police have said that the woman who called triple zero is a "person of interest". They said they want me to come forward to "assist them with their inquiries". That means I'm a suspect. That means they're going to arrest me.'

Sister Pat leaned forward, her eyes focused on Harper.

Harper steadied her breathing and continued, 'I'm never going to get out of prison. I'm going to be like Louise – I might take holidays on the outside, but jail is my home.'

Sister Pat smiled and stretched. 'Ah, Louise!' she said, and Harper could tell she was picturing the overweight prison regular with her dolphin-themed trinkets and slightly vacant smile. 'You know, I still have hope for our friend Louise. But you're not like her, you know that.'

Harper shook her head. 'I stuffed things up with my crochet group. They know everything. And I stuffed things up with Claire. I said it was her fault even though I know it wasn't. I wanted to hurt her. There's nothing left now. I just want to run away and keep running.'

Sister Pat surveyed Harper over the rim of her cup. 'I suppose that's one option.'

Harper stood up. 'I don't have options! There are no fucking options!'

Pat leaned forward. 'Harper, sit down. Let's talk this through.'

Harper shook her head and kept shaking it. 'I don't want to go back, I don't want to go back, but there's no place for me here. Nobody's ever going to believe me.'

Pat stood up and held Harper's gaze. She spoke slowly. 'I understand why you think that. Your whole experience has been of adults letting you down and breaking your trust and not believing you when they should.' Pat gave the words a delicate emphasis and smiled sadly as Harper looked at her in surprise. 'It's okay. I'm not a mind reader. It's just that your story is not unique.'

Pat pressed on. 'Here's what I suggest,' she said. 'Step one: I'll give the police a call and organise for the two of us to go in tomorrow to give a statement. I have lawyers we can call on if we need to, but seeing as though you've done nothing wrong, it should be enough for the two of us to go in there. If you're nervous about going into the station, I could even arrange for them to meet us in my office.'

Harper watched Pat warily, but she sat back down. 'What's step two?'

Pat smiled broadly and sat down too. 'Step two: we give this information to Andrew and work with him to write a feature exposing this group. He might even want to write a series with all of the dirt you've dug up. Eat a biscuit.'

Harper's mouth twitched briefly into a half-smile. She picked up a biscuit and studied it.

Pat also took a biscuit and munched thoughtfully. 'Step three: I'd really like it if you tried to patch things up with your crochet group.'

Harper coughed. A piece of chocolate Florentine had gone down the wrong way. 'I don't think so,' she said, once she'd gained her breath.

'Why not?' Pat said, pouring Harper a second cup of tea.

Harper shrugged. 'They know about me now. And I was horrible to Claire. It's all over.'

Pat passed Harper her cup. 'You're very judgemental sometimes. Did you know that?'

Harper raised her eyebrows. '*I'm* judgemental?'

Pat nodded serenely. 'You treat everybody like they are harsh and narrow-minded. You don't even give them a chance to accept you.'

Harper glowered into her tea. 'Like *that's* ever gonna happen.'

Pat refilled her own cup with the dregs from the teapot. 'When I first started at the prison, the ladies had to get used to the fact that a funny old woman was there trying to run programs for them. Wearing this nun uniform doesn't win me many friends, you know. There are plenty of people out there who will judge me before they've met me. All I can do is keep being myself, and eventually people get used to the fact that I'm a religious sister. They can live with it. After that, it's easy.'

Harper scoffed. 'I'm pretty sure there's a big difference between being a convicted criminal and being a nun.'

Pat gave a mischievous grin. 'True. People tend to be more forgiving if you're *not* a representative of the Catholic church. The point is,' Pat leaned forward, 'you just need to keep telling the truth. You are very good at it. Just keep using your voice and telling the truth. The truth is powerful. Use your voice.'

Harper looked away. 'What voice?'

Sister Pat stood up and walked to a set of shelves in the corner of the room. She retrieved a paper carry bag and walked back. 'The voice you've been using all this time,' she said, handing the bag to Harper.

Harper opened it. It was full of neon-coloured yarn. Harper looked at Sister Pat. 'How did you know it was me?' she said, after a pause.

Pat grinned. 'How could I not know? Those spiderwebs had Harper written all over them. I was so inspired when I saw them, I thought I'd hook up some of my own, to string along the convent fence, but you know I don't have your skill with crochet. I'm sure if I give you this yarn, you'll put it to good use.' Pat sat down. 'Harper, I want you to promise me you'll keep being yourself. Keep doing what you do. Eventually, people will appreciate who you are no matter what.'

Harper turned the balls of yarn over in her hands. Then she stopped, and smiled. She knew just what to do with them.

CHAPTER TWENTY-EIGHT

A walk. That's what she needed. A walk to clear her head. Claire had tried to settle down next to Peter and watch his film, but she couldn't concentrate. She had tried to clean the kitchen, but Peter had already done the dishes and Claire got the sense he didn't enjoy the stomp and clatter as an accompanying soundtrack to the movie.

Walking was good. She just needed to tire herself out. She had too much excess energy. She shouldn't have exposed Harper in front of everyone. She could see that now. It should have been a private conversation. But she had been so shocked when she realised just how deeply involved Harper was with the anti-mosque group and shaken when she'd heard what had happened to the imam. She replayed the scene again in her head, surveying it from different angles. What should she have done differently? When she got to the part when Harper stormed out of the meeting, she played the scene from the beginning again. She stomped uphill to the top of her street, then turned onto Churchill Street.

She understood how groups like the anti-mosquers attracted people who were disaffected and disenfranchised, people who were lonely and desperate for community. Coming out of prison could be a vulnerable and isolating experience. Who was Claire to judge what Harper did out of desperation?

But what about what had happened to Yasmin? How could Harper stay involved in the group after they poured live spiders over a pregnant woman? And the imam? Claire tried hard, but she just couldn't picture Harper bashing an elderly man. Then again, just how well did she really know Harper? And anyway, Harper had chosen to remain with this group after they had committed these acts. She sighed as her brain shifted fretfully to replay the scene another time. As she walked a circuit around her block, her brain walked another circuit around what had happened.

She had made two more turns as she walked and was now back on her own street, uphill again. From here she could see a person standing outside her house. Was it Peter?

As she got closer, she realised that whoever it was, it wasn't Peter. The person was too small, probably a woman. She was still standing in the street, looking up at Claire's house, unmoving.

It was dark. Claire was almost at her house when she recognised the person as Harper. She stood there with a beanie pulled over her ears, crouched against the cold. Claire deftly turned on her heel and started to walk in the other direction when Harper called out to her.

'Claire.'

Claire froze.

Harper called again. 'Claire! Come over here!'

Claire turned slowly and approached Harper. 'I don't want to talk to you right now,' she said, her tone flat.

Harper gave a small nod, as if whatever she had planned to say had died a quiet death on her tongue. Claire stepped back, about to go, but something stopped her. She drew a deep breath. 'I know that you're in pain,' she said, 'and I know I can't properly understand the kind of turmoil you're living with. But I do understand that pain causes fear, and a need for things to be simple.' She kicked at a weed growing out of a crack in the footpath. 'I think that's where racism comes from. You're so unhappy with yourself. You're in pain, so you find a group of people who look different from you to lash out at, to focus all of your anger on.' Claire made a small gesture, indicating that they could continue walking together up the street.

Harper fell into step beside her. 'You said you didn't want to talk,' she said. But her tone was missing its usual snark.

Claire kicked at a stone. 'It's not like this is fun for me. I'm not talking to you because I'm looking for some great way to spend my Tuesday night.'

Harper continued walking in step, her expression stony once more. 'Why bother, then?' she said at last, almost to herself.

'Because I care about you!' Claire exclaimed. 'It would be a lot easier if I didn't, but I do. And I need to speak out about the bashing. I don't think you did it. I know you well enough to know that at least. But Harper, when you align yourself with these people, you become a part of that violence. Having racist views is bad enough, but to enable racist-fuelled violence? I can't stand by without saying anything.'

They rounded a corner. 'I'm not racist,' Harper said.

Claire shifted her bag on her shoulder. 'Nobody thinks they're racist. But we all are, a little bit. The trick is, I guess, to recognise it for what it is. To question our assumptions, and—'

'Claire, you don't understand—'

'I do understand, Harper. You think you've found a community with these extremists, but they aren't your real friends. They don't really care about you. And here's what you need to understand: we're your real friends, Harper. The crochet group. We're your community.'

Harper made a scoffing sound, then continued to walk in silence. Halfway up the street, they paused. Claire thought Harper was going to say something, but instead she perched on the brick fence, pulled some yarn out of her satchel and began to crochet. Finally she said, 'Yup. I'm sure everyone is just itching to welcome me back now that they know I'm a criminal.'

'Give us a chance. If you're willing to work on challenging your racist thoughts then—'

'I keep telling you, I'm not a racist!' Harper barked in frustration.

Claire sighed. 'I know you think—' she began.

'No you don't. You don't know anything!' Harper interrupted.

'I KNOW ENOUGH,' Claire roared. 'People just assume that because I'm a mum with kids that I'm invisible, that my opinion doesn't matter, that I should stick to icing birthday cakes, but I'm a person too!'

'Okay, yes, I respect you, but look. Can you just read this?' Harper fished a piece of paper from her bag and thrust it at Claire. 'Andrew gave this to me a few days ago.'

Claire started reading, and stopped. 'What is this? He's saying that you should consider joining their cadetship program? What does this have to do with anything?'

'Not that bit. Read here.' Harper pointed further down the page.

I'm concerned about your methods. Remember, we only ever took you on as an internet researcher. The information you've brought me is gold, but NOTHING is more important than your safety. No more meetings. No more risks. Okay?

The amount of information you have hit upon here is astounding. I think this should be a series, not just a feature like we'd planned. I don't think I should be doing this, but I'm going to give you a shopping list of things that would be especially helpful to the investigation.

1. *Financial records. That house they're renting wouldn't come cheap. Where is all their money coming from?*
2. *Member names and addresses. If they are really 'concerned residents', how many actually live in Copeton?*
3. *Anything – minutes from a meeting, purchase records, emails – that links them to illegal activity.*

Hard copy is best. Just come by and drop it at the office. I know everyone thinks I'm paranoid, but I prefer not to leave an electronic record, if I can help it. Plus, if HR finds out what you've been doing, I'm going to be in a lot of trouble. Remember: NO MORE RISKS.

Claire blinked. 'Okay, so who is Andrew Northey?'

'He's a journalist. Have you heard of *The Faber Review*?'

Claire knew of the current affairs journal, though it wasn't something she read. She'd seen it at Peter's parents' house. Her father-in-law read it (or at least, he subscribed and kept a copy on display for credibility alongside his copies of *New Scientist* and *The Economist*).

Harper told Claire the whole story – about how she had worked for Andrew as an internet researcher, how this had led her to join the UCR, and what had really happened that afternoon with Imam Jamil.

Claire felt numb as she stared back at Harper. 'So that time you were riding in the van with ... with Mr Whippy: you were working undercover doing research for a reporter?'

Harper had switched yarn colours and was beginning a new piece. 'Actually, that time I rode in the van with Gideon, I was interviewing him and recording it on my phone. He was really happy to be interviewed for a magazine article and I thought Andrew might find it useful.' Harper shrugged. 'I wasn't supposed to be doing all of this stuff. It was meant to be a pity job. But the more I got into it, the more I wanted to bring them down.'

'And the men who assaulted the imam?'

'I'm going to the police tomorrow with Sister Pat to make a statement.'

'How are you getting there?'

'We'll get the 893 early in the morning. It runs past—'

'Please let me drive you,' Claire interrupted.

'It's fine. We're all set.'

'No. Please,' said Claire. 'Please just let me do this for you. Peter's working from home tomorrow, so it's easy done. I really want to do this.'

Harper swallowed. 'Okay.'

They paused, Claire lost in thought, Harper steadily crocheting.

Then Harper spoke. 'I'm really sorry, Claire. About … about before. I know you didn't tell the others. And I'm sorry I was mean. I just wanted to push you away.'

Claire gulped and shrugged. 'You weren't wrong,' she said with a small laugh. 'My life is pretty boring.'

Harper shook her head, almost fiercely. Her hands had stopped stitching. 'No. Your life is – it's everything.' She gave the yarn a savage yank. 'Sometimes I feel like I just want to go back in time. Before Dad left. Before Mum … got sick.' That tiny pause, that brief gesture. Claire wondered if Harper meant her mum had mental illness. 'Before her boyfriend moved in and everything went to shit.' Harper paused. 'I don't think your life is boring, Claire.'

Claire stared at Harper's hands as she worked, holding back tears. Then she blinked and focused; for the first time, she noticed what Harper was crocheting.

'Harper. You're making a spiderweb. Where did you learn how to do that?'

Harper looked at the neon-pink crochet work in her hands and then back at Claire. She shrugged. 'It's my own pattern. Making webs is kind of my thing.'

Claire stared at the web with her mouth open. 'But what about Siobhan? Do you know Siobhan? Did you teach her how to do it?'

Harper gave a small half-smile. 'I didn't know you read my blog. Do you like it?'

Claire continued her impersonation of a startled goldfish. 'Your blog? What? Do you know Siobhan? Are you her computer person?'

'Her computer person. Is that even a thing? Claire, I am Siobhan.'

'What … I mean … but Siobhan's got kids …'

Harper shrugged. 'I might have invented the kids. And the house. And, like, the husband.'

Claire shook her head. 'But Siobhan is my hero! I really want to be like her.'

Harper paused in her crocheting. 'That's funny,' she said, 'because I – I mean …' she trailed off and continued stitching. 'I like going to your house,' she said finally in a small voice.

Claire sat on the brick fence beside Harper. 'I can't wrap my head around it. Were you in prison when you started it? Is that even allowed?'

Harper nodded. 'Sort of. It was a special program they were trying out. We got one session with the computer on Thursdays. We were only allowed to post about a hobby, nothing personal, we weren't allowed to respond to the comments, and the prison, like, moderated everything. But it was my favourite thing. I would think about what I was going to post all week. I didn't even know if anyone was reading it until I got out and could access all the stats and everything.'

Claire shook her head. 'I still don't see it. You and Siobhan seem so different.'

Harper nodded. She was still stitching away. 'That's what I liked about her. She is perfect. She is nothing like me. She is always in control. And I'm a bit obsessed with, like, perfect homes and perfect families. Every Thursday I got to spend time in this beautiful world. It was everything to me.'

Claire was now mentally flipping through the blog archives, trying to piece it all together. 'But the photos …?'

'Some of them were lifted off the internet. But the crochet stuff was mine. I made a photo box to stage it with. And one time I took some photos of food some of the other girls made at their hospitality course. I said it was for my family's dinner.'

'And then you started this whole yarnbombing movement.'

Harper grinned. 'That was funny. Melinda and Jim couldn't work out why the spiders were getting yarnbombed so, like, efficiently. It's easy when you already have a full-on *map* of where the spiders are going to be.'

Harper's phone chimed. Her face clouded over as she read the message, then she resumed crocheting with greater urgency. 'Claire, I need your help.' She didn't slow in her stitching. 'The text thread for the UCR has been going off all night. What happened to the imam, it hasn't stopped them, they are doubling down. Tomorrow, they are thinking of going to the hospital to stage a protest alongside the people praying. They want to use their loudspeaker to drown them out. Like, so they can't pray or something. I have an idea to stop them, but I need your help. And it needs to be tonight.'

Harper quickly outlined her plans. Claire was shaking her head slowly. Harper frowned. 'Okay. I understand if you don't want to get involved, but don't try to stop me. This is something that I have to do.'

Claire realised she was still shaking her head. 'No. No. It's just that – this is brilliant Harper. You are brilliant. But it can't just be us. We need everyone.'

Harper looked up at her. 'Everyone?'

Claire nodded. 'All of the CCC. All of us.'

Harper shook her head. 'They aren't going to want to see me.'

Claire grinned. 'You need to trust me. Wait here. I just need to run home and grab some things. This is going to be epic!'

Claire launched herself at Harper, gathering her into tight bear hug, all elbows that she was, then ran off at a sprint down the road.

Lottie stood in Edith's kitchen, refilling the kettle. 'Please stay for another pot,' Edith had said. 'We still have so much to talk about.' Lottie was glad, but she insisted on being the one to make the tea this time.

She gazed out of the dark window and wondered how Yasmin was going. Dr Malak had looked apprehensive when he arrived. Was that the normal nerves of a first-time father, or was that his medical training telling him something was not right? She shuddered. Yasmin had, after all, had more than the usual amount of stress in her life over the past few weeks. What if that had affected the baby?

Then her phone rang. Lottie gave a start. Claire. Was Claire calling about Yasmin?

'Lottie!' Claire's voice was cheerful to the point of being hyper. Lottie started breathing again. 'Lottie, do you still have all those extra welcome blankets?'

'Yes. Five big garbage bags full. I can't get rid of them. Why?'

Claire explained the plan and gave directions. Lottie nodded vigorously, even though she was on the phone and Claire couldn't see her. 'We'll get there as soon as we can!'

Claire dashed back out of her front door and walked up the hill carrying a backpack, a jacket and a large shoulder bag. She had emptied the Drawer of Shame and stuffed some balls of yarn and spare hooks into her bags as well. On the way out the door, she'd grabbed Piper's ski jacket, the one that was still too big for her.

As she rounded the corner, she saw that Lottie and Edith were just arriving. Claire thrust the thick jacket at Harper. 'I hope this fits. It's chilly tonight,' she said. 'Oh – and you should have this back.' Claire handed Harper a small pile of wool – the half-unravelled tea-cosy.

Harper smiled sheepishly as she shrugged on the jacket and pocketed the cosy. Then she explained the full plan to Lottie and Edith. 'Of course we are on board,' Lottie said. She pulled out her phone. 'What we need now is some decent project management.'

CHAPTER TWENTY-NINE

Meredith had already washed the cups and biscuit plates in soapy water, rinsed them in scalding hot water and left them on the drainer to dry. She emptied the urn and wiped down the worn formica countertop. There was no stipulation in the scout hall's lease agreement that tenants deep-clean and sanitise the kitchen after every use, but Meredith wasn't ready to go home, not yet. She cast her eyes around for something else to do. There was a black spot on the bench. She scrubbed at it viciously for a full five minutes.

'You're fighting a losing battle there. That's a crack, not a stain.'

Meredith jumped in alarm, then cursed herself for doing so. Luke was standing behind her in the kitchen. She hadn't heard him come in.

Luke ran his thumb lightly over the black spot. 'I used to be a scout here. This mark was made when I dumped a big metal box full of pine cones on it. There's another scratch here, from the other side of the box, but you can hardly see it now.' As Luke pointed, he moved closer to Meredith. 'I have a particular talent for messing things up.' His tone was light. He could easily have been talking about the scratched benchtop, but when Meredith looked into his dark hazel eyes, she saw something else.

She looked away. Her heart was pounding. He really had startled her, walking in like that. She drew a breath. 'So, why did you come here?' She worked hard to keep her voice level, to keep that note of hope suppressed.

Luke jangled his car keys. 'Lottie drove Gran home. They're still in the kitchen, talking about what happened. I thought I might come here to see if – to see how you were going. And Lottie thinks she might have left her glasses case behind.'

Meredith rinsed the cloth, wrung it dry, turned the water off. 'She didn't. There's no lost property. I checked.' She gave the cloth a shake, folded it over. 'I think we're done. I don't think the group is working any more. I'm going to close it down.'

Luke gave a start. 'What? No! Meredith, you can't do that!'

She started wiping the clean sink. 'It's the only way. Everything went wrong. There was a big argument, and it all just finished.' She turned the cloth over in her hand. 'I think I need to give up. It's clear people don't want to be here. And I'm just no good at social things. I need to stick to what I'm good at.'

Luke opened a stiff drawer in the bench cabinet and retrieved a faded yellow tea towel. 'But you are good at this. You've created a little community and kept it going all this time. This group has meant so much to so many people. It *has*,' he insisted, as Meredith shook her head at the sink. 'I know it's been important for Gran.' He picked up a mug and began drying it. 'One of Gran's best friends died at the end of last year and her other best friend moved into a nursing home. It always used to be the three of them going out together. My sister was so worried she almost cancelled her big trip. As if Gran would let her!' He put the mug down and started on a new one. 'This group came at just the right time for her. It's given her a community, and new things to be excited about.'

Meredith said nothing. She continued wiping the clean sink.

'And it's not just Gran,' Luke continued. 'What about Claire? Claire has five kids at home. She's run off her feet. Coming here lets her do something that's just for her. It makes her a better mum. And Harper …'

'Harper is a criminal,' Meredith said shortly. 'She's in league with the UCR. And Lottie can't even crochet. You weren't here, you missed the big fight. It's all over.'

'So what if there was a fight? That's just growth. That doesn't mean the end.'

They stood side by side. Luke looked at Meredith. Meredith looked at the sink. 'It wasn't supposed to happen like this,' she said. 'This was never the plan.'

'This isn't just your group, Meredith. This is bigger than you. You can't control us the way you control your stitches. You can't write a pattern for our interactions and tell us to follow it. You need to trust us more.'

Meredith shrugged and turned back to wipe the bench. 'If you think it's such a great group, why did you stop coming?' Her voice faltered just a little bit.

Luke didn't answer straight away. He picked up the clean mugs, took them to the cupboard and put them away. It took two trips. Finally, he spoke. 'I didn't think you'd want to see me,' he said, 'but that doesn't mean I don't care about this group or about you.'

She carefully ignored the strange thrill threatening to burst out of her chest and turned to face him. She should say something. She didn't know what to say. Her heart was beating again, very fast.

He picked the tea towel up again and ran his thumb along the hem. 'I told my sister I was moving back home to help look after Gran while she was away,' he said. 'That was true, but it wasn't the whole truth. When I first joined the group, I was in a bad place. I was miserable, I'd had a bad break-up, I felt like everything in my life had gone stale.'

Meredith narrowed her eyes. 'I remember when you joined the group. You weren't miserable. You were *cheerful*.'

Luke smiled. 'You can be cheerful and sad at the same time. At least, I can. I was cheerful in the moment because I like meeting new people. The sadness was like a background noise.

'And then I joined this group and things started changing. I learnt new skills, I found new things to be passionate about, I started to see things differently. Except it wasn't just this group. It was you. You made me realise I could do other things. You pushed me out of my comfort zone. You even made me a better runner.'

The fridge hummed. Water dripped into the drain. Luke put the tea towel down, then picked it up. 'If you were a bloke, if you weren't Meredith, but you were … I don't know … Merv. If you were Merv and not Meredith, then I'd want to be your best mate. You're clever, you're funny, you're completely original. I'd definitely want to be friends with you. We'd have great times together.'

Meredith wrinkled her nose: *Merv? What was Luke talking about?*

Luke looked down as he traced the outline of the tea towel with his thumb. 'But the thing is, you're not Merv, you're Meredith.'

He looked up. Meredith was hit with the full force of his gaze. She felt as if the breath had been taken from her chest.

He turned towards her. 'You're Meredith and everything about you – the sound of your laugh, the way your hair moves when you walk, the way your nose scrunches up when you're thinking – it's, it's taken over my brain.' He ran his hand over his forehead and through his hair. 'You're so powerful and so passionate. It's all I can think about.'

Luke dropped the tea towel on the bench and stepped closer to her.

He was very close now. They were almost touching. She probably should have taken a step back, but she felt rooted to the spot. Staring up at Luke. Holding her breath.

'The thing is,' he said, 'I know the right thing to do is to give you distance. If you're not attracted to me, I should leave you alone.' He placed his hand lightly on Meredith's upper arm. 'But I don't think it's about that. Not really.'

Meredith said nothing. She felt like she had been paralysed and set on fire, but it wasn't a bad feeling. He let go of her arm. 'Maybe I'm imagining it. Meredith, I need to know: do you have any feelings for me at all?'

His eyes were searching hers. Those eyes would bring her undone. She did not know what to say. She didn't—

They both jumped at the shrill ringing sound. Her phone! Meredith picked it up, the spell broken. It was Lottie.

'Can you come to meet us at Churchill Street? We need you. Come quickly. And bring Luke.'

CHAPTER THIRTY

Five garbage bags' worth of blankets looks like a lot when they're all spread across the floor. Lottie tugged the corner of the last one straight, then stood up to survey the sea of crocheted colour.

It had been a good idea to call Meredith. Meredith had taken one look at the mismatched group milling around on the suburban street and come to a decision. They couldn't stay out here. They needed a staging area. Armed with measurements and photos, they decamped to the scout hall.

Of course, it was a pity to thwart the scheme she had going with Edith. She wondered if Luke and Meredith had managed any sort of conversation when they found themselves alone together. The missing glasses case was a ruse, of course, but Lottie and Edith wanted to make sure Luke went to the scout hall. The energy between them definitely seemed different. Luke watched Meredith with an inscrutable intensity as she gave directions, then buried himself in the task of sorting, avoiding all eye contact, while Meredith cast him furtive glances.

It was strange to see Harper back among them. She was wearing what looked like a child's coat. Durable fabric in pearly lilac-and-pink with shiny silver unicorns stamped over it. There was something incongruous about Harper's surly face peering out from the fluff-trimmed hood. She looked like she was wearing confectionery. Lottie still needed to hear the full story there. Claire seemed completely relaxed around Harper, who was as fidgety and defensive as ever, shooting glares around the room, as if daring them to ask why she had come back.

The door swung open with its usual creak-bang. It was Yasmin, smiling sheepishly. 'Claire texted me that you were all here,' she said. Her gaze fell on Harper and she frowned quizzically.

Lottie dropped her handful of crocheted daffodils and rushed across to Yasmin. 'What are you doing here? Shouldn't you be in the hospital?'

Yasmin tore her eyes from Harper, shook her head and swallowed, looking down. 'The midwives sent me home. They said I should rest and come back when the contractions are closer together.'

Claire rolled her eyes. 'It's the *worst* when they do that. I got sent home twice for Piper. Then with Harry, I was having regular contractions, five minutes apart, and then I go to the hospital and they literally just *stopped*. But they let me stay that time.'

Meredith clipped across the hall in quick strides. 'If the midwives told you to rest, why aren't you resting?'

The door creak-banged again and Dr Malak stepped into the room. Well, that was something at least, but Lottie had to stop herself from seizing him by the shoulders and giving him a good shake. 'Dr Malak. Why isn't Yasmin resting? Don't you think Yasmin should be resting?'

He gave her a tired smile. 'Lottie, it's Omar, please. We GPs like being on first-name terms with our patients. And if you have a method that can make Yasmin do something she's made up her mind not to do, please share it with me. It would be a scientific breakthrough.'

Yasmin made a face at her husband. 'I need to be a part of this.

I can rest later.' As her eyes met Harper's again, her lips parted in a question that hadn't yet found words.

Lottie looked across to Harper. Her pale face was flushed red; her fingers scratched at her forearms while her mouth worked silently, trying to force out the beginning of a sentence.

'What is it, Harper?' Lottie said softly.

'I need to tell you something.' Now that Harper had found her voice, it rang out clearly across the hall. Not that she needed to speak loudly. Everything was suddenly very still. 'Claire told you that I'm a member of the UCR and that I have just got out of prison.' Harper looked steadily at the Queen's Scout Award board as she spoke. 'I was a member of the UCR, but not in the way you think. And it's true. I did just get out of prison.' Harper shifted her weight on her feet and continued. 'Last year, I was sentenced to eight months at the Highton Women's Correctional Facility after I pleaded guilty to arson and destruction of property. I set fire to my mum's boyfriend's car. It was an expensive sportscar. I'm not saying he didn't deserve it, but I understand now that what I did ended up hurting me more than it hurt him.'

Harper took her eyes from the wall and looked down. Then she slowly and carefully looked at each member of the group. Lottie followed her gaze. Meredith, frowning and inquisitive; Luke, relaxed and open; Yasmin, piercing and intrigued; Edith, calm and steady; and Claire. Claire had the quiet smile of a young athlete's mum on school sports day. Lottie made a mental note to badger Claire with questions after this.

'Being part of this group ...' Harper's voice wavered slightly. 'I know I can be, well, you know how I get. But being part of this group meant so much to me. Even though I didn't show it. Thank you. I won't forget it.'

Luke frowned. 'Why are you talking like you're leaving the group?'

Harper shrugged. 'I told you. I was in prison.'

Meredith raised an eyebrow. 'So what? Are you planning on going back there? Or do you want to set fire to the scout hall now?'

Harper looked at Meredith. 'People aren't going to be comfortable with an ex-convict in their crochet group.'

Meredith sniffed. 'I don't know about that. It looks like we're letting Lottie stay, and she's a *knitter*.'

The room broke out into giggles. 'Meredith,' Claire gasped, 'did you just make an actual joke?'

Meredith gave a small smile. 'It's been known to happen.'

Yasmin raised her hand. 'Madam Chair, I'd like to forward a motion.'

All eyes turned to Meredith, who looked as if she were about to dispute the title, but then shrugged and said, 'The Chair recognises Yasmin Malak.'

Yasmin grinned. 'I move that the Right Honourable Harper remains in this group.'

'I second the motion,' said Claire, 'on the condition that she teaches us all how to make neon spiderwebs.'

'Excellent,' said Meredith. 'All in favour?' There followed a loud chorus of 'AYE's, as Luke, Claire, Edith, Yasmin, Omar and Lottie competed for the loudest response.

'The motion carries,' Meredith pronounced with a smug smile. 'I'm afraid you're outvoted, Harper. You need to stay.'

Harper glared sideways at the door for a moment. Then she drew a deep breath, glared at Meredith and nodded.

Meredith nodded back. 'Moving on. We need to get started right away. I propose that I manage logistics. Harper needs to be creative control. This is her vision and we need to honour it. Luke' – her voice squeaked a little – 'you are in charge of measurements and dimensions. Dr Malak can help you while he's here. Lottie, you are inventory and assembly—'

'And snacks!' Lottie interrupted, unable to contain her excitement.

'And snacks,' Meredith confirmed. 'Claire, Yasmin and Edith, I need you to consult with Luke and Lottie to construct any custom-sized pieces needed. I want you to use Luke's yarn for this because it makes up so quickly. All questions on the overall creative vision of this project must be directed to Harper. Questions on logistics and execution come to me. Now, let's get to work!'

Yasmin needed the measuring tape again. One more row and this triangular piece would be the right size, but she wanted to double-check. Just as she opened her mouth to ask Claire to pass it, she felt the beginning of a new contraction. She clamped her mouth shut again and waited for the uncomfortable cramping sensation to pass. She didn't allow the pain to show on her face. Lottie's flapping panic was more than she could handle right now.

Claire wasn't fooled. 'That was another one, yeah?'

Yasmin nodded. 'Thirteen minutes apart now.'

They were sitting in the corner of the scout hall. Luke had opened up the Venturer Den and he and Omar had carried some of the armchairs and bean bags into the hall. Claire and Yasmin now sat alongside each other on an ancient brown couch.

Claire was digging in her bag. 'I gathered together all of my unfinished projects. It's embarrassing seeing them all in one place. Some of them only need a few more rounds to be finished. I'll lay them out so Harper can see if she wants any of them. Oh, and look.' Claire pulled out a small crocheted ladybird. 'I've got all the bits from my yarnbomb efforts.'

Yasmin smiled and sighed. 'I wish I still had my poor little duck,' she said. 'It would take me ages to make a new one.'

Harper had come over to inspect Claire's assortment of crocheted flowers, granny squares and stuffed toys. On hearing Yasmin's comment, her face brightened and she rushed to the other side of the hall. Yasmin and Claire exchanged a look. Harper reappeared moments later, holding a black garbage bag. With a small smile, she produced Yasmin's spider-eating duck.

Yasmin gasped. 'How did you find that? I thought it was destroyed.'

Harper shook her head. 'I put myself in charge of cleaning up the yarnbomb installations for the UCR. I didn't want my spiderwebs getting chucked out. And of course I saved everything. It's all here. The stuff from the protest, too. I really liked your duck, so I decided it would take me an extra-long time to find out about it. But I had to take it down in the end. I didn't want anyone else to take it.'

Yasmin hugged the duck to her chest. 'Thank you, Harper. I'm happy to loan my duck to the project, but after this I want to keep it.'

Harper nodded emphatically and then ran off. Harper was hyper. There was no other word for it. Yasmin watched her as Meredith placed a sketch pad and a pencil case full of markers in front of her, along with a dossier of sorts she had compiled of measurements and an inventory of supplies. Harper sketched furiously as Meredith barked out commands. They made an odd couple. Yasmin would have thought Harper would bristle at what she saw as Meredith's overbearing manner. But tonight, something was different. It was as if, with Meredith running things, Harper was free to exercise her creativity. Yasmin smiled, and then winced. Another contraction.

Claire walked around the scout hall, taking in the scene. Meredith was putting masking tape down on the floor, to fit Luke's measurements. Edith had sorted their crocheted stock by size and type against the back wall. Lottie and Omar were sitting on chairs with a bag of blankets between them, busy sewing them together. Yasmin was still on the old brown couch, making custom pieces using Luke's yarn and a washcloth stitch. Occasionally she would have a quiet contraction and look at her watch. Harper was holding a crocheted lily in her hand, absentmindedly pointing it at the floor and at the stock of crochet, and sometimes at an imaginary object a few feet in front of her, muttering to herself the whole time. In a minute, Claire would go back to helping Yasmin, but there was something she had to do first. She stepped into the kitchenette and switched on the urn. Everyone was going to need some caffeine. She reached into her bag and pulled out a battered, but unopened, box of coffee sachets.

Meredith and Harper sat alongside one another discussing plans. When it came down to it, they had good working chemistry. Meredith was surprised. This almost never happened. She gave Harper a shrewd look.

'Do you have a portfolio of your previous work?' Meredith asked.

Harper squinted at Meredith. 'What?'

'Do you have any experience with interior design?'

Harper frowned. 'What's going on?'

Meredith sniffed. 'I've been put in charge of spearheading a new project at work. And I'm supposed to take on some more staff. Creative types. I'm dreading it, actually. I can never get a good read on a person

281

at a job interview. It doesn't really matter how many qualifications a person has if they're impossible to work with.' Meredith sighed and flipped the page on the sketchbook. She examined the sketches for a moment, then said, 'It would be a matter of designing and creating handmade pieces and installing them in display homes to create a sense of warmth and, well, homeyness.'

'Show her your blog!' Claire called from across the room.

'Get back to work and stop eavesdropping!' Meredith snapped.

Harper shook her head. 'I'm pretty sure I'm not the type of person who would fit in where you work.'

'Good. I'm getting pretty sick of the culture at Rivergum. If I need to change things one employee at a time, then so be it. Anyway, you'd be reporting directly to me. Come and visit me at work on Tuesday and we can talk about it some more.'

'I can be a reference! She did interior decoration on my house!' It was Claire again.

'Get back to work!' snapped Meredith and Harper in unison.

CHAPTER THIRTY-ONE

By the time they were finished in the scout hall, it was well into the small hours of the morning. Meredith didn't feel tired at all. On the contrary, adrenaline pumped through her veins; she'd never felt more awake.

She also felt acutely aware of Luke: where he was in the room, what he was doing. While her hands were busy cataloguing their accumulated crochet stock, her mind was following Luke, setting up the floor measurements. As she consulted with Harper on design and colour placement, her peripheral vision took in Luke, hard at work crocheting a custom-sized corner piece. After he left to get supplies and to drive Edith home, Meredith's eyes were drawn to the door every few seconds.

The first time the door opened, it wasn't Luke. It was Lottie. She had run home to fetch her hot glue gun. Then some women from Yasmin's Qur'an group dropped off food in foil-covered trays. Together with Omar, they convinced Yasmin it was time to go back to the hospital. Then a small group of *nuns* arrived! They seemed to know Harper.

When Luke finally did return, it was with a large carrier bag. 'Gran wanted me to bring these doilies to include in the project.' Luke handed the doilies to Harper. He had been looking at Harper as he spoke, glancing also at Claire and Lottie. Luke had not looked at Meredith. He had been avoiding her gaze for a while now. She swallowed and returned to her work.

Their last conversation played over in her head. Luke was right. She was attracted to him. But so what? Anyway, she'd blown it now. Which was good. Wasn't it?

Several weeks ago, Claire had shared an infographic she'd found online. 'Accommodating Muslim Co-workers During Ramadan'. Meredith had printed it off and laminated it, even though none of her co-workers were Muslim. It was so clear. It had little comic strips showing the right way and the wrong way. Examples of phrases you could use. Meredith wished the author/artist team would make some more infographics, to cover all social situations. 'Engaging in Small Talk', 'Discerning Correct Frequency and Duration of Eye Contact', 'Conversing with Domestic Tradespersons'. Right now, she could really use a set of comic strips to walk her through 'What to Do When a Person Has Taken Over Your Brain, but Also He Won't Look at You.'

'Drat it all!' she exclaimed, and pulled out the last row of stitches. She really needed to concentrate on her work.

Later, back at Churchill Street, whispering and giggling, they set to work on the final stage of their project. Meredith couldn't believe how much they achieved in such a short time. Lottie and Claire only stayed for a little bit, then went home, yawning openly. Harper stayed longer, tweaking and shifting and tying off ends. Meredith was impressed with her attention to detail. Only when Harper was convinced that everything was exactly as it should be did she hoist her bag up to her shoulder and stalk off into the night. Now it was Luke and it was Meredith. Somehow, it felt like everything had been leading to this point.

Luke was crouching down, tying two pieces of cord into a sheet bend knot, while Meredith busied herself filling up a bag with leftover supplies. She looked around for something more to do, but there was nothing. She didn't want to go home. Not yet. Luke stood up slowly and walked over to Meredith. He hesitated before pulling a piece of paper out of his pocket. 'I wanted to run something by you,' he said gravely. 'It needs your input and approval.'

She unfolded the piece of paper and squinted at it under a streetlight. 'This is an agenda,' she said.

He nodded. 'I've come around to your way of thinking. Agendas can be very democratic.'

She continued reading. 'This is an agenda for a *date*.'

He grinned. 'Surely a date is just another sort of meeting? This way, it's all on paper. No surprises.'

Meredith gave Luke an appraising look, then continued reading. She shifted closer to the streetlight, so that she could make out the fine print. 'I haven't been to that restaurant, but the specials sound good. I like that you've included them.' She offered Luke a half-smile. 'Wait: you've even included conversation topics!'

He nodded. 'They are suggestions only. All of this is subject to your approval, of course. We could even have a pre-meeting to sort out the finer points.'

She gave a cautious nod. 'So after dinner, you've suggested walking home, followed by – wait, does this say "a chaste kiss"?'

Luke shrugged. 'That's what I'm pitching for. But if you'd rather we make it a warm handshake, or perhaps a curt nod, I'm willing to negotiate.'

She folded the agenda carefully and handed it back to him. 'Look, I don't know,' she said carefully.

Luke smiled sadly and put the agenda back in his pocket. 'Well, it was worth a shot.'

Meredith drew a breath. 'I don't know,' she repeated. 'I think we might need to workshop this.'

He looked up sharply. 'Workshop?'

Meredith nodded. She concentrated on keeping her voice level and calm. 'Indeed. I'm going to need some more information before we can go ahead with this. This kiss, for example …' Her voice wavered ever so slightly, but she got it back under control. 'What was your plan of action here? What, exactly, is a *chaste kiss?*'

Luke looked at Meredith. He had stopped smiling. 'Let me walk you through it,' he said. He stepped closer and touched the side of her face. Leaning down, he brought his jaw just inches from hers. Their lips were almost touching. 'You see, I would move in, just like this,' he said quietly, 'and then …'

Meredith closed her eyes and parted her lips. Luke's fingers were in her hair. She tilted her chin upwards as he moved in to kiss her – to kiss her *cheek*!

Luke had kissed her on the cheek. It's true, the corner of her mouth, which had received a tiny portion of the kiss, was demanding her attention. But still, as kisses went, this one was *very* chaste.

She opened her eyes. He was still so close. He'd barely moved away at all. 'How was that?' he breathed.

She shook her head. 'We're going to have to work on that,' she croaked. In one swift movement, she pulled Luke's mouth to hers.

He responded immediately, pushing her against the side of the parked van with intense longing. She dropped the bag, spilling yarn in all directions. It was everywhere. They were stepping in it. And Luke was kissing her. He was *kissing* her and it was like nothing else. Her heart was thumping in her ears. Luke's hand was stroking her cheek. He smelled like coffee and sweat and soap and clean washing. And Luke was kissing her. The yarn was getting tangled. It was caught on her foot. And Luke was kissing her. He was kissing her. A dog was barking somewhere a few blocks away. The streetlight was flickering. And Luke was kissing her.

She pulled away abruptly. 'Stop,' she said.

Luke stepped back.

Meredith rubbed her hands over her face. 'This is a lot.'

Luke watched Meredith as she pulled the yarn off her feet and packed it neatly back into the bag. After she had zipped it closed and placed it against the streetlight, she swallowed and looked up. 'We might need to block out some time to go over this properly,' she said.

Luke's face broke into a broad smile. He took her hand and brought it to his lips. 'Whatever you say, boss!'

CHAPTER THIRTY-TWO

Gideon grunted as the alarm clock chirped insistently. Five-thirty a.m. The early mornings were tough on a man accustomed to staying up late on internet forums and chat rooms. But it was worth it. He was an important contributor. A righteous crusader. He heaved his big frame out of bed and got himself dressed. He wasn't good at organising people, like AussieMumma73, or arguing in public, like JimThePatriot, but he was good at computers and he was one of the top posters on the No Mosque For Copeton forum. Even now, when he knew AussieMumma's name was actually Mrs Keith, and JimThePatriot was Jim Thompson, he still called them by their forum handles in his mind.

It was good to meet so many of his online comrades IRL. It was good being a part of things. And he really liked the task he'd been assigned, despite the early mornings. It made him feel like he was really doing something. He was out there. He was a hero. He could be daring, and in people's faces, without actually having to engage with them or have a conversation. And he loved the cabin of his van. The microphone and the post-it note reminders on his dashboard. It was his nest, his own bubble. Perhaps today he would get himself some drive-thru breakfast. Or a bag of banana lollies from the servo.

He took a can of energy drink out of the fridge and made his way down the hall. When he stepped out onto the pavement, he stopped. Something was wrong. Something was very wrong. His van was there, parked in its usual place on the street, but … Gideon opened and closed his mouth like a startled goldfish. His van. What had happened to his *van*?

The shape was the same, but instead of its usual rusty white, the van was a blaze of colour. Had it been graffitied? As he lumbered closer, squinting through his transition lenses, he realised the colour was not from paint, but *wool*. The van was completely covered in some sort of woollen patchwork slip-cover, snug against the bodywork. The headlights had neon-pink spiderwebs stretched across them and crocheted flowers lined one side of the van, by the window, like ice-cream varieties for sale. The other side of the van was strung with lace doily bunting. Crocheted block letters in bright colours arched over the back window, or what would have been the back window, had it not been covered in navy yarn. Like a rainbow, they spelled '*HOME TIME*'. Was that message meant for him? Home, in a different state, in his parents' backyard flat, with no important job to do. Gideon wasn't ready to go home.

He couldn't get into his van. The outline of the door was there, and there was even a crocheted grey rectangle where the door handle should be, but the van was trapped within its snug woollen jumper. He stood on the pavement and stared forlornly at this strange and garish display. It was only then that he noticed he was not alone. It was one of his compatriots, standing there with her camera out. The young girl, with the tattoos. He couldn't remember her name.

'I came as soon as I heard,' the girl announced breathlessly.

The corners of her mouth were twitching in an odd way, but Gideon had bigger things to worry about than whatever might be wrong with the girl. His beloved van!

'I can't drive it!' he said helplessly. 'Should I call the police?'

'Do you have roadside assistance?' the girl enquired. 'Maybe they can send a van out.'

'I think I should call the police,' he repeated. 'I'm going to call the police.'

'You call the police. I'll let the others know.' The girl's tone was authoritative. He nodded mutely as she disappeared from sight.

Gideon was still standing in the street, scratching his head when the girl – Katy, her name was, he remembered now – reappeared. With her were two people, a man and a woman, he'd never met before.

'It's okay, they're with me,' she said. They were both older, middle-aged. Were they her parents? But Katy introduced the woman as Sister Pat. Was she a nun? A third lady, a woman in her thirties, was putting car keys in her bag as she approached them. Where were all these people coming from?

The man's name was Andrew. He was holding a large box of donuts, the good kind. When Andrew suggested they go in and eat them at the table, Gideon was quick to agree.

They had barely settled down, when Katy and the two other women stood up to leave. 'We're gonna have to eat and run,' said Katy. 'We need to chase things up with the police.' She grabbed two donuts and passed one to Sister Pat. The other lady was already wrapping her donut in a napkin. 'We'll be back a little later.'

Usually, Gideon would have frozen at the thought of being left to converse with a stranger, but Andrew made things easy and the donuts were very good. After a while Jim emerged, bleary-eyed, from his room. His eyes narrowed in suspicion at the sight of the newcomer, but his face relaxed when he heard Katy had brought him. He sat at the table with them. There were still plenty of donuts and Gideon felt proud to introduce these two intelligent men to each other. Then he had the pleasure of listening to them have an in-depth conversation. Gideon loved being involved in a rigorous discussion without the pressure of contributing to it. He munched his double-glazed chocolate donut thoughtfully and allowed the words to wash all around him.

At one point Andrew stretched, leaned back in his chair and surveyed Jim. 'You are a fascinating man, Jim. I'd love to write a book about you. Or at least a think piece.'

Jim laughed and puffed out his chest. 'Go ahead. You're welcome to try. But good luck getting it published anywhere!'

They were still sitting at the table, deep in discussion, when Mrs Keith arrived.

'Melinda, this is Andrew,' said Jim.

'Hi and bye, Melinda,' said Andrew, with a smile. 'I must be off.' He stood up. 'Thanks for a great conversation, Jim, and Gideon. You've given me a lot to think about.' He walked towards the door.

Mrs Keith blinked. 'What happened to the van? And who is he?' There was a note of panic in her voice.

Jim smiled. 'Relax, Melinda. He's with Katy.'

Mrs Keith's mouth dropped open. 'He's with – *what did you tell him?!*' She strode down the hall and out the front door. Gideon and Jim followed her out and through the front yard. 'Andrew!' she shouted. 'Stop!'

But Andrew was already in his car. He was driving away.

The police arrived soon after. Upon catching sight of the elaborately festooned van, the senior policeman was seized by a fit of coughing, while the young, foreign-looking policewoman with him rubbed her mouth and looked the other way.

When they had recovered, they took note of the time and details of the incident and discussed between themselves whether an offence had actually occurred ('Destruction of property?', 'Graffiti?', 'Trespassing?'). Then the policewoman put her iPad back in its case and addressed the group.

'We've taken a record of the incident and that will remain on our file,' she said, in a reassuring tone. 'Unfortunately, I don't think we will have any luck apprehending the offender in this case. It's not something we can commit resources to.'

'That's disgraceful!' Mrs Keith expostulated. 'Some very expensive property has been interfered with. Are you just going to do nothing?'

The senior constable raised his eyebrows significantly at Gideon. 'Sometimes we can't act, no matter how much of a *constant nuisance* something might be to others. At any rate, we have to go now.'

'Can I take a few photos first?' the policewoman asked. 'For ... uh ... the file ...'

'Oh. For sure,' replied the senior constable. 'I probably should take some too.'

At this, both police officers pulled out their phones and snapped the van from various angles One of them was taking a while to get a close-up picture of the little crocheted rabbit sitting on the windscreen, driving the van with a pair of reins, alongside a small hedgehog.

Mrs Keith asked if the stuffed animals held any forensic significance, in a very angry voice. The female constable was certainly interested in this detail.

The police officers put their phones away and nodded to Gideon and his comrades, standing bereft around the enormous, vivid, woollen van. Gideon was sure he imagined it, perhaps it was a trick of the light against the windscreen, but as the police drove away, it almost seemed as if they were *laughing*.

CHAPTER THIRTY-THREE

Harper had looked pale when Claire dropped her at the Highton police station. Sister Pat had given her a reassuring wink. 'We're okay, aren't we Harper?'

'Give me a call when you've finished,' said Claire. But later, after she watched Harper and Sister Pat disappear inside the station, she realised her phone was missing.

Not in her handbag, car console, pocket. Not on the floor under the car seat. When she saw the wrapped donut she'd stashed in her shoulder bag, Claire knew where her phone was. She'd left it at the house where they'd had the donuts.

'I just don't see why we couldn't get a coffee on the way.'

'I'll buy you a massive coffee after, Frank. But we're late. Yasmin said we should be here first thing. Is this the street?'

'I cannot operate heavy machinery without the aid of caffeine,

Rachel. This camera counts as heavy machinery. And yes. This is the street. Looks like it's about halfway down.'

Rachel didn't need her camera operator's directions once they got closer to the house. A glorious, multicoloured van shone out like a beacon, marking its place. This story was going to have excellent visuals.

She had not felt right about the way the last story about the Copeton Wars had been edited. Yasmin's interview had been impassioned and intelligent and they'd used almost none of it. The executive producer had been completely unapologetic about the whole thing. 'Loud-mouth racists rate better than clever Muslims any day of the week.'

It was vindicating to see the massive online response to the leaked footage of Yasmin's interview. Rachel would deny any involvement, of course. But when Yasmin had sent her a text message – *Was this you?* – she couldn't resist responding with a winking-face emoji.

It was on the table inside. Claire was almost certain. She would have set it down there when she was wrapping the donut, then forgotten to pick it up again. Oh, why was she like this?

A woman stood in the front yard. It looked like she was returning to the house from her car, having retrieved a pair of scissors. When she saw Claire approaching, she shouted at her, jabbing her finger at a sign by the door. 'No canvassers or solicitors! Can't you read?'

Claire smiled apologetically. 'I was – I just wanted to – I was here before …'

The woman narrowed her eyes at Claire. 'Who are you? What business do you have here?'

Claire could feel a blush creeping up her face. 'My phone – I left my phone in your house—'

'Did you plant a recording device at this house?'

Claire shook her head. 'I – no – I – it was just my phone. I—'

The large man with the beard appeared in the door. Claire appealed to him instead. 'Can I come inside …'

'You need to leave,' the woman cut across her. 'You need to leave this property before I call the police. You are currently trespassing. Go away.'

'Start recording now,' Rachel muttered to Frank as she parked the car. People from the UCR group were already outside, gaping at the van. She tried to maintain a relaxed, authoritative air as she stepped out of the car. *Don't mind me. I'm definitely supposed to be here.*

The woman – Melanie? Melissa? Rachel forgot her name – was wielding a large pair of scissors and berating the others. It's a good thing they hadn't stopped for coffee. It looked like they'd got there just in time. It looked like the brilliant van cover was about to be cut right off.

Rachel bit her lip. It would be sad to see the perfectly moulded, vibrant slip-cover destroyed. Then again, it would make great TV: the deranged woman hacking at the colourful crocheted masterpiece. It was exactly the sort of drama this story needed. Perhaps the report could make reference to 'social fabric' or 'fabric of society'? Yes, that was good. She signalled Frank to get a close-up of the scissors. Frank was looking the other way.

Two cop cars were driving up the street. One of them was a divvy van. Two uniformed officers got out of each car. 'Are you getting this?' she muttered to Frank.

Melinda was pleased to see the camera crew. They were the ones who had filmed their staged protest for that current affairs show. Good. Jim must have called them. They could film her cutting the cover to ribbons, liberating the van like they were liberating Australia. Then they could film the van driving triumphantly away to cheers and salutes.

She angled herself towards the camera. But the camera wasn't facing her any more. The police. Were they back to ask more questions about the van? Had they found the vandals already? But no. These were different police cars. These were different police. They stepped out of their cars, affixed their hats to their heads and strode to the front door of the Frat House. The scissors fell from her hand.

Claire watched as the four police officers marched past her into the house. The reporter and camera operator slipped in behind them. Claire couldn't believe the news team had actually come. Yasmin had said it would be a long shot. She hesitated, then slipped inside as well.

Her phone was right there on the table. Claire snatched it up. There were loud noises coming from the room ahead. The door opened and the police officers reappeared, with two men in handcuffs. One of them was only wearing underpants. A third man, the one Yasmin called Ned Kelly, was shouting.

One of the police officers firmly asked the news team to leave. The reporter nodded and made as if to leave without actually going anywhere. When the tattooed man in undies saw the camera, he gestured to the police with his elbow and started screaming about his freedoms and rights. One of the police officers was loudly explaining that they were being arrested for the aggravated assault of Jamil Khan. The whole group spilled out into the front yard.

The woman from before ran over and positioned herself between the camera and the police and projected her voice, demanding answers. 'What's your evidence?' 'Whose orders are you carrying out? Do you even know who's pulling your strings?' The police ignored her. As they continued towards the police cars, the woman became more desperate. 'Stop! You can't arrest them! They haven't eaten breakfast! He isn't wearing *pants!*'

EPILOGUE

Sister Pat had finished setting up the prayer space in the chapel room with cloth, a candle, their crucifix and a vase of early roses. It was the feast day of St Therese of Lisieux, the Little Flower, so the roses from the abbey gardens seemed appropriate. The young 20th-century French saint and her simple philosophy of doing small things with great love held a special place in Pat's heart, and she had made a point of getting up early to pick the flowers.

She still had time for a cup of tea before they met for morning prayer. She smiled as she fitted her new cosy over the pot. Harper had handed it to her a few days ago with a dismissive shrug, trying her best to look indifferent even as Pat gasped and cooed. It was a rich purple, worked in a chunky, textured stitch. Sewn onto the front was a grey crocheted skull motif. 'I love it!' Pat had exclaimed, hugging it to her chest. 'Oh! It reminds me of my years in Bolivia. Thank you. Thank you so much, Harper.'

They had met to look over the journal article, an in-depth exposé which was the first piece of what had developed into a four-part series.

Many saw it as the catalyst for the national conversation on racism, even while *Crossfire Report,* the commercial current affairs show, was trying to take all the credit. It had been described as 'empathetic, yet eviscerating', 'a disturbing insight into Australian Islamophobia' and 'groundbreaking investigative journalism'. There were even murmurs of it winning the next Walkley Award. She smiled when she saw the by-line: 'Andrew Northey and Harper Salmon'.

The article, thanks to Harper's research, had certainly put a cat among the pigeons. The formerly anonymous donors, including some high-profile businesspeople and corporations, promptly withdrew their support once exposed. As a result, the financial structure of the Patriots League collapsed. It was discovered that Jim Thompson had being abusing his position as a bank manager for many years to approve loans for the Patriots League without disclosing his involvement in the organisation. He was currently under investigation.

Crossfire Report managed to get several nights' worth of entertainment out of this, ambushing Jim as he took the bins out and gleefully interrogating him through his wire security door. It was a similar situation when Melinda and Dylan were investigated for the live spider incident, which was now being described as trespassing, assault and unauthorised filming on council property. They were now tied up in legal proceedings and *Crossfire Report* was loving every minute of it.

As a rule, Pat and her community never watched commercial news or current affairs shows. Their preference was always for SBS and Aunty ABC. Still, since *Crossfire Report* had started going after the UCR, a nightly dose of the garish, sensationalist program had become a shared guilty pleasure for the five women.

She breathed in the steam of her tea, still too hot to sip. Then she closed her eyes and recited the prayer of St Therese. *Jesus, help me to simplify my life by learning what You want me to be and becoming that person.*

Yasmin sat at the table with her journal and a cup of herbal tea. She had managed to get out of bed early and pray Fajr. It wasn't easy – sleep a rare commodity, and Omar so deliciously warm beside her. But Yasmin knew that if she gave herself this quiet time in the morning, alone with God, the whole day would be so much better.

Little Rani Esma slept peacefully in her bassinette. Her long lashes rested on her small, perfect cheeks. Yasmin's heart squeezed. She hadn't realised how intensely she would feel about this tiny person. So much love.

Her bullet journal looked different these days. In one corner, Yasmin wrote basic household chores, including 'have shower'. In another, she recorded Rani's feeds: the time, the duration and the letter 'L' or 'R'. Omar had hooted with laughter when he saw this. 'Don't let Leftie miss out! Rani fed an extra three minutes and twenty-five seconds on Right last time!'

Today, she would get a load of washing on the line and she would go to Lottie's music group. If she achieved both these things, the day would be a success. The music group would be Yasmin and Rani's big event of the week, apart from the maternal and child health nurse visit on Thursday, and driving Imam Jamil to his physical therapy on Friday. Her world had become so much smaller, and yet deeper and richer.

She remembered the first time her dad had visited after they had come home from the hospital. He was loaded with ready-meals and snacks.

'These biscuits are made with special ingredients,' he said. 'For the breast milk. And chocolate chips. But they don't help, they just taste nice.'

'Dad,' said Yasmin. 'It's obvious Noor cooked all of this stuff.'

Khalid shifted in his seat. 'Well. I did help with the lactation cookies. I looked in three shops to find brewer's yeast. I kept buying the wrong kind of yeast!'

'Dad,' said Yasmin. 'Next time, *bring her.*'

Last week they visited the new mosque for the first time. It was so fresh and new and welcoming. Yasmin smiled when she remembered the children's education room. It was decorated with a colourful spiderweb motif. We are all connected. *We have made you into nations and tribes that you should know one another.*

Khalid and Noor would be having the Nikah ceremony there in a few weeks. 'So soon!' Claire had exclaimed when Yasmin told her. 'I didn't think they'd get married for a few years yet.'

Yasmin had smiled. 'It's normal. Muslims don't really date. I'm happy for them.' She had said the words as a matter of course, but Yasmin was surprised to discover that they were true. She was happy for both of them. She genuinely wanted them to be married.

'Good morning, My-Darling-My-Love!' Omar emerged, freshly showered, in his linen shirt. He gave Yasmin a peppermint kiss and wandered into the pantry.

'How did Rani go last night?' Yasmin asked. Omar had settled her back to sleep after her 4am feed.

'Well, she gave me a lovely baritone burp, then I patted her for a bit and she went to sleep. And she slept through her twelve am feed again last night! I got a solid six hours. I feel like a million bucks! Ah! There we are,' he added, as the sound of Rani's squawking cries filled the room. 'She doesn't like us talking about her. No, no – you sit down and finish your tea. I'll get her.'

Yasmin drained her tea and set herself up on the couch with the feeding pillow. She could hear Omar chatting away to baby Rani as he changed her nappy. Soon, he carried her into the room and gestured at Yasmin. 'Look what Hero Daddy's organised for you! A nice morning feed. Isn't your daddy good to you?'

A full feed and another nappy change later, she dressed Rani in her nicest outfit, another gift from Noor, and packed her second nicest outfit in the nappy bag as a back-up. Claire had laughed the first time she saw Yasmin doing this. 'I used to do that when Piper was a baby,' she said, 'but standards drop for each baby you have. Now all I care about is if it's easy to change and easy to wash!'

The mums and bubs music session was in the living room of Cottage Three. The residents sat in armchairs eyeing the newcomers with mild interest. Mums were arriving with small children in tow. They were the new refugee families from the residential units. A lady in her sixties with pink-streaked hair was setting up a CD player and boxes of musical instruments.

Yasmin arrived and set the baby capsule down on the floor, rolling out a doily-embellished play rug and handing Rani her favourite toy, the crocheted duckling.

Lottie rushed over to her. 'Yasmin! It's so good to see you! Let me introduce you to the other mums. Claire's here already, and we have three of our new neighbours. Irma and Maryam are still learning English, but Fatima is fluent and can translate for us.'

Yasmin smiled and nodded to the three other mums. Claire hefted Lily up onto her hip and walked over, Hope in tow. 'You came! Well done getting out of the house. It's tricky when they're so small. Irma has a baby as well, but he's a little older than Rani.'

Irma smiled and indicated the seven-month-old playing on a flannelette rug. They had just embarked on a conversation about

305

teething (a subject which, six months ago, Yasmin would have found deathly boring, but now followed with avid interest) when Lottie called them to order.

The lady with the pink hair's name was Rosemary. Rosemary's program was a strange mix of nursery rhymes, simple games and jaunty wartime melodies. And yet, it worked. Yasmin bounced Rani on her knee, clapped Rani's hands and pumped Rani's legs. She watched as one of the three-year-olds, a little boy named Jack, tried to guess which one of the adults was hiding a maraca behind her back (the culprit was a ninety-two-year-old named Bev).

Afterwards, they moved to the dining room for morning tea. Lottie pressed a mug of peppermint tea into Yasmin's hands. 'What did you think?'

Yasmin grinned. 'Can we come every week? I had so much fun!'

Lottie gave her a relieved smile. 'I'm glad. This has been fantastic for our residents. It really brightens up their week when kids come in. Look there,' Lottie nodded across the room to where an old lady sat in an armchair. A toddler boy, Maryam's son, was passing the lady a toy train and the lady was passing it back to him. 'Those two are the best of friends. Gianna sits in the courtyard of a morning when Akif and Maryam walk past on their way to the shops. You should see him rush over to Gianna to say hello. Little Akif chats to her in Arabic and Gianna chats back in Italian, but they seem to understand each other just fine.

'My next scheme,' Lottie pointed with her lamington finger, 'is to build a little playground opposite that courtyard. I'm going to see if we can apply for a grant to build it.'

Claire joined them. 'I've had my fill of imaginary tea, now I'm going to drink a real cup.' Lily and Hope were playing with Fatima's four-year-old, Aisha. Aisha had set up the toy tea set and was running a cafe from the corner of the room. Lily and Hope were obediently delivering plastic cups and saucers to the adults in the room.

Lottie handed Claire a steaming mug. 'Has Fatima gone to set up?' she asked.

Claire nodded. 'Yes. She's in the community room right now. I said I'd watch Aisha for her.' She turned to Yasmin to explain: 'Fatima runs an English class for the refugee families with a bunch of volunteers. She was an English teacher in Syria.'

There was a crash. Lily and Hope were struggling for possession of a toy tea cart. Lily had pushed Hope over. Hope reached up to yank Lily's hair. Claire rolled her eyes. 'Please don't kill each other while Mummy's drinking her tea!'

The running sheet for tonight's meeting was all drawn up. Meredith had formatted it to fit onto a couple of index cards. Then she thought better of it and cut the index cards in two. Now they were more like business cards. Small. Unobtrusive. Just the right size to consult without anybody else seeing that you are consulting them.

Technically, Meredith was not in charge of the meeting tonight. Technically, Meredith had not been in charge of a meeting for a few months now.

When Luke and Meredith had taken a holiday together to the snow, Meredith had assumed the meeting that month would be cancelled. Instead, Luke had arranged for Edith to run it in their absence. Edith had apparently managed everything very well, giving everyone a tutorial on crochet fancywork. If Meredith had known that this was to be the meeting where three new members joined, she might have cancelled her trip entirely. But thankfully, Fatima, Maryam and Maryam's elderly mother, Urwa, had come back to the meeting the next month and were now regulars.

After Edith's success, the new plan was to let members take turns running the meeting. Which was an excellent idea. Meredith wouldn't have to keep thinking up new content each month. It was good for the other members to do it. It was good, so long as they knew how to do it *properly*.

At the meeting after their holiday, Luke had taught everyone how to make a stash-buster beanie. He had laughed when he'd seen Meredith's running sheet for that meeting. 'You don't need that,' he'd said, giving her a lingering kiss and easing the paper from her hands. 'I'm in charge of this meeting. You can relax.' Meredith had smiled. That copy was meant for Luke anyway. She still had the master copy in her bag.

The new members had been asking to be shown how to make the spiderwebs, so Harper might need to give a workshop soon. Would Harper appreciate a running sheet placed casually on her desk? Probably not.

Tonight it would be Claire presenting on amigurumi gifts and toys, those cute animals and characters made Japanese-style with tight stitches to hold the stuffing in. Claire planned to show them a cactus in a flowerpot, with round black eyes and a tiny smile. You could use it as a pincushion.

The pin-cacti were charming. And they hadn't done a workshop on amigurumi yet. And Claire was good at it, she really was. But did Claire know how to run a meeting efficiently? What if she forgot something important? What if she ran over time? Meredith would just feel better if she could quietly tick each section off as they occurred . She could do it very surreptitiously. Nobody needed to know.

'Two school lunches, a kinder lunch and a cappuccino?' Claire loved Luke's cafe. It was her happy place. She parked the stroller and browsed the cubby shelves stacked high with luscious balls of yarn and delicious haberdashery. Best. Decor. Ever. Luke's beanie kits were also for sale and the broad front counter acted as a little gallery for handmade gifts by local artists. She had set up some of her crocheted ladybirds next to the register, but they'd sold out already. She needed to make some more. The sales could fund her new coffee habit. Luke took the lunch boxes from Piper, Ben and Harry and chatted to them about what they wanted in their sandwiches.

Claire had just grabbed a ball of bright red yarn and was inspecting the rolls of lace and grosgrain ribbon when Harper jangled through the door. Since Harper had been earning money, Claire had noticed a distinct upgrade to her wardrobe. Today she was wearing a navy A-line print dress with red tights and Mary Jane shoes. Her dark hair was drawn back from her face with a red scarf and she wore bright red lipstick. With her vintage ladies' briefcase in hand, Harper would have looked like a secretary from the 1950s, if it weren't for the tattoos decorating her arms, or the fact that her navy dress was printed all over with repeating images of the grim reaper. Claire smiled broadly at the sight of her.

'Harper! Are you coming to the meeting tonight?' The CCC meetings were no longer held at the scout hall, but at Luke's cafe, a change of which Claire thoroughly approved.

Harper grinned back. 'I reckon I'll come straight from work. Meredith's going to sweet-talk Luke into cooking us both dinner.' She paused, then went on, 'I have a new blog post ready to go. I'm thinking I'll publish it tomorrow.'

'Oh, great! I can't wait to read it.'

Harper bit her lip. 'Please, maybe could you look at it now? I want to know what you think.'

Claire tucked the yarn under her arm and took the iPad Harper was handing her. The draft post had photos from 'a dear friend's house'. There was a close-up of a child's posy of orange nasturtiums and pink fuchsias in a jam jar. A piece of banana cake on an antique plate. A group of coffee-stained mugs in cheerful colours. 'This person has the same cups as me,' Claire murmured as she scrolled through. And then she stopped. The next photo showed a wooden train set on a rug. Her rug. The couch leg in the corner of the shot had the same moss-green stain that looked kind of like Daryl Somers. It was *her* couch. And the following photo, of pea sprouts growing out of an egg carton filled with soil, was of her kitchen windowsill. Claire looked slowly up at Harper, who was watching her carefully. 'These pictures are of my house. They are all of my house.'

Harper bit her lip. 'I hope it's okay. I won't publish it without your permission. I was careful not to give too much away. I mean, there are no photos of bills or the kids or anything.'

Claire looked helplessly back to the screen in front of her. She read the text that accompanied the photos. *My friend's home is a constant source of inspiration to me. This is not some sterile showroom. Colour and life burst from every corner. Where my friend sees mess and clutter, I see warmth. I see welcome.*

'Harper's here!' Ben, Piper and Harry rushed over to Harper and began vying for her attention.

Luke, meanwhile, had stacked the lunch boxes on the counter next to the takeaway coffee. 'So each lunch box has a sandwich, fruit, muesli slice and a monkey face biscuit. Oh, except Piper's: she has a spotty biscuit.'

Claire smiled, a little absently. 'Luke, you are a lifesaver! Can I get this too?' She indicated the red yarn. While Luke rang up the purchases, Claire took another peek at the blog post. Then she handed the tablet back to Harper. 'I love it, Harper. Thank you.'

Harper chatted to Luke as he made her a double espresso, Harry on her hip. Claire gazed out of the window. She could see the yarnbombed van, perched on the top of the hill, welcoming all visitors. Meredith had purchased the body of an old ice-cream truck from the wrecker's yard and dressed it in the patchwork slip-cover Claire had salvaged after the two men were arrested. *Home Time.* Visitors took photos beside the van, and the van appeared on all of Rivergum Estate's promotional materials. Meredith had figured out some sort of royalties system where Rivergum paid the creators for use of the van, but Claire was happy enough just to see her work on display.

Claire sipped her coffee and sighed. Life could be pretty wonderful.

ACKNOWLEDGEMENTS

My favourite place is the centre of attention. Sitting at the table, telling an elaborate story while my parents, brothers, sisters and grandmother laugh and tease and interrupt – this is what I've always loved. It is impossible to describe all of the ways in which my family of origin has helped me. Felicity Walter has been my writing coach throughout this whole process. She is the reason this book happened. Emily Walter read scenes for me and provided feedback, from the earliest days.

My beautiful mum and dad, Kathleen and Alan Walter. Thank you, Mum, for being the reason I am so close to my siblings, and thank you, Dad, for coming up with 'subterfuge'! Daniel Walter helped me with plot logistics. James Walter sent encouraging texts from random bookshops. Michael Walter told me to stop self-identifying as an 'author-stalker': 'You're an author, too, Kate!'

My irrepressible grandmother, Aileen Moriarty. Thank you for being a human spell-check, for insisting that I enter writing competitions, for being my first and favourite publicist.

I don't know how to thank Cate Kennedy. For many years, you've been 'the kindest person I never met', yet through email you supported me practically and emotionally. Thank you for providing insight, for teaching me the industry, for introducing me to the right people, for sending me helpful articles and podcasts. And (this is huge) thank you for championing my manuscript to Affirm. Also, thank you for turning out to be even more lovely in real life!

Cate introduced me to Demet Divaroren. Thank you, Demet, for helping me with Yasmin.

While I'm busy name-dropping, the ever-charming Toni Jordan helped me during the edits stage. Thank you for being so generous, warm and encouraging.

To Fr Andy Hamilton SJ and the best-ever writing group. Thank you for shared meals and evenings in your cosy living room reading scenes and eating penalty chocolate.

Thank you to my magazine editors, especially Michael McVeigh and David Halliday, who put their faith in me from the start and helped to form me as a writer.

To Kelly Doust and Armelle Davies at Affirm Press, you have been magnificent. Thank you also to Kevin O'Brien, Susie Kennewell and Dana Anderson.

To my editors, Sonja Heijn and Anna Thwaites. I have learnt so much from you. To Kirin Nabi and Zainab bint Younus who provided thoughtful and incisive feedback as sensitivity readers. To Louisa Maggio, who designed the cover, thank you.

For sharing expertise and/or writing space: Najma Sambul (a brilliant writer herself), Chris Farrell, Sergeant Peter Northey, Andrew and Katrina Solly, Bob and Nola Solly, Cathy and Josh Simons, Lia Ray, Michael 'Hatchy' Neeson, and Julian Sargeant, of Julian's Kitchen.

Thank you to Nina Kelabora, Gillian Essex, Jane Williams and the Welcome to Eltham movement. Marie Wood shared her experiences volunteering in Eltham. I won't name the refugee who also helped me, but I'm eternally grateful for her assistance.

I'm only going to name a scant few of my wonderful beta readers, but I am so grateful to each one of you. Special mention to Rachel Enright, Mark O'Dowd, Scott and Jane Gould, and Will Mithen.

To Simone, Wendy, Carissa, Monica and the GC parkrun cheersquad. And to Tracy and her lovely book club.

I don't have the words to thank David Solly, the love of my life, who would engineer family logistics to find time for me to write, who always had an unquestioning belief in my ability, who would take the children camping to give me a writing retreat at home and for being so attractive. That last part has nothing to do with writing books, but I AM very grateful for it.

To my gorgeous children! Thank you for allowing me to document our chaotic life in fictional form.

This book was a group effort. Thank you to everyone, even to those not named here. Thank you to those of you who faithfully comment on my blog and socials. I am so grateful. And is it corny to say thank you to my readers? I don't care. It means everything to me. Thank you. Thank you SO MUCH.

BOOK CLUB QUESTIONS

1. Which member of the CCC do you most relate to and why?

2. At the beginning of the novel, Claire is searching for community. What other characters share this need, and what role does community play as a theme of this novel?

3. Do Luke and Meredith make a convincing couple? Do you think their relationship will last? Why or why not?

4. Meredith is an only child. She believes if she'd had siblings she might have grown into a different person. Luke is the youngest, and Yasmin has a sister who is very different from her. What role do sibling relationships play in shaping these characters?

5. Meredith asks Harper, 'Why do you even come here? It's clear you aren't enjoying yourself.' Why does Harper join the group, and why does she stay?

6. We see casual microaggressions and overt bigotry in the novel. Do you think this is an accurate depiction of racism? Can Claire ever understand the nature of Islamophobia to the same degree that Yasmin does?

7. Is there any character you would describe as 'evil'? Who do you find the most dangerous?

8. Claire reads Siobhan's blog as an escape from the relentless mundanity of her life with small children. The aspirational beauty soothes her but also makes her feel bad about herself. Do you think this is a common theme in real life?

9. Both the UCR and the CCC use installation art to champion their causes. What role does this form of street art play in influencing public opinion?

10. Compare the group dynamics of the CCC to the UCR. In what ways are they similar or different?